Aubrey Rhodes was born in Ennistymon, County Clare, Ireland and raised in Cornwall. *The Secret of Provence House* is her first novel. She currently lives between Dublin and Middlebury, Vermont. Her passions are literature, swimming, Arabian horses, and Tibetan Terriers. Her guiding authors are Marguerite Yourcenar, Virginia Woolf, Mary Ann Evans, Elena Ferrante, James Joyce, Edward Gibbon, and Sigmund Freud. She is also an admirer of filmmakers Ida Lupino, early Godard, Michael Powell, Yasujiro Ozu, and Michelangelo Antonioni.

The Secret of Provence House

Aubrey Rhodes

OneMoreChapter

One More Chapter
a division of HarperCollins*Publishers*
The News Building
1 London Bridge Street
London SE1 9GF

www.harpercollins.co.uk

This paperback edition 2020

First published in Great Britain in ebook format
by HarperCollins*Publishers* 2020

A catalogue record for this book
is available from the British Library

ISBN: 978-0-00-837603-1

This novel is entirely a work of fiction.
The names, characters and incidents portrayed in it are
the work of the author's imagination. Any resemblance to
actual persons, living or dead, events or localities is
entirely coincidental.

Set inBirka by Palimpsest Book Production Limited,
Falkirk, Stirlingshire

Printed and bound in Great Britain by Clays Ltd, Elcograf S.p.A.

For Piquie
And in Loving Memory of
Omero

'Put sadness and melancholy aside. Life has but a few days, and we've only the here and now to enjoy them.'

'But one day all the stars will disappear.'

'Don't think of that, dear friend. Enjoy what the dawn brings us.'

A conversation between two insects
from *The Butterfly's Evil Spell* by
– Federico García Lorca

'There is no murky pit of hell awaiting anyone. Mind cannot arise alone without body, or apart from sinews and blood. You must admit, therefore, that when the body has perished, there is an end also of the spirit diffused through it. It is surely crazy to couple a mortal object with an eternal.'

– Titus Lucretius Carus

Chapter 1

Laura turned off the narrow main road onto an even narrower one marked as a dead end. For the last twenty minutes she had not seen another vehicle or human being. Early autumn winds were blowing in from the Celtic Sea, and as she shifted gears to take a curve, she caught sight of grey waves below. They were spewing ivory manes, rolling in toward a beach strewn with driftwood. Further along, jagged bluffs blocked the shore from view, sea-dampened, mossy bluffs veined with ores of metal. It was almost impossible for her to imagine that anyone might live at the end of such a road, until she saw the massive house suddenly looming in the distance. Where the asphalt stopped, an elegant gravelled courtyard began that belonged to a regal estate. The gates were open and she drove in, parking off to the side next to an old Land Rover. She got out and breathed in air that was tinged with brine and clover, and she marvelled at the fact that just two days earlier she had been jogging around Washington Square Park before getting her bialy and coffee, that last night she had been in London carousing with Fiona, and that now she was here at what seemed like the end of the world.

She had looked up the estate on a National Heritage website. The twenty-six-room mansion, known as Provence House, had been constructed in the fifteenth century and had belonged to the same family ever since. It was Tudor in style, built with grey granite stone, and flanked by formal Elizabethan gardens. Its 600 acres formed part of Cornwall's World Heritage Mining Site.

Retrieving her suitcase and imagining herself a protagonist in a Daphne du Maurier novel, she made her way to the huge front door and used a heavy brass ring to knock. She wondered who might open it. A dour maid perhaps in a starched white apron, or a haughty butler in waistcoat and tails. Maybe it would be a relative of the woman she had travelled all this way to meet – a handsome bachelor in twill trousers with an ascot. But the door was answered by the owner herself, a woman she immediately observed to be thin, chic, close to seventy, and who had the exotic name of Camilla Trevelyan de Figueras.

'You must be Laura,' the woman said.

'Mrs Figueras?'

A thin, jewellery-free hand was extended as the door opened wider.

'Camilla, please.'

Laura was expecting a sombre interior to match the mansion's façade, but the entrance hall was airy and white.

She left her suitcase next to a large Chinese urn filled with sturdy umbrellas and silver-handled canes.

'I'm sorry to be late,' she said. 'I took the train to Truro and rented the car there and I'm not used to driving on the left side of the road.'

'It's not the most convenient place to reach I'm afraid.'

'I only arrived in London yesterday and spent the night with Fiona.'

'You must be exhausted.'

'A little.'

They moved into an immense living room.

'You're just in time for tea.'

'That would be great.'

'Or perhaps you'd prefer coffee?'

'Tea would be perfect. Is there some place I might freshen up?'

'There's a powder room there, just under the stairs.'

The stairs in question were wide and grand with an oriental carpet running up the middle, held in place by brass fittings in need of a polish. The powder room was a windowless but cheery space that smelled of mildew and of the large, unused bar of vetiver soap that was resting on a porcelain dish. There were embroidered hand towels, a sink and a mirror, and an old-fashioned water closet with a wooden seat that had a pull-down chain. She confirmed her bloodshot eyes in the mirror and took note of the nail she had chipped trying to get the car's seatbelt to enter properly. Sitting down to pee she applied Visine drops to her eyes and went to work with an emery board. She was still a little woozy from last night's London binge. Fiona's idea of dinner was mostly a liquid affair. They had gone to the Groucho Club where Laura had been unable to get any more useful information about this mysterious interview that Fiona had arranged for her. Looking to her right, she appreciated how the leading edge of a full roll of loo paper had been carefully folded into a triangle.

Back in the ample hallway it took her a bit to find Camilla. They were served a proper tea with scones, jam, and clotted cream in a yellow and white breakfast alcove too brightly lit under a crystal chandelier. To get there they walked through a large library lined with two levels of leather-bound tomes. The round table they sat at faced one of the gardens that was divided by a long reflecting pool edged in boxwood. A stone bench was at the far end of the pool and a wall hiding the garden from the road had an elaborate beehive sitting in a space carved out for it.

'I found some Bed & Breakfasts and made a list,' Laura said. 'I was hoping you might recommend one.'

'Whether I end up hiring you or not,' Camilla replied, 'I've no intention of making you stay at some grim inn. Unless you are opposed to it you shall be my guest. There's no one else here to bother us, except the Irish couple who work for me who are quiet and harmless.'

'That would be great,' Laura said, before promising herself to try and never use the word 'great' again during her stay.

'Splendid.'

She tried to place Camilla's accent. Despite friends from various strata of British society, two years at Oxford as a visiting fellow, and a year lived in London with a beau, Laura was no Henry Higgins and could only, at best, separate the intonations of the rich, well-educated, Tatler crowd, from those of the *vox populi*. In addition to all Fiona had told her she had googled Camilla and knew she was upper class and then some, related to old royalty. But there was something else in her voice, a particular timbre that made it distinctive. It was almost as if she were from another country. Perhaps it was the influence of Spain, for Fiona had mentioned that Camilla, an old family friend, had lived there for many years. Or perhaps it was just a local lilt, a relic from what *olde* English might have sounded like, the sort pronounced by Milton or Tennyson.

'I'm grateful to you for giving me this opportunity.'

'Not at all,' Camilla said finishing her tea, 'despite the affection I have for Fiona, and for her mother especially, I wouldn't have asked you here unless I thought you might be suitable. Your resumé is impressive.'

'Thank you.'

'I'm talking to some other people too. Two gentlemen from Oxford to be precise.'

'Of course,' Laura said, trying to mean it. 'Might I ask who they are?'

'I'd rather not say.'

'It's just that some of my first translations were published there, and it was at Oxford where I became enamoured of thirteenth-century French literature, there and at the Sorbonne. Anyway, it's quite possible I know them.'

'Yes. I know all that. But, even so.'

Laura looked down at the carpet that had a mustard colour with flowery designs and a thick border in royal blue. Camilla continued.

'It seems you're fluent in Italian, Spanish, Hebrew, Arabic, Aramaic, Ancient Greek, Latin, and French, old and new – which I must say is quite extraordinary.'

'That's very kind.'

'My son looked at you online and all of that. You seem extremely competent. Though it appears you no longer actually teach at New York's University.'

Laura felt her heart tighten even as she was amused by Camilla's original way of identifying NYU.

'That's right. I transferred there with the man I live with. He was offered an important position and they gave me a post in my area of expertise to sweeten his deal. But it was a three-year, non-renewable lecture job that finished in May, which is why I'm free at the moment. So, the timing of this, this possible job, is good for me.'

'I see.'

'What sort of document is it you need to have translated? Fiona didn't seem to know much about it.'

'That's because I didn't tell her.'

'Actually, she didn't even know if it was a document.'

'It's something that's been in my family for a very long

6

time. To be honest I'm really not all that sure what it is, what it contains, but I've been told it's very old and possibly very valuable.'

'I'm intrigued. I'd love to see it.'

Camilla looked away, as if distracted. Her hair, dyed a rich auburn shade, was plaited at the back into a single braid. Then she looked at her guest again and found her unusually pretty. Knowing photographs to be deceptive she had worried the girl might look different in person or have one of those overly bouncy personalities characteristic of many Americans. But in addition to her attractive looks she was stylish and seemed refreshingly low-key.

'If you can spare the time,' she said, 'and having come all this way, I'd like to have a day or two before making up my mind, before getting into more detail – if that's all right? We can have a nice bit of supper this evening and get to know each other and take it from there.'

Laura was shown upstairs by Bidelia, the stout, red-cheeked Irish woman who had served them tea. The room that had been prepared for her, located at the far end of the second floor, was large and grand with floor to ceiling windows that took in a view of the Cornish coast. It had grey walls adorned with old family portraits and high, white ceilings festooned with ornate plasterwork. Two armchairs faced a stone hearth she could practically walk under, and a massive canopied four-poster bed aimed at the ocean had a mattress so high off the floor a small set of mahogany stairs was required to access it. Her clothing filled a fraction of the walk-in closet that had a full-length mirror and a built-in bureau with numerous drawers, each containing its own sachet filled with dried lavender. In the adjoining bathroom that also faced the sea, there were two sinks under a vast, time-stained mirror, a cast-iron tub coated in white enamel, and a separate, roomy, multi-spigot shower with a thick glass door.

Enchanted, she permitted herself to relax for the first time that day. Though frustrated by Camilla's withholding tactic, and more certain by the minute that Nathan would prove to be irritatingly accurate in his assessment of this trip, as being useless and a professional folly, she stood by one of the windows and felt generally pleased. Even if it turned out that all she was going to get for her effort were a few nights away from New York, sleeping in this room, it would be worth it.

Trading her boots for a pair of espadrilles she went into the bathroom and filled the tub. A hardly touched bottle of an expensive Italian body wash sat in the bath caddy, and she squeezed some into the steamy water. Then she stripped, and with the lights off so she could watch the boisterous ocean in all its glory, she got in and soaked, savouring the miraculous change of light taking place as the sun sank below the cloud line. Part of her regretted that Nathan was not there to share it with her, and part of her was thrilled to be alone. They had been finding each other increasingly irksome this past year, especially as her lecture position came to an end and it became clear that

New York University was not going to offer her anything else. It was humiliating for her and doubly so because Nathan chose to feel humiliated by it as well, worried it might be a reflection of some diminishing influence on campus after all the fanfare his presence had been regaled with when they first arrived.

Before she got to know him better, she'd been bewitched by him, by his intelligence, his bullish ways, his celebrity connections in the Political Science arena, his occasional appearances on the News Hour and the BBC, and the invitation to join the Council on Foreign Relations. She had been amenable to leave London with him and go to New York where she had the apartment her stepfather had given her, an apartment she loved, an apartment Nathan was more than pleased to move into.

But she had never felt at home within the NYU culture, or with American academia in general. She often had the impression she had arrived on the scene a generation too late. The few remaining stars and rebels in her field had been driven out, and an MLA-approved, buttoned-down, post-structuralist crew had taken their places, politically correct militants whose skill at playing the system drove her mad. Nathan had learned to swim in that world and her criticisms of it had been at the root of many of their fights. When she was not asked to stay on, he all but blamed it on her attitude that, according to him, was out of sync with the academy's current realities. She knew he worried that she had become a liability for him.

On the other hand, living with her provided him with a prized address and, in the beginning at least, a devoted admirer. He loathed the life she had led in London as a single woman, and he hated it whenever she spent time with Fiona or even spoke with her on the phone. He thought the girl frivolous and superficial, which, Laura had to admit, was basically true. Fiona was not the sort of person he wanted his partner to be seen hanging out with. That was the world he had 'saved her' from. That this new, potential job offer had come through Fiona was all he needed to know about it.

Letting the water out but continuing to lie there, she wondered why she was still with Nathan at all. She knew part of it was her own stubbornness, something inherited from her late mother, a refusal to admit defeat and acknowledge that the relationship would end in just the way so many of her friends had predicted. There had been some chemistry between them at first. The age difference, with all of its Oedipal implications duly noted in therapy, plus the difference in professional status, had collaborated to release the appropriate endorphins. But time 'had darkened it'. What had Fiona's sweet gay friend said to her last night? 'Having someone in bed with you every night can be a wonderful thing, but it ain't necessarily love.' 'So, what is love?' she had asked him from the eye of a Grey Goose hurricane. 'It's the thing that grabs you by the heart and won't let you go,' he replied – sincere, corny, and undisputedly true. 'Well, not everyone gets to have that,' she said.

Her parents hadn't. Her mother and stepfather hadn't. None of her friends had either. Who even admitted to wanting such a thing anymore?

Chapter 2

Finn served supper. The tight-lipped husband of Bidelia was tall and lean with an almost invisible comb-over, and he had a pinched but not unfriendly face with a veined, hawkish nose. During the meal – roast chicken with fingerling potatoes and a chilled red wine – Camilla, as promised, avoided any specific mention of what it was she might require Laura's help with. At first, she avoided conversation in general, which made Laura nervous and caused her to talk too much about herself.

'While I studied for my doctorate at Columbia in New York I went out with a poet.' Camilla's forced smile diluted Laura's confidence, but she forged on. 'Much to my mother's chagrin, I moved in with him down in Greenwich Village just before graduating, and after saving for a year we took off for Europe and ended up staying almost three months with my Uncle Manolo – the black sheep of my mother's family who lived like a Bohemian Pasha in the hills outside of Málaga.'

She could see her hostess beginning to fidget with her

napkin, a clear cue for Laura to wrap things up quickly. But lemming-like, she kept on full tilt toward the cliff's edge. 'He had this glorious house, surrounded by lemon trees, that was filled with books and cats and dogs, and he was involved in an explosive *ménage à trois* with two Finnish sisters. There was a constant stream of visitors that ranged from California drug runners to louche Euro types, including a not terribly good painter, gaunt and balding, who was a descendant of the Marquis de Sade.'

She included this last detail hoping it might at least raise one of Camilla's eyebrows, but the woman, displaying the composure of a Zen monk, remained immutable. 'Everyone appreciated Manolo's wine and whiskey and his politically incorrect conversation. And as much as I sometimes like to ignore it, the truth is that he had an important influence on me. Apart from being an outwardly amoral man who hid a Catholic, guilt-ridden core, he was a polemicist of the first order. His specialty was aggressively debunking the most cherished beliefs of true believers, be they political or religious. But he also would become especially obnoxious when anyone began to agree with him – at which point he would instantly change sides just to spite them. Fiona spent some time there with me that summer and loved it. And it was at Manolo's that I began to read, voraciously, tons of literature. He had an amazing library and it was there I picked up the Bible, a lovely old, King James edition.'

This last detail did seem to breathe some life into

Camilla's face. 'I could tell he was pleased that I was taking on such an unlikely book for someone my age, and his way of showing his approval was by taunting me and telling me why the text was corrupt and leagues away from the originals. This, coupled with a trip Saul – the poet – and I made to Paris where I got to see some ancient manuscripts, stayed with me. When we returned to New York we soon split up. He was appalled at my interest in Hebrew, a language that had been an integral part of his nightmare of a childhood. I got my PhD from Columbia and then began studying for a ThD at Harvard where I began seeing a professor who was a curator on leave from the department of Greek and Roman Antiquities at the British Museum. We lived together in London for a time until I had to admit he was essentially gay – but I also realized that areas related to his field fascinated me and I ended up being invited to Oxford as a visiting fellow and then went on to the Sorbonne – like I told you earlier.'

She stopped, out of breath, enveloped in a wave of self-loathing, and reached for her wine, hoping she wasn't blushing. What was that all about? She thought to herself. She would never have done such a thing at a conventional job interview. Then Camilla confirmed her worst suspicions by simply ignoring it.

'Where are you planning on working next?' her hostess asked.

'I've applied to a number of places,' said Laura, 'but I have my own income, a modest trust fund my stepfather set up for me that gives me enough to get by on, so I'm not absolutely desperate.'

She took another sip of wine, a large one.

'And when did you meet Fiona exactly?'

'After her mother got divorced and moved to New York for a while, Fiona went to my high school, a private girl's school called Chapin. We were in the same class. She spent a lot of time doing homework at our apartment that was practically across the street from school.'

'Ah yes. I visited with them once during that time.'

'And then when I lived in London, we became good friends.'

'You mentioned a current beau I believe. I don't mean to be a busybody, but might that relationship be problematical in terms of how much time you could stay here?'

This was the first indication that the unsolicited revelations of her personal life might not be held against her.

'I have a boyfriend, a man I'm with. But that won't be a problem – at all.'

'At all?'

'Let's just say I'm glad to be here, and not there, at the moment.'

'How old are you Laura?'

'Thirty-five.'

'And you've never married?'

'No.'

This line of questioning made her uncomfortable. And

here she had been thinking that Camilla could not have cared less about these kinds of things.

'Why is that?'

'Maybe I'm too much of a romantic?'

'In what sense?'

'I've a notion about the way I'd like to feel with someone before marrying them – and that hasn't happened to me.'

'Yet.'

'Yet. Yes. That's the spirit.'

'And how about children?'

'I don't want to have them enough to have them alone or have one with someone I'm not truly into.'

'No. Quite right. Well I wish I had been more like you. Perhaps I was born a bit too early, or in the wrong ambiance.'

Laura sensed a slight crack opening in the woman's elegant veneer.

'So how did you get to Spain, Camilla? Fiona told me you've spent a lot of time there.'

'I was born there, for one thing.'

'Well, that will do it.'

'I'm sure she's told you all the rest as well. How my mother fell in love, at seventeen, with an Irish boy, Irish-English, and just before he went off to war – World War II – he got her pregnant with me, and before he could do anything honourable about it he got himself killed in Belgium in a V-2 rocket blast.'

'How terrible.'

What she knew from Fiona was that it hadn't been just any Irish-English boy. She admired the woman's style.

'And in those days such things were far more dramatic, socially I mean, than they are now. In any event, my grand-parents shipped my mother off to Mallorca. Have you heard of Robert Graves?'

'Yes, of course.'

'His father knew my grandfather and Graves' house in Mallorca was still empty at the time. Graves had left it with one wife when the Spanish Civil War began and was still some months away from returning there with a new one, and so my mother and an aunt that we all loved rented the house from him and I was born there, with a midwife, like something out of Chaucer; and when Robert and Beryl arrived we got our own place just across from them and lived there throughout much of my childhood. I grew up as a wild child in Deià but surrounded by books, like you at your uncle Manolo's, and Graves took an interest in my education and so all of that went rather well.'

'I would imagine so!' Laura was floored.

'And then I went to university at Cambridge. But I met a man one summer near Cádiz, a Catalan on vacation who seemed a good enough sort, and we married – I was eager to escape my mother's orbit really. He and I lived in Barcelona mostly, where my children were born, my son, and then a daughter who died when she was still very little. After that happened, I began to spend more time here.'

'I'm sorry to hear that.'

'That I began to spend more time here?'

'No. Oh no. About your daughter I mean.'

'It was ... very sad.'

Camilla looked away and it was clear to Laura that a change in the conversation was called for.

'My mother's story was a bit similar to yours.'

'How so?'

'She came from a very conservative family, from Granada, Spain. Her father was a super-Catholic Franco supporter and an important professor at the medical faculty where my mother also studied. But she made a point of falling for a fellow student who was from Palestine. She did it just to spite her parents. I mean she told me as much. She even converted to Islam, married him in a mosque, and after they got their degrees, moved with him to Hebron on the West Bank, where I was born.'

'I'd no idea. I thought you came from New York.'

'It's a long story. Well, not that long.'

'Proceed.'

'In Hebron she discovered that her in-laws were even more conservative than her own family. "I told you it would be like this," my father apparently said to her. "We should have remained in Spain. Married to you I could have become a citizen and practiced there. We could have had a good life there. We still can." But my mother could not bear to admit to failure, or to face her family, so she divorced my father, took me, and moved to Madrid. She got work there as a gynaecologist in a doctor's suite that catered to Americans, which is how she met my stepfather, a State Department official attached to the Embassy. He came from a waspy, wealthy, New York, New England family. When his stint was over, he asked my mother to marry him. She said yes, became a Presbyterian of course, and we moved to Manhattan. I took my stepfather's last name. When my mother died, suddenly, fifteen years ago, she was buried in the Protestant cemetery in Southampton, Long Island, far from the Roman Catholic *campo santo* behind the Alhambra where her parents, my grandparents, are interred.'

'That's quite the tale. And yes, I do see the similarities. What became of your father?'

'He died when I was little, after we'd left Palestine.'

'Oh dear.'

'He was hit with a stray bullet during the first intifada while trying to help someone who'd been injured.'

Camilla was about to say something, but then Bidelia came in to clear the dinner plates and right after that Finn served dessert and replenished the wine. By the time they were alone again the moment had passed.

After they said goodnight Laura went outside for a walk. A damp sea breeze moistened her face. She liked the gentle crunching sound her boots made on the gravel. The Land Rover and her rented car were covered with night dew and sat snugly by a large hedge that grew flush to a brick wall. All of the talk about her family and past had left her agitated. Though once upon a time she had thought to recover her father's last name – Hourani – she rarely spoke or thought about him. That side of her gene pool only came up at dinner parties when Nathan liked to brag about that part of her heritage as a way of bolstering his own cultural cred. She had a craving for a cigarette and rummaged around in her bag for some gum to stave it off. She felt particularly virtuous resisting the temptation without Nathan there to scold her.

Venturing out past the gates onto the road, it was very dark. It was difficult to make out the low bulwark of irregular stones on the narrow lane's far side that marked the border of a scruffy field where, when arriving that afternoon, she had noticed sheep grazing. The field sloped down and ended in dunes, beach and sea. The sound of the waves breaking was exhilarating. Her phone rang. She had forgotten to turn the ringer off before dinner and thanked the stars it had not blared its rap-song ringtone during the meal. It was Nathan. She hesitated to take it, but then she gritted her teeth and did.

By that time, Camilla had changed into a flannel nightgown – not worn since the previous winter – and got into her gondola-shaped, Renaissance-era bed where, as she sometimes commented, 'Two kings had been born and where, no doubt, all manner of rakish activity had been indulged in.' She was pleased with how the evening had gone, and generally pleased with Laura. The idea of having to interview two Oxford professors had never thrilled her. Putting up with a strange man wandering about the property in tweeds with a pipe and bad teeth was not something she thought she could stand for very long.

And she congratulated herself once again for the decision to have the codices properly translated before alerting Sotheby's. Though the scroll remnants and the codices had been handed down within her mother's family for close to a thousand years, lost sometimes for over a century before being recovered, only to be lost and recovered again, she felt no emotional connection to them. If it had been a painting or a house, a piece of jewellery even, she might have felt differently. But a trio of objects so foreign and inscrutable did little to warm her heart. She was only grateful for their existence and grateful to her disaster of a mother who remembered where they were just before the Alzheimer's had done her in. With any luck their sale might avail her of a proper nest egg for her son and his girls – just in case.

Turning off her reading light she lay in the dark and thought about her mother who had slept, had affairs, and died in that same bed. She remembered coming into that room many times not all that long ago, or so it seemed, to say goodnight, and how more often than not her mother was inebriated, her face covered in night creams. Her mother, who had never tired of complaining of how Camilla was the first woman in the family's history not to marry into a fortune. Complaining incessantly about how Camilla had run off with a member of Spain's middle class instead, an attractive but provincial businessman without a title. Whenever Camilla had countered with the observation that her mother had never married at all, she would then watch her take another sip of wine before saying, 'But your father my dear was the Viscount Elveden, Arthur Onslow Edward Trevelyan, who would have been a millionaire many times over, and if you had been a boy instead of a silly girl your paternal grandfather would have taken more of an interest and bequeathed us a lot more hush money than he did.'

Chapter 3

L aura came down for breakfast just before eight thirty and was told by Bidelia that Camilla had already eaten and left for a good part of the day to attend to a horse. Laura wondered if it was something her hostess had already planned and chose not to mention the night before.

'I didn't know she had a horse.'

'Oh yes, Miss. There's a stable full of them out back. One of the girls came in this morning to tell her about the one that's ill and they loaded the creature into a trailer and off they went. She told me to apologise for her.'

'No matter,' Laura said. 'What time does she normally take breakfast, Bidelia?'

'Seven if it's in her room, seven thirty if she comes down here, miss.'

And yet she had encouraged Laura to sleep as late as she wished. Might this have been some sort of test she failed?

Two perfectly boiled eggs with soldiers and a cup of Irish breakfast tea settled her. She decided to try and relax and enjoy herself, if only to contradict Nathan's certainty last night that she was wasting her time, that she should be attending conferences and looking to publish if she was serious about her career. 'You'll see,' he said. 'She'll string you along for a few days, positive that she is in possession of some unique treasure – keeping you captive there at Wuthering Heights – and in the end it will be, at best, some bad poetry from medieval France.' There was always the unstated implication in much of his criticism that she was somehow lazy, that she lacked the necessary discipline, or fire in the belly, that she was *en fin*, a spoiled girl too easily put off by the sort of demands that real academics, like himself of course, took in their stride. He called her from the apartment on West Tenth Street where once again he had forgotten to water the plants on the terrace and he actually had the gall to get angry with her when she gently chided him about it.

She browsed in the library and thought to call Fiona who would be eager to hear Laura's first impressions, but she knew Fiona would not be up for hours. She sent her a text message instead:

Camilla gone for the day! Amazing estate – going out for a hike – seeking Poldark.

But rather than go out just yet she went back to her room to brush her teeth and retrieve the book she was reading. Then she explored the house, peeking into each of the twelve immense bedrooms, including Camilla's with its bizarre, boat-shaped bed that she found a bit kitsch.

Downstairs she settled into a cavernous and comfortable sofa in the formally appointed living room, the sort found in many grand houses that were rarely used. She looked at a family photo album there, large and brown with sheets of onionskin paper between the pages. Though she saw no hints of royalty, the pictures depicted a century of family life lived, physically at least, in a state of grace. Large lunch tables under trees and grapevines in what was surely Mallorca, with Robert Graves presiding, a teenaged and vivacious Camilla sitting next to a woman who was certainly her mother – a woman with an arresting aristocratic head but thick wrists and hands that Camilla had been fortunate enough not to inherit. Patio life at a villa on what looked to be Lake Como. Riding and hunting parties there on the Cornwall estate – a lot of fly-fishing – a young, dark-haired boy, probably Camilla's son, being offered a taste from a silver flask as two older men stood by grinning. Pictures of Camilla with a little girl, probably the one who had died.

She fell asleep reading, woke an hour later and went for a long walk. The weather had been calm and sunny early in the morning, but clouds were rolling in from the sea by then and once again a brisk wind blew. The countryside along the road to the mansion was magnificent and had nothing to do with the moors of Wuthering Heights. It was all hillocks and green pastures, fast-running streams, stands of trees broken by gentle glades, and then the beach and the cliffs curving their way north. She wandered about wide expanses of grassland and heather, resting now and then on boulders of granite. Arriving at the edge of a marshy valley, she looked down into it and saw stands of gnarly, ancient, oak trees. Stonechat and Wheatear songbirds accompanied her, and near the sea cliffs gulls rose on currents of air without having to flap their wings.

By noon she was starving but too embarrassed to ask the Irish couple for anything, so she took the car and drove to the nearest village, bought some newspapers, and had a glass of beer and a Croque Monsieur at a gastro-pub. By and large the townspeople were doughy and white and reserved with her, but she was still glad to be there. The sudden break from New York continued to feel invigorating and before returning there she would be able to give London its due, shopping and seeing old friends.

When she got back into the car, she called and reached Fiona.

'I told you she was a bit mad,' Fiona said, laughing. 'But Mother loves her; says she can be a lot of fun once you get to know her.'

'Fun?'

'Not in a social way. She's a bit of a hermit, I think. But in a quirky way.'

'I just wish she would get to the point.'

'You just arrived. It's gorgeous, no?'

'Oh my God.'

'A bit lonely I expect.'

'Lonely is not so bad after the last five months with Nathan.'

'Lose him. Do yourself a favour.'

'You mean do you a favour.'

'Do us both a favour. It would be nice to have you around without a jailer.'

Laura was reluctant to go on arguing about Nathan because it often had the effect of drawing her closer to him.

Jet lag and the beer got the best of her and she was sound asleep when Camilla returned that afternoon, something she feared might put another check mark into the negative column. But Camilla showed no signs of disapproval and they had a pleasant drink before dinner during which Laura learned all about Camilla's passion for horses.

That night it was a rack of lamb, cream of spinach and mashed potatoes, with a twenty-year-old Burgundy of the sort that Nathan would never allow her to order even if she were paying.

'You mentioned that you have a ThD,' Camilla said at dinner. 'What is that exactly?'

'It's the equivalent of a doctorate degree, but in theology.'

'So, you must be religious.'

'Not really, no.'

'You've no spiritual feelings?'

'Yes and no.' She wanted to tread carefully here. 'I understand, in general terms, how religions came about. I mean it's one of my fields of study. And I can sympathize with why people seek comfort in them, and I find many religious paintings and texts extraordinarily beautiful. I adore churches and temples and mosques, just sitting in them, for the peace they offer, but I also find it ... well, curious, in an age when we know so much, to see religion still having such a powerful sway in so many parts of the world. It astonishes me really.'

'You don't believe in any sort of deity.'

Laura decided to throw caution to the wind.

'How could one really?'

Camilla smiled, a real one this time. 'I appreciate your honesty.'

'Did I just give the wrong answer? I don't mean to be disrespectful to anyone.'

'No. I quite understand your point of view. What I may believe, or wish to believe, is probably determined by my background.'

'Growing up with Robert Graves surely exposed you to all the great mythologies, no?'

'More than I could count.'

'I devoured *The Golden Bough* in college.'

'I'm glad to hear it,' Camilla said.

They finished their wine.

'I find most people's religious beliefs come from a very emotional place,' Laura went on, 'and that they're cultural, and that people really don't spend all that much time thinking about what it is that they profess to believe in.'

'So, I suppose it's science you believe in then?'

'I don't believe *in* it; I mean I guess what I "believe in" might be the scientific method.'

'But many of the texts you've translated have been religious in nature, no?'

'It is paradoxical, I admit. But what I love most about what I do is the uncovering, bringing back human thoughts written down in code, as it were, deciphering actual feelings that were put down and then lost.'

Camilla refreshed their glasses without waiting for Finn.

'Have you ever signed a confidentiality agreement?'

That seemed to come out of nowhere.

'Once before, yes.'

'Good.'

'Why? Is that going to be necessary?'

'I'm afraid so. But it would be just a formality. Well – tomorrow we can continue.'

Camilla rang a small bell by her plate and rose from the table. Laura followed suit.

'Can you just tell me one thing?' Laura asked, almost biting her tongue.

'Yes?'

'Where did the ... whatever it is, originate?'

'I'm not entirely sure,' Camilla said, stealing a glance at herself in a mirror. 'I'm hoping that's something that can be deduced. I mean I know the story I've been told over the years. But the amazing thing is that no one in my family, myself included, ever had the curiosity to try and find out for sure.'

Chapter 4

Though she could have slept til noon, Laura made a point of appearing at the breakfast table at seven thirty sharp. Camilla came in a minute later, greeted her, and placed a folder next to Laura's plate. It was the NDA.

'If you could read and sign it, I am prepared to offer you the position.'

'Really? What about the Oxford professors?'

'I spoke with my son last night and we both agreed we'd rather go with you. To be perfectly frank, I'm not terribly good at this sort of thing and the idea of having to meet two more candidates, perfect strangers, is beyond me.'

It was not the most ringing endorsement, but Laura took it. She began to peruse the document.

'You should read it carefully,' Camilla said.

She did and saw nothing she had not seen before; she made sure there was a provision allowing her to publish her findings once a possible auction had gone through. She signed it with the pen she had been using to solve a crossword.

'There you are,' she said, handing it to Camilla.

'Splendid. Oh, and we have to speak of terms, of remu-neration.'

'All right.'

'What do you normally earn, say over the course of a year?'

'Hard to say, maybe, oh, like sixty-five thousand dollars – for a full year.'

'I'm willing to pay you the equivalent in pounds of a hundred thousand dollars for as long as it takes you, which shouldn't be more than a month or so I imagine, and with the option to renegotiate if it goes on too long. How does that seem?'

'Very generous,' Laura replied, even though the word 'extremely' was what came to mind. It would be what Nathan made for a full year.

'Good.'

'I have to say, I thought I was failing the audition.'

'Why?'

'Insecurity I suppose – not about my competency – but about selling myself. I hate doing it and I'm not any good at it. And then the fact I've come to you through a friend rather than through more official channels. That sort of thing.'

'For me, that is just a pleasant coincidence,' Camilla said. 'We shall see of course, but my general impression is that you'll do a perfectly good job of it.'

As Laura tried to conceal her glee at the rate just agreed

upon, Camilla poured herself more tea and looked out at the garden, one she had been contemplating all her life. She felt a sudden pang for the only house she considered to be truly her own, far away from the windy sea down the hill: her hideaway in the pines of Mallorca. Laura felt another craving for a cigarette, so she helped herself to an additional piece of toast. Camilla rang the bell again and stood up.

'Shall we have a look?'

'By all means.'

They made their way into the library. Camilla went up to a section of shelving at shoulder level and removed an end volume. 'You'll find this amusing – straight from the movies.' She reached her hand into the shelving and Laura heard a distinct click. Then Camilla pushed against the shelves and the whole section became a door that opened inwards. 'Voila.'

'Amazing.'

'I've been coming to this house since I was six and only found out about this five years ago. This part of the house dates from the sixteenth century. These secret spaces were originally made for priests to have a place to say mass during the reign of Queen Elizabeth.'

'A priest hole,' Laura said.

'Exactly. Many of the passageways were sealed when they put in central heating between the wars, but this chamber proved to be an ideal place to hide the family treasure apparently.'

She flipped a light switch. The room was square-shaped, fifteen feet wide by fifteen long, the floor carpeted, wall to wall. On a wooden side table there was some electrical monitoring equipment, some of it with a dated look featuring dials and indicator needles, some of it more recent and digital. In the middle of the room stood a large, glass display case containing the remains of an ancient scroll and a pair of leather-bound codices.

'Oh my goodness,' was all Laura could think to say.

They approached the case and stared into it.

'Let me turn off the alarm,' Camilla said, moving to the side table and punching a code into a keypad. Then she retrieved two pairs of sterile latex gloves from a dispenser full of them. 'The case is kept as free from humidity as possible.'

Laura just kept staring. Even as she took her set of gloves and put them on, she could not tear her gaze away.

'Do you have any idea how old they are?'

'My son James looked into that for me. I gave him samples of the parchment, of the papyrus and the vellums and he took them to a place called the Oxford Radiocarbon Accelerator Unit, who were most thorough about it.'

'What did they say?'

'Approximately 60 CE for the scroll, around 390 CE for the older codex and 1285 or so for this one that's written in old French.'

'Really!'

Camilla carefully removed the top of the display case.

She reached down and untied satin ribbons dyed a Lenten purple hue that had been added a century earlier to hold the leather cover of the codices in place. Then she removed the cover and put it gently to the side, away from the scroll, revealing to their eyes the top sheet of vellum parchment and its sea of ancient French. There were no illustrations, just script.

'This is very exciting.'

'I'm glad you think so.'

'Do you have any idea what they are?'

'The only thing my mother told me,' she said, pointing, 'was that a great-great-great-grandmother of ours, who was French, tried to make sense of this one and declared it to be "a sea yarn," as she called it. But that was the most she could glean from it.'

The older codex was written in ancient Greek. From the small scraps available to her and without doing any further damage to the scroll that was in a sorry state, Laura could see that it was written in Aramaic. Camilla gave her the alarm code and left her to it. After doing an intensive comparison that took up the rest of her morning, she determined that the Greek codex was probably a faithful translation of the Aramaic scroll. But the old French codex, copied from the Greek, had introduced some changes. This being the case, she decided to first translate the Greek codex, the carbon date of which placed it in the same year that, upon the decree of Theodosius, the Serapeum library was destroyed in Alexandria. Might it have come from there? And if so, how had it happened that these three versions of the same text came to rest in Cornwall? It boggled her mind.

Chapter 5

Laura translated the opening pages from the ancient Greek codex in the following manner:

In light of my advanced years, the pains in my heart, and of what befell my nephew in Jerusalem, I feel compelled to put an end to the rumours his death has given birth to. My scribe shall put down here what I know. Word has reached me that the Mashiah story runs like fire through dry brush, argued by the Pharisees in the Sanhedrin. Perhaps the tale shall fade as time progresses and be cast into the pit of superstition where it belongs, these Mashiah dreams that keep men from watching the sun set in peace, that keep men in caves of ignorance.

I failed, in the end, to persuade Yeshua to keep hold of the simple beauty of flesh and blood. After his wife and their two children passed away, he returned to Jerusalem, to resume his earlier dream of being a teacher. He left behind the young life of his one remaining son. I have forgiven him, concluding he was mad with grief.

His was a good and loving soul, who turned away from the world I offered him with its pleasures and woes, and returned to the darker world of superstition, sin, and suffering. I am told his followers claim he came back to life after his execution, and that he rose into the heavens. They say he was divine, that he was the son of God. But I know what I know, and I have seen too many men die vile deaths and seen what becomes of their bodies, the very same thing that happens to beasts and fowl. Therefore, I shall make this testament, and tell of things that I have lived, and do my best to celebrate my nephew's humanity.

Laura was riveted. Excitement pumped through her heart; excitement mixed with deep suspicion. She was tempted to call an expert she knew and ask some key questions. But given the restraints of her agreement, she would have to put that off. What was clear to her already was that, even if the content of the texts was false, her career in the field, simply based on what she had before her, on how old the texts were, would be guaranteed. The three documents resting in the glass display case would merit decades of study, all over the world.

Unable to resist translating the next section she skipped lunch and continued working through the whole day.

My niece, Miryam, invited me to her home. She was the fairest of three sisters and the one who had displeased her mother and my brother by marrying a simple joiner. Yeshua was her eldest son and she was fraught with concern for him. She said to me 'We are pained for he continues to argue with the Sadducees and the Pharisees of the temple. He tells us he is a prophet. When he finishes working with his father each day, he studies the books of the Tanakh, and since the first signs of manliness have settled upon him, he shows scant interest in any of the maidens who live nearby.'

I sat down next to her and said to her, 'Is he negligent in his work with Yosef?' 'No,' she said. 'And does he argue well with the Sadducees and the Pharisees at the temple?' 'Yes,' she said. 'And does he learn the texts of the Tanakh?' 'Yes,' she said. 'And does he show interest in other young men?'

'No!' she said, putting a hand to her mouth.

'Then you are graced,' I said to her.

She went for a pitcher of water and poured me a cup and said to me, 'Though we be graced we fear for him, for already the Pharisees and their Rabbis speak of him.' And I smiled at her and rested my hand on her simple cloak and said, 'The story you and Yosef often told of the three foreigners who rested in that stable when you fled the dictum of Herod, and of the star that shone so brightly, and the lambs that lay about you on the night Yeshua was born, has brought this upon you.'

'Do not be cruel with me,' she said. And I said to her, 'I only wish to see you smile as you did before you

became a mother and a joiner's wife.' 'It is too late for that,' she said, and as she said it, I hoped it was not so, for she was still fair and beguiling, and little changed from when she had been a maiden. 'What would you have me do?' I asked her, already knowing her response, for her husband had visited me and told me of their wishes. 'We would ask that you take him with you when you next set forth for the Cassiterite Isles, so that he might see more of the larger world for a time and less of this one.'

Chapter 6

When she was able to calm down and accept the probability that the texts were apocryphal, the last thing she did before resetting the alarm and closing the chamber was to meticulously photograph each fragile sheet of both codices and the available scraps of Aramaic written on the disintegrating papyrus scroll. Then she copied the photographs onto her laptop before erasing them from her phone for security's sake. Working from the photographs, she would not have to risk damaging the originals any further. She went upstairs, took a bath and, before coming down to dinner, sent a brief email to Fiona, simply saying that she had been offered and had accepted the job.

That evening's meal was a shrimp cocktail, filet of *sole meunière* with rice, and a bottle of white wine.

'It's a Pouilly Fumé, La Doucette; it was my mother's favourite for everyday use.'

Laura took a sip. 'It's wonderful,' she said, even though she found the taste a bit too acidic.

'What, if anything, have you been able to discover?'

Camilla asked, as Finn stood by holding the bottle for all to see.

Laura shared only some of what she had gleaned.

'So, they are three versions of the same text,' Camilla said.

'I'm almost certain.'

'But the most recent one, the one in French, is altered for some reason?'

'That's how it seems at the moment.'

'And you understand what you are reading. I mean, do you think you can translate them?'

'Yes, I do. I can translate the codices. The scroll requires a level of professional care and scrutiny beyond our resources here. But I can supervise that when the time comes.'

'Splendid. And, do you suppose they might be as valuable as my mother seemed to think?'

'Regardless of what they contain,' Laura said, 'they have great value just as objects. I've never heard of a text available in three different periods of antiquity gathered together in one place. And if it turns out that the subject of the text or its author have significance, well the value would increase significantly.'

'I suppose it's too early to know anything about that.'

'It is,' said Laura, and because she could not be certain of the author's true identity yet, she did not feel she was lying. 'But I'll get there. You mentioned last night that you'd been told 'a story' of how they came to be here. Could you tell me what you know? The whole issue of provenance will end up being important.'

'Like I've said, they've been in our family for a very long time.'

'Fiona told me, in passing, that you were related to royalty in some way.'

'On my mother's side, we're descended from Plantagenets, Henry II, Eleanor of Aquitaine and all of that, Richard the Lionheart, King John and the Magna Carta.'

'I see.'

'The official language at court in those days, as you probably know, was French. Do you know anything about Edward I?'

'Nothing springs to mind at the moment.'

'He was the eldest son of Henry III – very tall, severe, all in all considered to be a good king for England. His mother was French, Eleanor of Provence, which is how this house got its name. Edward brought Wales into the realm, mostly by force of arms, did much legal reform and reinforced the legitimacy of Parliament. He also spilled much blood and coin waging a brutal war with Scotland. But before all that, when he was still a young prince – and I am simplifying things considerably – in order to resolve a problem that arose between Henry III and the King of Spain, he married the King of Spain's daughter, Eleanor of Castile. She was thirteen and Edward was fifteen.'

'It's extraordinary how common that was back then,' Laura said.

'As you know, such marriages were about property and propagation and not at all about affection,' said Camilla, continuing. 'The English royal family, even then, was a randy bunch, and keeping a bevy of mistresses about was *comme il faut*. But the marriage between these two blossomed, and it quickly turned into a real love match. It apparently remained that way until Eleanor, who was known for her love of culture and literature, and who kept many scribes employed, died when she was forty-nine years old. Edward was beside himself with grief, and though he remarried, again for political reasons, he never got over her.'

'And she was Spanish.'

'Her father was the Spanish king, her mother, like Edward's was French, Joan, Countess of Ponthieu. When my mother told me where the documents were hidden – for up to that point I had just considered it all to be a family legend – she also said that it was Eleanor of Castile who had acquired them, and who left them to her descendants, along with many other things. Luckily for us, this particular part of her personal fortune stayed together, and was passed down generation after generation, while most of the rest of it was squandered.'

Though she would check the history being thrown her way, on the face of it the story seemed to hold together. Even so, Laura held on to some healthy scepticism.

'Is there any particular reason you've waited until now to look into it?'

'My mother's father told her that if she were ever to find herself in financial straits, selling these things might solve the problem. She said it had almost come to that for her on more than a few occasions but she was lazy and unorganized – characteristics that run in the family – and she never got around to it. But I would like to have some extra funds now.'

Camilla finished her shrimp and rang for Finn to return.

'If you're in that kind of difficulty,' said Laura, 'perhaps you are paying me too much.'

'Not at all. I have done a budget and that is what I have allotted for your position. I am going to need your absolute attention and your absolute discretion, so I mean to make it worth your while.'

'All right.' Laura said, relieved. 'It's astonishing to me that something so rare and unusual could be kept out of view all this time.'

'It's probably not that unusual.'

Finn entered the room keeping his hands behind his back.

'If you knew more about my family,' Camilla went on with a slight smile, 'it would be easier for you to grasp – their tradition of proud and aggressive absent-mindedness, their uber-British, self-destructive snobbery. Anyway. That is neither here nor there. The important thing now is that the documents will, I hope, speak for themselves.'

Chapter 7

The following morning Laura translated the next segment:

What I valued most in those years was independence, the freedom from having to explain my movements, my whims, or the company I kept. The idea of having any person along on my travels was irksome, having a youth with me for whom I would be responsible was worse still, but that the youth in question be difficult and judgmental, felt especially odious and put me into a sour temper.

On the morning of our departure he embraced his parents and three younger siblings. His father wept, but neither he nor his mother did. The little ones looked at us as if for the last time. Given the perils that often occur on these lengthy journeys, they may well have been right.

We travelled on tall, well-shod mules, with a line of smaller but stronger pack mules behind us bearing casks filled with coins, provisions, extra clothing, and the oils I traded for tin. Two guards accompanied us, men I had done business with for many years. They were Roman soldiers on leave, one an aristocrat and former Dux, the other a fierce legionnaire, two men who had formed an unusual friendship given their respective ranks, both of them enamoured of the region and fearsome with their swords. They rode before us on handsome Arabian steeds.

A plague had taken hold in Acre, so we set out for the port of Tyre. When the Roman road ended and a rockier, unpaved route began, we had to leave the mules and the horses and arrange to travel by camel in caravan. The caravan merchant I normally paid was not to be found. I was forced to haggle with a group of other caravan leaders. All of them were related and the level of argument and rivalry flowing between them, speaking a tongue unknown to me, was exasperating. My Roman guards smirked and waited, indifferent under the shade of a date palm. My nephew, who up until that day had been silent and uncooperative, suddenly spoke to me in a whisper. 'They are trying to cheat you,' he said. 'What you call cheating, they call business,' I replied. 'The one on the left, the one who is missing an eye, he is ashamed of the others and is telling them to be more reasonable,' he said. 'Do you pretend to understand them?' I asked. 'Yes,' he said. 'It is a local dialect my father's woodcutter uses. How much do you usually pay them?' I told him the price and he said to me. 'The lowest number I have heard thus far is twice that. How was the man called? The one you are used to dealing with?' And I told him that as well, and he went over to the man with one eye and began to speak quietly to him. The others at first grew more furious until Yeshua turned to them and yelled back at them in their own tongue. Some of them looked to be chastened, some of them angrier still, but their furore diminished. He then resumed his dialog with the more reasonable one until they each put their hand upon their breast and lowered their heads. Then he came back to me. 'He will take us for the usual price.'

I am certain he did not speak with the camel drivers that day in order to help me. He spoke, I believe, to show me his intelligence and guile, in a manner many youths his age would, youths who strut about like cockerels preening before a clutch of hens. Nevertheless, after that day, things began to improve between us.

Chapter 8

Laura spent most of the next day working and reworking the first two instalments, trying to achieve a prose style that was not too literal, but not too contemporary either. In bed in the dark that night, over-excited and anxious for sleep to relieve her, she made a note to herself to work on them yet again, to get it right, to avoid the evangelist tones popular since St Jerome's thirteenth-century *versio vulgata*, or the lush, Jacobean, Tyndale-influenced prose style of the 1611 King James edition of the Bible. Once again, a whirlpool of fantasies spun within her brain, immediately followed by heart-stabbing worries tinged with paranoia. If the scroll and the codices were authentic, she would undoubtedly become famous. The story was being told by Josephus of Ha'Ramath, meaning Josephus 'of a high place or plateau', the Hebrew version of Arimathea. Joseph of Arimathea was the uncle of Ieēsous, the Greek form of the Hebrew name Yeshua, more commonly known as Jesus Christ.

She thought it curious that, at the time this was written,

which must have been around 60 CE, Joseph of Arimathea would have felt the need to set the record straight as he saw it. The Christian religion hardly existed then. Although there were some people taking Jesus' story forward, it was still pretty much unknown, and the parts that were known were varied and conflicting. The more controversial Christian beliefs didn't come about for another fifty to 200 years, which is what led to the Council of Nicaea in 325 AD. But here it was in front of her. The carbon dating procedure done at Oxford was surely accurate. Once revealed, news of it would capture headlines around the world. What would that be like? And what if it turned out to be false? Which was more than likely the more she thought about it.

She heard a train whistle in the distance and imagined a line of freight cars moving along the outskirts of some mill town miles away. She pictured the engineer unshaven and awake, peering ahead, a lit cigarette in the hand that rested on the throttle. And she saw the iron wheels turning on rusty rails flanked by sentinel weeds and broken brush. It was a sound that, coming as it did through sea-moistened air, reminded her of her youth, in bed at night, cosy in her room at her stepfather's summer house on Great Plains Road in Southampton, where she had sometimes awakened to hear the milk train from Penn Station carrying the morning papers to East Hampton and Montauk.

She drew a sensorial connection between Camilla's baronial home in Cornwall and her stepfather's house within the Cuddihy compound on Long Island; the rich scents of wood resin in the hallway, the civilized dampness, the appealing contrast of the good linens and furniture kept within, the semi-agricultural seascapes without, and how the main bedrooms faced the ocean. She imagined the Southampton house across the Atlantic at that very moment, five hours earlier along the Earth's curve, uninhabited, closed up for the season, with some of her mother's clothing still folded in dark drawers, musty raingear and tennis racquets in the entranceway closet; the old TV set in the maid's living room where she had watched cheesy American sitcoms with Pat and Clara, the couple her mother had found on Martha's Vineyard. The bedroom that had been hers was upstairs facing the ocean, like this one, where as a girl and then as a teenager she had slept all those summer nights protected, a Chinese red bureau against the far wall, the dainty mirrored wall sconces at either side of her bed.

She thought about her mother, who after her conversion to Islam and her embracement of the Palestinian cause, had – once she fell in with Gerald Cuddihy II – converted just as fiercely to the Protestant faith, and sworn solidarity with the State of Israel as well. Such had been her determination to distinguish herself from her Spanish parents who had kept a photo of Francisco Franco in their living room. She remembered those grandparents, the gloomy trips she and her mother made once a year to visit them in Granada for Christmas. Despite their rigid morals, ugly politics, and the tension in the air between them and her mother, they had been kind to her and loving.

By dawn she had the library bookshelf open, the security system disarmed, and she was back at work. As Camilla had said, the scroll was in a lamentable and more than understandable state of decay. Placing a towel upon the side table, she unfurled the scroll just enough to see a further section of script. She wanted to verify one more time that the two texts were the same. She did this a few times, scanning from place to place.

She had never handled anything so old or fragile and at one point she removed one of the latex gloves and touched the papyrus with her bare finger. It was not the same as touching old rocks or peering into a prehistoric cave. This was an artefact of distinct and miraculous human ingenuity. Living hands had harvested the plant and prepared it for writing. Human hands had made the ink and honed the reed pens. Human hands had written down the symbols while listening to another man speak, recording his thoughts, observations, and emotions.

She saw enough to satisfy her that it was indeed the same text that had been later translated into Ancient Greek. It had the same voice, the same tone. It was shockingly distinctive, not the sort of verse found in the Old Testament, nor the poetic cadences found in the Psalms, nor the disembodied meter authored by the evangelists hundreds of years after the fact. It was freer than that, conversational and personal, more akin to the tone found in the letters of Paul. She decided to share her thoughts with Camilla. To sit on them any longer would not be ethical.

'Something to do with Christ you say?'

'Quite a lot to do with Christ. It's hard to believe.'

'So it might be very valuable.'

'Very. Not to mention sensational. Which probably explains why the codex in old French was altered. Whoever did it censored it some, or was told to. But it is still difficult to figure out why these texts never saw the light of day, as far as I know.'

'You are asking the wrong person,' Camilla said. 'I've no idea. Maybe because not many people knew how to read back then? Perhaps by the time reading and scholarship were more common, these artefacts were already put away somewhere, out of circulation.'

'I'd like to see the carbon dating study done at Oxford.'

'I'll show it to you this afternoon.'

'We should get a second opinion too.'

'James was most thorough about it, and it did cost a small fortune to have it done properly.'

'I'm sure. It's just that the level of scrutiny this will receive once word gets out is going to be intense.'

'All right,' Camilla said.

'Remember what happened to your Robert Graves with his translation of the *Rubaiyat of Omar Khayyam* in 1967 – based on a manuscript the Shah brothers claimed had been in their family for 800 years and that later turned out to have been a forgery.'

'Good lord. This is the first I've heard about that.'

'It was a terrible blow to his reputation for a while. It probably wasn't talked about much around the dinner table.'

'I'll show you the report James had done, and you can see if you think we need a second opinion. But I don't want you to worry about that now Laura. Just work on the translation, doing the best job you can. Let's see what we really have, no?'

'I will. You're right.'

The technical report was lengthy, detailed, and reassuring. It calmed Laura's nerves, giving her the necessary peace of mind to continue translating. She employed a stop and go rhythm that seemed to produce the best results. She set herself up in a corner of the library near the breakfast alcove where there was more natural light and sat at a Louis XV Tric-Trac game table that had a chessboard inlaid into the surface. It seemed appropriate for the task. She put the photos into a desk file on her laptop that she labelled 'Fall Project', and then began to translate the next segment.

Chapter 9

We travelled through a desert-like terrain. Its effect upon Yeshua was powerful. Its austerity, its cleanliness, the sensation it imparts to one of insignificance, most especially at night when the sun that has been relentlessly searing disappears, giving way to a cold and empty darkness and when the stars and their constellations seem perilously close.

His state of rapturous wonder and continuous pronouncements about God irritated me. I felt closer to my sardonic Romans who only referred to their gods when cursing, or when marvelling about the pleasures of flesh or food. For them that terrain was an infernal nuisance that made them wary of scorpions, a geographical aberration to be traversed as quickly as possible. Whenever my nephew would remark 'Heavenly Father, what feat hast Thou wrought to lower the stars so close to we your minions?' I would say to him, 'What brand of arrogance is it to think your heavenly father is paying us any mind at all?'

And when he would remark, 'Look upon the mountains and the craters of the moon, uncle, seen so clearly on this night, where surely souls shall gather to rest, as if at an oasis, upon their way home to our Heavenly Lord.'

I, who had more in common then with the Sadducees who do not believe in an afterlife, would say to him, 'It seems to me, dear nephew, that the moon is cold and empty. One has only to regard the expression of melancholy on its face. Woe be the soul inclined to rest there.'

But he travelled well, and he did not complain, and it seemed he confined his urge for teaching mostly to me. No doubt he had learned from his mother the fame I had in the Sanhedrin as a doubter, a man more concerned with profits and earthly welfare, someone who chafed at the religious rules that pushed too far into a man's life.

Apart from the one-eyed Bedouin whose company he enjoyed, he took to speaking with my Roman guards as well, and when I made light of it, he said to me, 'Love thine enemy.' 'This is a new opinion,' I said to him, 'but an easy one for someone who has yet to face a sword. What do the men in your temple answer to such a proclamation?'

'An eye for an eye, and a tooth for tooth is what they say,' he answered. The mixture of youthful gentleness and brashness was not without its appeal.

When I was younger than he and already trading

with my father, we were set upon by thieves one night. They slit his throat before I was able to do anything. My cries roused our servants and made the thieves flee, and seeing my father dead I pursued them and captured one who was broader and slower, and I dug my knife into his back until he too was dead, and I am glad to have done it. Since that time, I have never been able to slaughter a beast without recalling the noise my father made as his life slipped away from him. I told my nephew this story that night under the heavens as we rested our heads upon our packs far from the foul-smelling camels, our fire all but extinguished. Every campfire I have known since that terrible night brings the memory back to me.

Laura took a break. She was tired but exhilarated. The laic, personal, almost suspiciously modern sensibility coming through the ancient Greek, was uncanny. She made her way to the kitchen, and glad to find it empty, made herself a sandwich and a cup of tea. Then she went outside and walked along the bluffs. The Cornish landscape, so verdant and distinct from the one she had been reading about, seemed especially invigorating because of how she felt inside. An hour later, calmed and refreshed, she continued.

The Roman guards, Lucca the legionnaire and Octavius the Dux, taught Yeshua the rudiments of Latin. Lucca, by far the fiercer of the two, was a lover of boys and from the very first day his adoration of Yeshua's beauty was evident to me. Octavius, an aristocrat, slighter and better mannered, was a womanizer. They worked for me because I paid them well. Lucca offered to instruct Yeshua in matters of self-defence, the use of the sword, the dagger, the throwing of the spear and wrestling. It was clear to me it was this latter art the brute was most inflamed about. The boy took a sword in one hand and a dagger in the other, gazed upon them, and then handed them back. Octavius kindly saved the boy from embarrassment by saying, 'Lucca, the young man is a philosopher, not a soldier. It would be like thrusting a scroll upon thee to interpret or asking thee to perform an enactment of verse.' We all made merry of these remarks, and though Yeshua sought them out less often afterwards, the Romans still behaved protectively toward him, displaying a depth of character unnoticed by me until then.

Early one morning, just before the sun rose, the gait of the caravan quickened. The stones were still slippery with dew, the air was filled with the scent of wildflowers, and there was another scent, almost imperceptible, as well. The camels and dogs raised their heads. I knew and sensed what the animals did, for I too caught the unmistakable presence of the sea in the atmosphere. The sea and the shores of Tyre would soon be visible through the morning mist. The food and the wines, the fruit trees and brothels, the gardens, the spice markets, the ships with their purple sails at anchor upon crystalline waters.

That was more than enough for the day. She saved her work and stretched. She too knew what it was like to sense the nearness of an ocean before it came into view. She shut down her laptop and decided to take a walk along the bluffs overlooking the sea.

Chapter 10

At supper she took Camilla through what she had done so far. The Cassiterite Islands mentioned in the text were how the ancients referred to a legendary land somewhere along the coast of Spain or Britain, long associated with Cornwall given its connection with the tin trade. It was clear to both of them that if the scroll was to be the story of Christ's visit to England with Joseph of Arimathea, it would draw an enormous price.

'But like I said,' Laura insisted, 'the level of scrutiny that will be applied to all this is going to be off the charts.'

'I've no doubt as to its authenticity,' Camilla said, pouring herself a second glass of wine.

'And I can already see,' Laura continued, 'the articles and the theories that will sprout forth, for and against it. The fact that these manuscripts have been sitting here all this time, not two hundred kilometres from Glastonbury, confirming one of the most fanciful myths of British Christendom, is going to encourage every kind of kook known to man.'

'I'm sure. But that will not impinge upon their profit-ability.'

'No, of course.'

Though she tried to understand Camilla's unrelenting focus on the project's financial implications, it astonished her to see how relatively uninterested her hostess seemed to be in the scroll and codices' contents. She had hoped to find more of a kindred spirit in Camilla.

'I see only one down-side,' Laura said, 'and, potentially, it is not a small one.'

'That being?'

'The stated intention of the scroll's author seems to be that of disproving his nephew was the Messiah.'

'But that is something for theologians to argue about, no?'

'No doubt,' Laura said. 'All I mean is that there is bound to be a popular reaction too, and if there is anything in there ... off-colour shall we say, or something convincing, many people will be inflamed by it. I mean, Christ having a wife and children has already been alluded to.'

'It's not like we're living in the times of the Inquisition, Laura. I'm not too concerned.'

'You might consider changing your name after it gets released.'

'I'll do no such thing.'

Laura laughed. 'I like your spirit.'

'You are part of this too, young lady.'

'I know!'

Bidelia entered the dining room to fetch some dessert plates from the sideboard.

'Look at it this way,' Camilla declared. 'This will be a test of that faith. This tale we have, no matter how it ends, will not contradict the New Testament or the Christian Church's basic tenets. They shall just have to find a way to incorporate it.'

'It doesn't bother you – religiously I mean,' Laura said.

'God no.'

They both laughed at that. Bidelia was still in the room.

'But there is a fanatical element out there that will view you, and me, as emissaries from Mephistopheles,' Laura said. 'I'd just hate to have you wake up one morning to the sound of angry locals wielding crucifixes and pitchforks.'

Laura noticed Bidelia making the sign of the cross as she went back into the kitchen.

'I remember,' Camilla said in a dreamy tone of voice, 'when they showed *The Life of Brian* at the cinema in Palma de Mallorca, ages ago, in Catholic Spain, and though there were some priestly protests, most people found it very amusing. And Graves, you know, wrote that book *King Jesus* in which Christ was clearly not the son of God, and nothing much came of that.'

'But this is different Camilla. If these are real, they are historical documents, not fiction.'

Laura was in bed by eleven and got up the gumption to call Nathan who had not bothered to call her since their last conversation. He had been sending her articles he thought might interest her but that was it.

'Hello there,' he said, picking up on the first ring. 'How's life at Downton Abbey?'

'Very agreeable,' she replied. 'I'm having an affair with the dashing Irish chauffeur. How are *you* doing?'

'Fine. It's a gorgeous day here, too nice to stay in slaving at the keyboard. Blue skies, great energy on the streets. I'm just about to head up to the Union Square greenmarket.'

'I'm jealous,' she said, lying, 'but you'd better hurry. It closes at six. Oh, and I've taken the job.'

'Ah-hah. And what pray, is the job?'

'It's more interesting than we feared. Some thirteenth-century documents pertaining to Eleanor of Castile.'

'Never had the pleasure.'

'She's too old for you.'

'That would explain it. And what, might I ask, are they going to pay you, and for how long will it keep you away?'

'The terms are very generous actually.'

'You can't kid a kidder, kiddo.'

'No, they are.'

Part of her was dying to tell him, but she thought better of it.

'It's too soon to tell how long I'll have to stay here.'

'That sounds rather vague. What's the chauffeur like?'

'Alas, there isn't one, not really. Just a couple in their sixties who do just about everything.'

'I miss you.'

'That's what I wanted to hear.'

'Do you miss me?'

'Of course I do.'

She knew both of them were fibbing on that count, that they did and they didn't, that what they missed was the illusion of being a happy couple. Both of them, inside, knew that was where they stood, but neither of them was prepared to face it yet.

After saying goodbye, they were beset by contradictory feelings. He was mildly peeved she had been offered an actual job, one that might be perceived as exotic and interesting, and that could make her just as appealing as him at whatever social functions they might still attend together. He had always sensed, if only unconsciously, that the balance between them was just right: she a minor scholar, younger than him, in an obscure but alluring field – and then he, who by virtue of his drive, charm, and brains, had climbed toward the top of his much more relevant field. Despite their problems he liked the way they presented as a couple in the New York intellectual scene. At the same time, he was relieved to learn she would be gone for a while, thus green-lighting a flirtation he had recently begun with a beguiling Ukrainian waitress at Veselka's restaurant who was all of twenty-two.

Laura felt lonely, more empowered than usual, but lonely. The loneliness did not derive from missing Nathan's company per se, but rather from the realization that the relationship was probably doomed and that it would require work to finish it off; that, once again, she would be alone in the world, five years from reaching forty and wondering if this was how her life was going to be. But then she also knew that the best way to distance herself from such depressing thoughts, the best way to forestall any wrenching decisions, was through work.

Taking advantage of her affiliation with NYU that had yet to expire, she consulted some journals on the Internet and learned that Eleanor of Castile accompanied her husband on the Ninth Crusade to the Holy Land. They travelled with an army of knights and retainers from England, down through France, and from there to the Kingdom of Sicily where Eleanor befriended an aging Thomas of Aquinas, the Dominican friar who was the Catholic Church's most esteemed philosopher and intellectual. From there they sailed to Acre, the town Joseph of Arimathea and Yeshua had almost left from.

Acre at that time was the seat and stronghold of what remained of the Christian Kingdom of Jerusalem. From there Edward sent trusted emissaries into what is modern day Turkey and Iran to meet with the Abaqa Khan, ruler of the Mongols, a Buddhist and a Christian, where they successfully secured his help. Various battles were waged, but none of them decisive. The only thing Edward was able to do was forge a peace that held for many years after they departed.

While they were there, a daughter was born to them and Edward narrowly escaped an assassination attempt.

Though he managed to kill his attacker, he suffered a bad wound to his arm from a poisoned dagger, the painful treatment of which caused Eleanor great emotional strife. They returned home by way of Sicily again, where they lived for a year while Edward recuperated from his wound and where they learned that Edward's father had died. Edward would now be king. Nevertheless, they took their time returning for the coronation, stopping in Rome to meet with their friend the new Pope, moving up through France again but at a leisurely pace, spending large amounts of time in Gascony and in Paris with members of Eleanor's family.

Laura saw that the period of time she needed to focus on was from September 1271 until September 1272, when Eleanor was in Acre, the most logical place she might have obtained the scroll and the Greek codex. Then again, Edward had been accompanied on the Crusade by Theobald Visconti who shortly after became Pope Gregory X. Perhaps Visconti had given Eleanor the scroll and codex in Rome as a devilish gift from the vaults of the Vatican.

She tried to imagine it all. What would it have been like to be married at the age of thirteen in thirteenth-century Spain to a fifteen-year-old boy introduced to you only days before? They would have spoken to each other in French. How and where did they actually get to know each other? What were their carnal relations like at such an age? How would Eleanor have felt leaving her home – crossing the channel by ship – travelling to London for the first time? It seemed luck was with them if in fact they were mad for each other and stayed that way. Eleanor accompanied him on many of his most rigorous and dangerous campaigns. Laura had never thought of the Middle Ages in these terms. In her head it had been a time when men went forth into war while women stayed behind. Was their arrangement a common one among sovereigns, or just as rare as it seemed? What manner of woman was this Eleanor of Castile who became the Queen of England? And how did she come to be so adventurous and passionate, a patron of the arts and the written word, while giving birth to sixteen children?

Laura fell asleep and then woke again two hours later with a new worry about the scroll and the codices. Could Camilla really prove their provenance? For an estate you have a deed, for a car a title. But what did Camilla have to show she was the rightful owner of something that all manner of vultures would be sharpening their beaks for in the not too distant future?

At breakfast the following day Camilla got through her half a grapefruit, labouring meticulously with a dainty, monogrammed grapefruit spoon, before responding.

'I see you are a worrier Laura.'

'I guess I am. I can't help it. It would be so awful to have these extraordinary objects taken from you after all this time.'

'Taken by whom?'

'I don't know. The government, the Royal Household, an act of Parliament, the British Museum.'

'Nonsense. But I take your point, and I shall call James and ask him, and I will have a look about. I do believe I have substantial proof.'

'Good,' Laura said. 'I think, according to the UNESCO convention, all you really have to show is that they have been in your family, that they have been your legal property, since 1970.'

'There are a chain of wills going back at least two centuries,' Camilla replied, 'some of them more rigorously inclusive than others as I recall. Some of them simply refer to the estate and all its contents, some of them specifying everything, with catalogues indicating every plate and dust bin, that make concrete reference to the 'Acre' scroll, the Greek and Amiens Codices. But James has a better mind for these kinds of problems. I shall call him after my bath.'

'Did you say 'Acre' and 'Amiens'?'

'Yes.'

Chapter 11

A disagreeable incident occurred before we set sail for Greece. I had already paid Lucca and Octavius in full and taken my leave of them. I who am only human was eager to install myself in a paradisiacal brothel in the hills above the city that commanded a fine view of the port. I encouraged Yeshua to accompany me if only so that I might keep an eye on him, but he set himself against it. His attitude was prudish and tedious, and after attempting all manner of argument to soften his rigid young mind, I turned my back on him and left him to his own devices. He assured me he would stay with the caravan Bedouins until it was time to board the ship.

Rather than enjoy myself as I was accustomed, I passed an almost sleepless night due to the worry the boy was giving me. Early the following morning I ordered a litter and was carried down to the city and when I arrived at the bazaar my worst fears were confirmed. The caravan had departed, and he was nowhere to be found. An informant I was pressed to compensate told me the one-eyed gentleman who had proven so reasonable when Yeshua proudly negotiated the price for our journey, was a well-known trafficker in slave boys. Clearly, he had had his one good eye on Yeshua from the beginning and had now kidnapped my nephew to sell for a price as handsome as the boy himself.

I proceeded directly to the port where my provisions were being held and availed myself of some additional money. I then set out to find my Romans. I hoped they would still be nearby, visiting a family they had told me about. During the trek to the north of the city, into an area of low hills and farmland that gave way to virgin beaches, I could think of no other thing save the horror weighing upon me. I repeatedly imagined myself having to tell Miryam that her prized son, left in my care, had been sold into slavery – with all that such a condition implied – for he would be bought for his beauty, not his brawn.

I found the Romans engaged in swordplay on the beach, putting on a demonstration of their skills. A young man and a young woman sat near to them in rapt attention. The house built by their parents sat low and white upon a hill behind them surrounded by oleander shrubs and two palm trees. The Romans stopped as soon as they saw me lifting my robes, removing my sandals, making my way to them as hastily as I could over the hot sand. On that day a gentle Mediterranean sun shone and the beach and the surf there were clean and calm. The entire tableau I was about to disturb spoke of leisure and harmony.

Lucca seemed especially angered by the news and he went over to the boy and spoke to him before thanking him and returning to us. 'I think I know where to look,' he said. 'Stay here and wait for us to return.' What else was I to do?

I had been prepared to plead with them and to pay them well to go after Yeshua, and yet it seemed this unexpected call to action gave them pleasure, allowing them to revert to a state that had formed a part of their life for many years.

The family did their best to entertain me that day, trying to distract me. They were very kind. But the state I was in made me an irksome guest. I went for a long walk along the shore. The evening star was already in view and the sound of the surf as the tide rolled in comforted my weary soul, a soul that over the course of the day had searched for a way to harden itself against the worst outcome. I knew that under the beautiful view I had of the sea, predators fed upon prey. What seemed majestic and inspiring on the outside, so in concordance with God's grand design, also contained savagery and an absolute dearth of pity.

I walked and thought of all these things even as I was forced to marvel at the great beauty surrounding me. As I retraced my steps I could hear, over the noise of the breaking waves, cries coming from the direction of the house where a large fire had been built out front. I hastened my step and was rewarded by the sight of Yeshua, alive, sombre, his robes stained with blood. He was dismounting a horse behind Octavius. Lucca was already standing by them and helped Octavius down who seemed to be wounded. It was from a dagger that had caught him between his ribs, but it was not deep. I put my arms around Yeshua who allowed me to embrace him for the first time. 'I beg your forgiveness uncle,' he said to me. 'Are you well my son? Have you been harmed?' 'Here I am,' was all he was able to answer. I embraced the Romans as well who seemed calm and who expressed a ravenous hunger. The girl helped Octavius into the house to clean and tend to his wound. Her father said to me, let us prepare the boy a bath and give him fresh robes. My eyes filled with tears of relief and gratitude. Once Yeshua had gone into the house, Lucca took me aside. He said the boy had already been sold by the time they found him. His face had been painted so as to liken him to a woman. I am sorry for that, he said, but he is alive and shall recover. We gave the curs a taste of Roman justice. Though we were vastly outnumbered we ran them all through with our swords, cursing them as we did. They were so surprised by our arrival they offered scant resistance. I considered bringing you the head of the one-eyed man, but the boy was too upset by the sight of it.

I was in no position to reprimand them. They had brought him back to me and done it in their manner. It was not a moment for moral quibbling. This fierceness was, after all, the reason I had hired them to begin with. I embraced Lucca and said to him I would be forever indebted to the both of them. The following morning both Romans approached me and offered their services for the duration of our journey. They were restless and had no desire to return just yet to Jerusalem. I told them I could not pay them their customary fee for such a lengthy period of time, but we came to an arrangement and I felt greatly relieved because of it. They were eager to see more of the Empire they said, and now they felt protective of Yeshua.

For days Yeshua refused to speak and I did not insist. It was only when we had been at sea for two sunsets that he was able to address it. He seemed older, tougher, but less sure of himself and more suspicious of others. These were all good things. He spoke in low, quiet tones, staring at the sea. Lucca and Octavius were below deck casting dice for money with members of the crew.

'Ahmed,' he said, 'the man I thought I had befriended, was the one who betrayed me. He sold me, like a rug, or a camel. The man who bought me, a soft fat man, had them strip me and paint me, as if I were a woman. The shame I feel has no limit.' 'There is no shame Yeshua,' I said. 'It has no meaning. The important thing is that you were rescued.'

'My rescuers are wild beasts,' he said. 'They killed everything that lived. I shall never forget it.'

'There is no need to forget,' I said. 'There is only the need to go on. Think of what your life would have become had they not found you. The world is a dangerous place and terrible things can befall us and now you know these are not just words from a fable but something you have witnessed and survived. It will make you stronger.'

'I have seen animals slaughtered for food,' he said, on the verge of tears. 'But never have I seen human innards. Now I have seen too many. I do not know what I expected, but inside we are the same as sheep and goats. I do not know what to make of it.'

I could think of no other thing to say to him that day. I put my hand on his shoulder and looked out on the sea with him. I too felt shame for having driven him away and into the hands of his captors. It was good to be under sail and heading west, and it was my most fervent wish that no further calamities would come our way. Alas it was not to be the case.

Laura typed the last sentences onto her screen. Then she saved the file and turned off the computer. Her eyes were filled with tears, just as Joseph of Arimathea's had been. How, she thought, had this extraordinary document come into her hands? Such a thing would never come her way again. Nothing else she would do in her professional life would ever come close to this. She vowed once again to do her very best by it. All of these precious hours she realized, working there at Provence House in Cornwall, would be fondly recalled someday as a blissful calm before a probable storm. Then Camilla appeared, knocking gently on the doorframe. Laura turned in her chair, drying her eyes.

'Have you been crying dear?'

'Tears of joy.'

Camilla was tactful enough not to insist. 'Feel like a bit of fresh air?'

'Love some.'

'Do you ride?'

'A little.'

Chapter 12

Six Arabian mares were housed in stables Laura had not noticed before. They had first been built in the sixteenth century and then Camilla had renovated them considerably. An old Morris Mini Traveller that belonged to Finn and Bidelia was parked next to them, along with two motorbikes belonging to the women who cared for the horses. As they crossed the gravelled courtyard behind the kitchen, she realized the extent of the myopia that had taken hold of her since seeing the scroll and the codices. Up until then all of her walks had taken place in the garden off the breakfast alcove or along the bluffs, back in the direction she had first come from. It had never occurred to her to explore or even to think about anything behind the house and, lo and behold, just past the stables, were hundreds of acres of rolling hills, copses, and streams, all of it Camilla's property.

The paddocks were spacious and there was a fine tack room filled with English saddles, reins and bits, blankets and riding boots and knockabout coats hanging from pegs.

There was a bathroom near an office that was decorated with an oil portrait of Camilla's mother, at age twelve, mounted side-saddle on a towering steed. The walls and flooring were made from wood that was well oiled and varnished, and all of it was tended by a young lesbian couple who lived two villages away, Gin and Jen, both of them with short hair and smiling ruddy faces.

'How much riding have you done?' Camilla asked Laura after making introductions.

'I took lessons as a young girl, mostly to please my step-father. He was Master of the Millbrook Hunt in upstate New York for a time. This was when I was fifteen and I kept at it for, say, three years. But I had a bad fall that kept me off horses for a long time. Then in France, a few years ago, I went for a long ride in the Jura Mountains and I loved that.'

'Let's put her on Daisy, shall we girls?'

'Daisy it is, ma'am,' said Jen, and off they both went, even walking in unison, to saddle up Daisy and Camilla's horse, Dorsey.

'What size shoe are you?

'A thirty-seven in Europe.'

'Just like me,' said Camilla, pleased. 'Let's get some good boots on you as well then.'

The earth was damp and the temperature mild. Throughout the morning the sun had burned off what had been thick cloud cover. A thin mist remained that was rising as they rode over rolling pastures that had the sort of luminous look that often follows a storm. Camilla did not like to ride alone, and she found the conversation of the stable girls tedious. Her son, who did enjoy it, rarely visited. She was pleased to see Laura looking more comfortable and assured than she had expected. Laura too was enjoying herself, the suddenness of it, the recovered familiarity of it, the rush of fresh air and the beautiful scenery that she had unknowingly cloistered herself away from; the contrast it provided to the work she had been immersed in all morning, the *Country Life* Britishness of it all, and the odd physical connection it provided with the ride of Lucca and Octavius that she had translated less than an hour ago. They dismounted at a stream bank, allowing the horses to drink.

'James arrives this evening in time for dinner, along with his wife and two little girls.'

'Really? My goodness. Well, how nice.'

'I'm sorry for the disruption. I shall endeavour to keep them out of your hair.'

'I can go to a hotel. No problem.'

'What on earth for? He far prefers the cottage anyway. It reminds him of when he was a boy and that sort of thing. That's where we're going now.'

'Are you sure? I didn't know there was a cottage. Isn't it too far from you?'

'It's only far on horseback and I am taking us on the scenic route. By car you're there in five minutes. I love my grandchildren, but they are best enjoyed in small doses.

So the cottage solution works out splendidly. I've you to thank for the visit.'

'You mean what I said to you about provenance?'

'Yes. They've had a trip planned to London for a while now and I was to go up there and join them. But James says he wants to make sure the papers I mentioned are where he remembers putting them – I confess I've not been able to find them. So, they are coming down here for two nights instead before returning to Barcelona. The only nuisance is getting the place ready for them. I'm meeting the woman I usually use now.'

'If I can be of any help, just say so. I'm quite good with a mop and pail.'

When they first stopped at the stream Laura had thought to use the pause to tell Camilla what she had translated that morning. But she decided to wait.

'Have you told him what's in the scroll?'

'No. Not in any detail. I trust him with my life, but he might say something to Carmensina, his wife, a girl brought up with a Catalan silver spoon in her mouth who loves to gossip.'

Laura did not say so but the idea of having a woman around closer to her age sounded good to her. She could use some gossip and idle chatter, if only as a counterweight to the momentousness of everything else going on.

The 'cottage' was a proper house standing at the edge of a small forest, all white on the outside with many latticed windowpanes and a roof thick with layers of wooden shingles. There was a matching garage behind it. Inside, the dark wooden walls were covered with still-life paintings, mounted antlers, and framed dry flies. All of the furniture was large and wide and comfortable. There were no dainty antiques. The bedrooms upstairs were airy and simple. It was a storybook house, a hunting lodge for Jane Austen's Mr Darcy, smaller and much less formal than Camilla's mansion, but more conducive to merrymaking. It was easy for her to imagine a son of Camilla's, mostly brought up in a dark apartment along the Avenida Diagonal in Barcelona, jumping for joy at such a place where one could picture Robert Louis Stevenson penning a pirate yarn before the massive hearth.

The maid was there waiting for them with another woman she had brought along to help. Absolved of any responsibility, Laura allowed herself to ramble about the property. She went through the bedrooms and then came downstairs and admired a proper snooker table in a games room where framed Punch magazine covers from the 1850s were on walls painted a scarlet red. In a small study she browsed through old books that described the minutia of hunting and fishing in the area down through the ages. Some of the pages had rose petals and sprigs of honeysuckle pressed into them. Then she studied a slew of family photographs in silver frames, all of them in need of polish, that were gathered upon a vast table pushed up against the back of the living room's largest sofa. A baby grand piano sat closed in the corner.

She went outside and fed the horses sugar cubes she'd found in the kitchen and then walked into a small forest filled with ferns where a path had been cleared. At the end of the path the forest gave way to a soft meadow that sloped gently down to a lake, and next to the lake by a wooden bench were the remains of some sort of dolmen. She walked down and examined it and saw it was authentic. Seating herself on the bench and placing a hand on one of the old stones she contemplated the lake until a call came in from Fiona. They had exchanged news via email over the past few days but had not spoken since the day she'd had lunch at the gastro-pub in the village.

'It was during my sport-shagging spree.'

Laura had listened to Fiona make reference to this period in her life many times and had even witnessed some of it in person when the two of them were in their late twenties, but this was the first she'd heard about the James Figueras episode. After pleasing her mother by marrying Jeremy Wynter, Earl of Somerset, it had taken Fiona two years to divorce him. Wynter's penchant for threesomes with other men and his increasing need, when it was just the two of them, for her to cane him before he could achieve tumescence, had got tiresome quickly. 'My life was a third-rate parody of upper-class English depravity,' she said. But she had got a lovely house out of it and was possessed for a time afterwards with a yearning to prove to herself that she was attractive to 'normal men, whatever that means.'

'What's he like?' Laura asked.

'He's smashing. Wonderful looking. Very proper on the outside but fun once you get to know him.'

'Sort of like his mother.'

'Exactly.'

'So how did it all go?'

'Badly. I tried every trick in the book to get him into bed and though he once came close, he ran off at the last moment. Set me back considerably.'

'What happened?'

'I always sort of fancied him since I was a teenager, but the opportunity really didn't present itself until I was divorced, by which time he was married.'

'What's the wife like?'

'That was the problem. She eats him for breakfast. Has him right under her sexual thumb. He kept on saying he felt too guilty to cheat on her, but it felt more to me like he was just scared to death of her.'

'Is she pretty?'

'Yes. In that Mediterranean way, like you. Good figure, massive amounts of healthy hair, almond-shaped eyes. I don't know about now but back then she drank and smoked heavily. I'm amazed their girls weren't born with three eyes.'

'So, you'd think he'd fall head over heels for a raven-haired beauty like you.'

'Well exactly. And he did, just not enough. I mean, in the end I really threw myself at him. It was so humiliating.

Anyway, that was years ago, thank god. Maybe he and his wife are both obese by now. That would be nice.'

'What does he do?'

'He works for his father-in-law who owns half the newspapers, publishing companies and magazines in Spain – another reason he sticks by her so faithfully, I guess.'

Fiona was seeing another married man now, one who had had the good sense to give into her. After what had been a year of drama filled with explosive ultimatums and furious bouts of make-up sex – all of which Laura had had to hear about while incurring the petulant disapproval of Nathan – Fiona and her fellow, Giles, who Laura had never met, had settled into an amicable and stable arrangement that suited them both – and that probably suited Mrs Giles as well.

The conversation, like so many others with Fiona, left her feeling out of sorts. The prospect of having some new people in the house, people who lived in a world more like her own, had given her a buzz that was now diminished.

When she got back to the cottage, she found Camilla coming out of the front door pulling on her riding gloves.

'I walked through the woods down to the lake. It's so pretty,' Laura said.

'My mother put the bench there next to the dolmen,' Camilla replied.

'I didn't know there were any dolmens in Cornwall.'

'Oh yes,' Camilla said, 'there are nine or ten that have been documented. I'm starving. Aren't you?'

'Yes, I suppose I am,' said Laura.

'Well back we go then. I was a fool not to pack us some sandwiches.'

'How is it going in there?'

'Wonderful. Hard-working women from Romania. The older one's lived here almost five years now.'

They freed the horses, mounted and headed back, breaking into a brisk trot both horses tried their best to push into a canter. Laura, close to Camilla and trailing her by just a few yards, admired the older woman's poise, her still shapely figure and straight back and the dyed hair swept into a French twist that day. English-Irish Camilla, she thought, stereotypical perhaps, but real, with one foot firmly planted in the early years of the last century while the other was holding its own in this one.

Laura took a nap in her room after lunch and when she awakened, she decided to work some more before the arrival of Camilla's family. Running a search connecting 'Amiens' with 'Eleanor of Castile' proved fruitless until, fine-tuning her terms, she discovered that one Gerard of Amiens had written a *roman*, called '*Escanor*', that had something to do with the Arthurian cycle, and that Eleanor had received a copy of during a later visit to France. Then she found an article about Eleanor that revealed that after she succeeded her mother as Countess of Ponthieu in 1279, a romance was written for her about the life of a supposed ninth-century Count of Ponthieu.

Situated in northern France, Ponthieu's most notable

town was Abbeville. According to a book she also found online, *Studies in the Italian Renaissance* by Berthold Louis Ullman, Gerard of Amiens lived in Abbeville and even started a college there where he was a collector of rare books, including a complete collection of 'pagan' Latin poetry. If Gerard of Amiens was the author of the book written for Eleanor in 1280, it made sense that Eleanor might have shown him the Greek codex containing Joseph of Arimathea's text, and that he would have pleaded with her for permission to translate it. And even though Gerard was also known for his opposition to the Dominican and Benedictine orders, Laura reasoned that he still would have thought twice about faithfully translating such an explosive text for fear of persecution – thus the censored version. She put all this in a food-for-thought category, making a few notes, and went back to the work at hand.

Chapter 13

It was midmorning in spring with a gentle sun. The floor of the sea was clearly visible as we approached Rhodes. Lucca stood by the railing with Yeshua and pointed out the remains of the Colossus that once dominated the harbour entrance. Yeshua asked what the Colossus had represented.

'Helios, the god of the sun,' Lucca replied. 'A handsome god who drives his flaming chariot across the sky each day, giving us light. He is brother to the moon and to Eos, the dawn.'

'And yet it was a mere earthquake that brought it down?' Yeshua asked.

'It was a statue,' said Octavius coming up to them, 'made from stone, not the god himself.'

'Have you ever been in an earthquake?' Lucca asked the young man. 'You would speak of them with greater respect if you had.'

'The Lord our God shall not be represented by idols,' Yeshua responded with irritating certainty. 'These other

93

gods you speak of are false gods, who crack and tremble from the wrath of the Almighty Father.'

'And what sort of Almighty Father might that be?' asked Octavius, 'who feels the need to knock down statues?'

'One who will not tolerate the worship of false idols.'

'You would think he had better things to do,' Octavius said.

'The Colossus was brought down by an earthquake,' said Lucca. 'But countless temples and statues remain throughout the empire, intact, dedicated to all manner of gods and mysteries, and people go to them and worship there. Why does your Almighty God strike down some icons and not all of them? What you are saying makes no sense.'

'I do not question the will of the Almighty Father,' Yeshua replied. 'I am but his humble servant.'

'The earth is much more varied a place Yeshua,' Octavius said, 'than the version of it taught in your temple. Life is hard enough without having to go about castigating people for their beliefs. A true Almighty Father, like Rome herself, would hold all people and all of their beliefs in his embrace.'

'You do not understand,' the young man said, his face reddening.

I stood back and listened to this exchange, content to let the Romans say things to him I myself was thinking. Better to hear it from them than from his Epicurean uncle who only pretended to be a devout Jew for appearances' sake.

When our vessel left Rhodes in the early evening, Yeshua was weary from a day filled with so much variety. 'I am too far from home uncle,' he said. 'I was happier there, living in a place bound by the same faith. The world is too wide for me.'

'I can promise you one thing Yeshua,' I said, 'that when we return to Jerusalem, all that you will have seen during our travels, all of this that tires you so now, and all that is still to come, will give you deeper wisdom.'

'I do hope this to be true,' he said, 'but I do not feel it now.'

Chapter 14

This last section, though not a long one, took more time for Laura to translate because the parchment was damaged with moisture stains and her photo was unclear in places. Furthermore, during the final sentences she was distracted by noises coming from the rest of the house, sounds announcing the arrival of James and his family. Just as she was rising from her chair, leaning forward to turn off her computer, the door to the library opened and two identically dressed little girls came in. One of them was slim and blond and looked to be around twelve years old. The other was two or three years younger, smaller, with lustrous dark brown hair pulled back into pigtails. Both wore beige Shetland pullover sweaters, dark brown corduroy jeans and short, lace-up, riding boots. They came just a few steps into the room and stared at Laura without saying anything.

'Hello,' she said to the both of them.

'Hello,' answered the older girl.

'Are you the teacher lady?' asked the younger one with a thick accent.

'Something like that.'

'What is your name?' the little girl asked.

'Laura. And you?'

'I am Anna,' said the older one whose accent was less pronounced.

'And I am Montse,' said the littler one.

At that point a slight but strong looking woman with short hair came in looking for them. She spoke to them in Spanish, albeit with a heavy Brazilian Portuguese accent. It was clear the girls had been told not to enter the library and disturb 'the professor'. Laura told them that she had finished work for the day and that in any event they could come and visit with her whenever they wished. Noelma, the Brazilian nanny, began to protest, in bad English, saying that Camilla, '*la señora de la casa*,' had given strict orders. Just as Laura began to answer her, Carmensina came into the room. As soon as they saw each other Laura and Carmensina were beset by feelings of tension neither of them had any control over. Both little girls picked up on it, as did Noelma.

Laura had hoped to find an ally in Carmensina, someone she could chat with, let off some steam with, and from whom she could perhaps learn some things about Camilla and her family. Even with Fiona's description of James's wife still fresh in her mind she had imagined another sort of Spanish woman, more cosmopolitan looking, and with a younger take on fashion that a number of women from Barcelona she had met in London espoused. What she saw standing in front of her was something else: a stylish but more conservative woman from the upper-middle class of Barcelona society. The impressive hair that Fiona had mentioned, no longer dark, was dyed a golden blond, and it had turned slightly brittle. She had suspiciously large breasts, wore too much make-up for someone her age, and used aggressive body language. There was something provincial about her, like the wealthy girls her mother had described growing up with in Granada.

Carmensina, in no need of any new friends and whose philosophy, on meeting new females not of her circle, was almost entirely coloured by a determination to ward off potential threats to an already semi-comatose marriage, had hoped for and expected someone plain or even ugly, someone whose superior knowledge in academic matters could be easily nullified by what she still considered to be her own Mediterranean sex appeal and charm. But Laura was very pretty and appeared relaxed. She seemed sure of herself, and she was well dressed, evincing a hybrid New York-Parisian sense of style that Carmensina admired in magazines but never thought of attempting herself. Both women picked up on these things immediately. In an instant, Carmensina grasped that the mere presence of Laura was going to ruin her two-day stay at the estate. She was already irritated by the way her two girls were capitulating to 'the American,' for that was how she saw her. Before even saying hello she barked out something terse and effective in Catalan to Noelma and the girls who left the library without a whimper. Laura realized that Carmensina was wearing the same outfit as her daughters.

'They weren't bothering me at all.'

Carmensina chose to ignore the incident and answered in an English more heavily accented than she could ever admit to.

'But you are not the professor, no?'

'I'm Laura. And you must be Carmensina.'

Neither of them made a move to shake hands or exchange kisses.

'Laura the professor? No, no, no. This is not possible. You are a top model!'

'I wish,' smiled Laura even as she knew the other woman's remark was meant as an accusation rather than the witticism it came awkwardly disguised as. Camilla entered the room.

'Ah, I see you two have already met. I hear the girls have been in here bothering you.'

'Not at all,' said Laura, feeling a sliver of irritation entering her voice.

'Camilla,' said Carmensina, lighting a cigarette, which only added to Laura's state of funk, 'surely the real professor is down in the basement sharpening pencils or some such thing; this woman is a top model!'

Camilla laughed and answered her daughter-in-law in Catalan, a language she clearly missed and was glad to have the chance to speak again, unaware of or not sufficiently concerned yet about the alienating effect it might have on her translator who was only able to understand the occasional phrase.

A fire had been lit in the living room and an assortment of drinks set out. The three women walked in, waiting for James to appear.

'I'm sorry I never learned Catalan,' Laura said, making herself a gin and tonic.

'This is fine with me,' said Carmensina, running a hand through her hair in what was a well-practiced gesture. 'It's good for me to practice my English.'

Carmensina poured herself a Highland Park on the rocks and Camilla went for a Pimms Cup Number 6. They clinked glasses, Carmensina saying 'Chin-chin,' and went to their respective easy chairs.

'Where are the girls?' asked Laura, in all innocence.

'Having dinner,' Carmensina replied, as if firing a gun, feigning surprise at the question.

'That's too bad,' Laura said before taking a sip of her drink. 'I was hoping we were all going to dine together.'

'Carmensina is old fashioned,' Camilla piped in. 'And I'm all for it. It's better for the girls too, I expect.'

Laura felt another wave of irritation but thought it wise to remain silent.

'My brothers and I never sat to the table with my parents until we were fifteen,' Carmensina said. 'It was much happier for us, and much better for our parents as well.'

'That was my experience too, mostly,' said Camilla.

'I was brought up in the crazy, child-spoiling United States,' said Laura, trying not to sound defensive, raising her glass and then downing the rest of her drink in two swallows. What most annoyed her was the realization that she in fact had no good memories at all of the meals she had to sit through with her mother and stepfather, and that the most relaxed meals she could recall as a little girl had been in the kitchen with Pat and Clara when her parents were out or away.

'It is hard to have an adult conversation when the little ones are there,' Carmensina continued. 'Even when they are behaving at their best one has to keep them too much in mind.'

Desperate to change the subject, Laura let it go. 'Whereabouts do you live in Barcelona?'

'We live in a house just off the Avinguda del Tibidabo.'

'It's beautiful there.'

'You know it?'

Laura could tell this too bothered the woman for some reason.

'I stayed at a hotel in that part of town last year, the ABaC hotel.'

It had been with Nathan, who always prided himself on finding the new, cool place, no matter how expensive. Then Carmensina said something to Camilla in Catalan that made them both laugh; a detail that annoyed Laura further.

Laura could see that Carmensina was feeling quite in command, pleased with the power she was wielding as a Spanish woman of her ilk, and as the future Lady of the estate at which the way-too-pretty Laura was just a transitory guest. They heard the rear kitchen door open and close heralding the arrival of James. Carmensina stood up, suddenly displaying an actress-like smile of anticipation, and left the room. Camilla and Laura stared at each other.

'Wow,' Laura finally said.

'I do apologize. I suppose she finds you threatening.'

'But that's preposterous.'

They could hear the two girls reacting as their father entered the kitchen to pay them a brief visit.

'She grew up the only girl with four brothers, the princess and apple of her father's eye.'

'So in theory,' Laura said, 'she should be brimming with confidence – which she certainly seems to be, by the way.'

'But she had, *has*, an atrocious relationship with her mother.'

Laura sensed the theme was a complex one for Camilla and that it was none of her business. 'The girls are adorable,' was all she said.

The married couple entered the living room, Carmensina with her arm locked around one of James's, like a teenager in love. James Figueras Trevelyan was as handsome as Fiona had described, with a full head of black hair greying here and there. He looked to be trim, in a relaxed way, not overly muscular. He had on a pair of grey flannel trousers with old loafers, a blue oxford dress shirt open at the collar and a navy cashmere sweater. Over that he wore what could have been an antique tweed sport coat that was charming for being somewhat tattered. It was probably a garment he loved, thought Laura, one that spent most of its time hanging in a closet at the cottage. She stood up to shake his hand as he gave his mother a kiss on one cheek.

'Oh, please don't get up,' he said, turning to Laura, looking very briefly into her eyes and taking her outstretched hand with surprisingly little force. Carmensina watched all of this transpire, her arm no longer entwined with his, standing just behind him.

'Do you see what I mean James?' she said. 'She's an impostor pretending to be a serious professor.' And then she said something to him quickly in Catalan that only she found amusing. James looked uncomfortable.

'I don't know what to say,' he said to no one in particular.

He had an odd accent somewhat akin to Camilla's. He went to the drinks table and poured himself a single malt whiskey, addressing Laura but not looking at anyone.

'I understand you're being an enormous help to my mother.'

'I'm trying.'

Then he did turn to face the three women, raising his

tumbler in their general direction but finding it wisest to settle his eyes upon his mother. 'Cheers.'

At dinner, Carmensina's desire to demonstrate her intimate connection with Camilla by speaking to her in Catalan overruled her common sense. It only served to nettle Camilla and it drove James into conversation with Laura. When he realized his mother was not going to intervene – Camilla had opted for the kind of passive paralysis often observed in people watching an accident occur – he was then forced, twice, to intervene himself. On the second occasion he simply said, 'Carmen ... please.'

'Ah,' she said, reddening slightly, as evidence of her error suddenly tripped off a micro spurt of adrenaline, 'I'm sorry. I get so carried away and your poor mother has been deprived for months of her second tongue.'

'If you don't want to speak in English, we can speak in Spanish or French or in Italian,' Laura said pretending to be helpful.

'No, no, no. I'd much rather speak in English,' said Carmensina, lighting up another cigarette, something which visibly irritated Camilla.

'Carmensina has issues with Castilian Spanish,' James said before he could stop himself.

'No,' Laura said, looking at Carmensina just across the table who held her Marlboro Light in a vice-like grip between two nail-bitten fingers bejewelled with gold rings, 'That can't be true.'

Carmensina gave James a glance of accusation. Then

she took a drag on the cigarette, stubbed it out on her butter plate and finished her drink. 'James exaggerates. My family, some of them, have roots in ancient Cataluña and so there was always a feeling in our household that Spanish was a conqueror's tongue. There was great resentment during my parents' generation when Franco had the language banned.'

At the end of this soliloquy Carmensina affected a faraway look of historical victimization, solemn and almost teary-eyed, that so annoyed her husband he had to fight the temptation to say something, to try to lighten things up. But he knew it would anger her in a way he had no appetite for.

The anger came anyway as they were driving back to the cottage after dinner. Noelma and the girls were half asleep in the back seat. Carmensina was well oiled with Scotch and wine.

'Why were you so mean to me?'

'I wasn't mean to you.'

'You were horribly mean. You couldn't take your eyes off the American woman, speaking with her the whole time.'

'Someone had to speak with her. You were being rude talking with Mamá the whole time in Catalan.'

'What did she want with you after dinner?'

'She said she'd like to speak with me in private tomorrow, for five minutes.'

'What for? It's your mother who's paying her. What is that all about? I don't trust her.'

'You don't like her. That was pretty obvious for all to see.'

'What – and you do?'

'I've very little idea of what she's like. She seems perfectly nice.'

'So, you are standing up for her.'

'Carmensina, what is wrong with you?'

'Nothing is wrong with me. We've come here to have a nice visit with Camilla and all because of this American girl everything has gone wrong.'

'Gone wrong because of you.'

'So, it's my fault.'

'Yes. Frankly.'

'Stop the car.'

'Don't be absurd.'

'Stop the car!'

He stopped the car. Noelma and both of the girls were wide-awake at this point. Montse began to whimper. Carmensina swerved around in her seat and yelled at her to be quiet. And as she yelled James hit the button by his left hand that locked all the doors. Carmensina then tried to open hers.

'James, let me out.'

'Will you please calm down? We'll be there in two minutes.'

'I want to walk. I don't want to be in the same car with you if you think so little of me.'

'That's not true.'

'Open the door.'

Then she leaned over him and released the door locks herself. For the second she was suspended over his lap, and through the smell of smoke and liquor wafting from her, he also breathed in her own particular scent that had drawn him to her since they first met. It caught him by surprise and filled him with an odd mixture of sadness and arousal. She straightened up, opened her door and got out, slamming it shut again behind her.

'Mother-of-God,' Noelma murmured to herself in Portuguese.

James turned around and looked at his daughters. 'I apologize girls. I'm sorry Mummy is so upset. She's just having a bad night. I don't want you to worry. All right?'

They both studied his face for a few seconds before assenting.

'Where is she going?' Montse asked.

'She's angry with me and wants to walk. I'm going to get out too and see if I can change her mind. OK? I won't be but a minute.'

He had to jog to catch up with her as she strode along the side of the road entranced by the sensation of having the world against her.

'Carmensina,' he said, coming alongside her, making a point of not touching her. 'Please. The girls are upset.'

She stopped, turned and looked at him with tears in her eyes, 'I'm upset. You've upset me.'

'I'm sorry. I truly am.'

'Go fuck her if you want to.'

'*What* are you talking about? You've had too much to drink.'

'Thanks to you. I need to feel you are there for me. That you are on my side. That I never have to worry about that.'

'I am. I am on your side. I'm sorry. I was just trying to be polite. Please come back to the car.'

'I don't want you to talk to that girl in private. If she has something so important to say, she should say it in front of Camilla, and me. I'm your wife. Camilla is my mother-in-law. Who the hell is she?'

'All right,' he said. 'You're right.'

Then she started to cry, and he took her in his arms and kissed the side of her head and rubbed one of her shoulders as he turned them both back toward the car.

When they reached the cottage, she went up to their room straight away and ran herself a bath. James and Noelma tried to put the girls to sleep but they were both too agitated and so he sent Noelma away to her room across the hall and he stayed with the girls, reading to them and talking with them until they drifted off. He watched them for a few minutes in the light of the bedside lamp he had promised to leave on for them. The fact that Carmensina's drunkenness and unhappiness had prevented her from making the effort with him to put the girls to sleep made him angry. But he knew that if he expressed that anger it would set her off again. He also knew that after her bath she would want him to make love to her, as proof of her continuing power over him, to show him and herself that everything was all right. He recalled the suggestion he had made to her some months earlier, that she 'see someone, a professional' and the torrent of derision she had spewed at him, deriding anyone who, in her opinion, was foolish enough to consult '*escuraments*' for problems best solved 'as my father used to say' by an extra whiskey and common sense.

He stood up and resisted the urge to give his girls a parting kiss for fear of waking them. Then he turned toward the door, preparing himself to go down the hall and face the music. They had all known happier times in that house and he only wished such times might someday return. At the moment it was hard to imagine how that might come about. He remembered taking Carmensina there once, before they were married, much to the recently widowed Camilla's disgruntlement – and how different a time that had been, the couplings they had subjected the cottage to. The idea of making love to her now felt impossible, even as he knew she would be unbuckling his belt sometime in the next half an hour. He hoped his body would ignore his emotional state and rise to the occasion if only so that this trip might be salvaged. It occurred to him, and it came seemingly out of nowhere as he placed his hand on the doorknob to their room, that one thing he might attempt in order to accomplish the task, would be to fantasize about the person at the root of this latest disaster. Carmensina had been correct on that account, for he had thought the professor very beautiful.

Chapter 15

For three days and nights there was no wind. Lengths of cloth were strung along the deck for shade. Lucca and Octavius were stripped down to their loincloths. The slaves kept below where the heat was infernal were put to the oars. The ship's captain fumed in a permanent state of ill humour for he was carrying perishables that needed to reach port as soon as possible. Drinking water was rationed. The Romans gambled and traded complicated, ribald stories of amorous misadventure. We few passengers passed the time telling tales as well, while dreaming of cool autumnal rains.

I was telling Yeshua how many of my fellow tin merchants obtained their product from ports in Iberia, where tin and lead were brought from mines worked inland, but that I still preferred the longer journey to Belerion, what his mother had called the Cassiterites, where I could visit the tin streams and deal with the miners directly. Over the years I had come to know them, a peaceful and colourful people, and I saw no reason to change.

'The land I am taking you to is green and cool. The stones grow moss. It is a land of sea mists, sheep pastures, cold rivers and winds.'

It was then we heard the commotion below deck, an argument, loud but brief, followed by the unmistakable cracking sound of a whip. Then the noise of a man protesting, of a man being flogged and then being dragged against his will toward the stairwell connecting the lower and upper decks. The man's protests turned into screams, terrible screams that all of us on the upper deck listened to transfixed, screams that pierced the deadly, still air.

The captain and his mate pulled the screaming and all but naked slave up from the hold onto the deck. The captain yelled at the dark and wiry muscled little man with all his might, yells that were just as loud as the victim's screams of protest. The mate held the man down and the captain went for his sword. He then began hacking away at the man's wrists, terrifying the mate who was ordered to hold the slave still – an impossible task – and in whose vicinity the slicing sword came perilously close. The captain, crazed by his rage, was inept and clumsy in his vile castigation, but finally the poor slave's hands were separated from his body with great spurts of blood spewing forth that covered the wooden planks of the surrounding deck. 'Don't look,' I said to Yeshua. But it was impossible not to stare at such an eruption of savagery. I looked to my Romans to gauge their reaction and found them taking in the spectacle with what might have been a combination of curiosity and contempt.

The slave fainted and went limp. The captain took him by the ankles and ordered the mate to grab him by what was left of his bloodied arms and they tossed the fellow into the sea. I made an effort to restrain Yeshua, but he broke free from my grasp and went to look. Octavius joined him. Lucca and I looked at each other until the legionnaire jutted out his chin and shrugged his shoulders. We later learned his transgression had been to remove his hands from his oar in order to tell a joke to those around him.

Seagulls alighted upon the deck and pecked at the pools of drying blood. Hours passed, and in the afternoon a cool breeze arrived bringing clouds and, in their wake, a steady wind that filled the sails, breaking the tedium, bringing relief to the spirit, bestowing upon the slaves below a merited rest, and justifying to the captain his brutality.

Chapter 16

There was a knock on the library door, followed by James stepping into the room.

'Laura?'

She put her computer into sleep mode and turned, expecting to find him alone, but Carmensina and then Camilla came in behind him.

'Hello,' she said, standing but staying put by her work table.

She thought he appeared both better and somewhat worse for wear in the morning light. He had a rugged aura about him that she liked, and he had nicked himself shaving. Carmensina looked hungover and was wearing a navy blazer with gold buttons. Camilla looked sweet but sheepish.

'I know you wanted to have a word with me alone,' he said, doing his best to radiate a confident and much-ado-about-nothing tone, 'but we thought, given the importance to my mother of the work you're doing, that we should all hear what you wished to say to me.'

In an instant Laura realized Camilla had been right about not telling James too much, for fear of his feeling compelled to share it with Carmensina who, clearly, was behind this awkward ambush. Laura sought to nip things in the bud.

'Well I can understand that,' she said. 'But I think there's been a bit of a misunderstanding, which is probably my fault. All I wanted was to fill you in on some of the concerns I have about this project, as a courtesy really, concerns I've already shared, in full, with Camilla. We can talk about it some other time. I'd never think of keeping anything related to this project from her. We're as thick as thieves, aren't we Camilla?'

'That's just what I told them dear.'

James looked relieved and unhappy at the same time. Carmensina, irked by this confession of mutual complicity, would not be put off.

'What is this secrecy all about?' she asked, taking a pack of cigarettes from her pocket. 'Neither James nor I really know what it is you are doing.'

'Surely Camilla has told you something.'

'I have,' said Camilla.

'What?' said Carmensina, 'That you are translating some old document, some old book that belongs to the family.'

'Exactly,' Laura said. 'It's a text that might end up being quite valuable and I just wanted James to know that, and for him to know how important it is that he and Camilla can prove that it legally belongs to them, to all of you.'

'I found the papers I was looking for early this morning,' said James, 'in the cottage, just where I'd hoped they'd be.'

'Oh good.'

'I'll leave them with Mother.'

'That's great.'

Laura then decided to cease being quite so cooperative and she just stood there, silent and composed, leaving it to the intruders to find a way to extricate themselves from a situation that was costing James a number of points in her estimation.

'Well then – what is it you need to speak to James about "some other time"?' Carmensina asked, taking out a cigarette but not yet lighting it.

'Just some details,' Laura said.

'Well, why not now?' Carmensina insisted, 'I mean, here we all are.'

'Because it is not a good time for me. I'm in the middle of something I should get back to.'

She said these last words looking beyond James and his wife, resting her eyes upon Camilla.

'Quite right,' Camilla said. 'Out we go then. We'll leave you to it.'

'Sorry for the intrusion,' James said, sounding like he meant it. Carmensina, who had no choice but to leave with them, began venting again to her husband and mother-in-law in Catalan as she marched out.

Laura sat at her desk wishing the married couple would leave the estate as soon as possible. The idea of having to sit through another meal with them felt impossible and she resolved then and there to go into the village that evening for a pint and some shepherd's pie. She was too unnerved to resume work right away. She had imagined what her talk with James was going to be like, a meeting of minds, the acquisition of an important ally, a hoped-for degree of understanding that would have allayed her worry that she was going to have to organize a response to what might happen when word got out about the project all on her own. But nothing of the sort had occurred. The man had caved quickly and disappointingly to the capricious needs of his jealous spouse.

Hearing the two girls playing in the garden, Laura went to the window to look at them. To her relief they were not wearing matching navy blazers. As Noelma hovered nearby, lost in her own thoughts, the girls squatted down by the edge of the reflecting pool. Laura imagined they were looking at the large goldfish that swam about under lily pads. She imagined the strings of genes wrapped and enfolded within their cells, inherited from Irish and English and Catalan stock. Then she thought about her own, and how everyone was a mongrel, but a mongrel that more often than not showed off the best traits of each parent's contribution. Or so it seemed to her looking at the girls and seeking to inject a bit of optimism into a day that had started so bleakly – the depressing piece she had translated, followed by the awkward confrontation. There they all were she thought, gathered in Cornwall that morning, a group of Spaniards and half-Spaniards, probably not half an hour's drive from the tin mines Joseph of Arimathea was en route to back at her desk. She noticed the girls turning in the same direction and then saw James and Carmensina walking diagonally across the lawn towards them. Instinctively she stepped back from the window, but she kept on looking.

Chapter 17

As we approached the eastern coast of Sicily the volcanic mountain surged up from the mist. The ship docked at Siracusa and we were grateful to bid farewell to the foul-smelling vessel and its violent captain. Octavius, a distant descendant of the consul who wrested the city from the Greeks two centuries earlier, invited us to stay with his father and mother in their villa.

Octavius's father was an elderly, open, worldly man, eager for new minds to converse with. The palatial home was near Akragas, up in the hills and the luxury of its appointments was notable. Yeshua was given his own room with its own bath and assigned a servant. Gardens and patios with mosaics and pools abounded providing privacy and sweet-smelling plants and tiny birds, and there were well hidden niches from which to contemplate the sea.

The wedding of a nephew was planned and the family was grateful to me for bringing their son to them at such a propitious time. No effort was spared to put us at ease.

Out walking one morning I rested on a stone bench

placed under the shade of a tall palm tree. Below me was a small garden with a fountain at its centre dedicated to the nymph Arethusa. Seated near the fountain were Claudius – Octavius' father – and Yeshua. I listened to the following:

'I would like to know more about Judaism,' Claudius said, 'about this Almighty God of yours.'

'We do not preach it to others,' Yeshua answered.

'But,' Claudius said, 'what if I have been in error all my life?'

'I'm sure you have been,' Yeshua said.

'So,' said Claudius, 'I have foolishly been making sacrifices and donating alms to our many Gods, each with their own temple, their own province in our lives – all for naught.'

'Yes,' Yeshua said, 'all for naught.'

'Might we bargain Yeshua? I will come here each day and learn what I must of your Judaism. But in return you must sit with an instructor of my choosing each night before retiring and listen to how life and the afterlife are regarded in the Roman manner.'

At this Yeshua remained silent. Part of him surely rejected the prospect of having to listen to someone extol the virtues of sinful icons. But I imagine part of him relished the opportunity to convert an influential Roman. 'I accept your proposal sir,' he said.

The instructor that Claudius chose was a beautiful young woman called Daphne who tended the family's private shrine dedicated to Minerva. It stood at the highest part of their property. Daphne's beauty mirrored Yeshua's and from the first moment he met her – for he told me so one night in Carthage during a fierce storm when we were unable to sleep – he felt unsure. He had expected his teacher would be a man. Little did he suspect that bets were being tallied throughout the household based on what Claudius truly intended to happen. The only ones to wager against the patriarch and his family were Lucca and myself.

Claudius dutifully appeared each day as Yeshua held forth on numerous matters regarding the Talmud and the Torah. Yeshua was a natural teacher so it came easily to him and it gave him pleasure, and Claudius, not entirely a cad, listened well and asked serious questions.

And in the evenings, after the meal, listening to music while smelling lemon blossoms, telling tales, hearing my hosts discuss the intrigues and rumours that reached them from Rome, Yeshua would leave us and walk along a steep path under stars to the clearing high above the villa where Daphne awaited him. On the evening of the wedding feast Yeshua did not come back down to the villa. When I expressed my concern to Octavius and to his father, they told me not to worry, that he was in good hands.

Before we boarded our new ship Lucca and I paid our debt, for everyone knew what had happened and everyone was kind enough not to make light of it in his presence. This is how Yeshua described it to me that blustery night in Carthage ...

'Despite my mother's concern, I have taken notice of

young women since I can remember. On the day of the wedding feast, I was asked to visit Daphne earlier than usual. The sun had barely set and such was the pleasure I took during my climb, the rosemary, the pines, the sea views that were no longer hidden in a shroud of darkness, that a scorpion climbed my leg and reached halfway up my thigh before I took notice of it. Not knowing what it was I swatted at it through my garment, only to feel its angry sting. By the time I reached the temple I was feverish. Daphne bade me recline and with the aid of her young servant girl they removed my garment. She recognized the wound at once and lost no time kneeling upon the ground beside me, whereupon she commenced to suck out the venom, spitting it away. Lifting my head to observe her, feeling her fingers gripping the bare skin of my upper thigh and knee, feeling her lips, teeth and tongue concentrated upon the intimacies of my affliction, I was, despite the pain, unable to control myself, and I felt myself hardening in a manner that was most embarrassing. It was soon impossible for either of the women to ignore it. But Daphne seemed unperturbed. She simply turned to the servant girl and said, 'Attend to him.' And then she looked up at me and said, 'It will help distract you from the pain.' The servant girl then proceeded to unwrap my loincloth. Both women paused a second to stare before getting on with their tasks, Daphne to empty my lesion of poison, the servant girl to empty me of something else. I swear to you uncle, nothing like this has ever happened to me before. 'And there is an excellent chance,' I said to him, 'that, free of charge, it will never happen to you again.'

I let him be for a few moments. And then I said to him, 'That was not all that happened, was it?' 'No,' he said, quietly. 'I was given something to drink that put me to sleep. And when I awakened night had fallen and I found myself upon a comfortable bed in a simple, narrow chamber that was new to me, lit by tapers placed along a small ledge that ran along one of the walls. Daphne appeared wearing a short and diaphanous garment new to me as well. She brought me some water and lay down beside me.

'Where am I?' I asked her. 'This is where I sleep,' she said. 'How long have I been here?' I asked. 'Many hours,' she said. 'I was worried about you at first, but now you are well.' 'I have caused you to miss the wedding feast,' I said, 'and I must go. My uncle will be concerned.' 'Your uncle, and everyone else in the villa are either drunk or asleep by now,' she said. 'And I had your uncle advised some time ago. You should continue to rest, here. The gods decree it.'

'My god forbids it,' I said.

'Your god forbids that you lie with me, not that you sleep next to me. That is all that shall happen here tonight.'

After that we lay there in silence. As time passed some of the tapers died out. The bed was not wide, and it was difficult to sleep or even to turn without touching her in some way. I remained silent for fear of provoking something. We fell asleep until some hours later when I awakened again. It was deep into the night and colder and all but two of the tapers had gone out. She was turned toward me on her side and her garment had opened and I saw her breasts only inches away. I leaned into them and softly kissed them, softly kissed their gentle swell and then she awakened and kissed me back and we spent the rest of the night and early dawn together. I sinned mightily and though my Heavenly Father may have been angry with me and ashamed of me, her gods were not, for Eos brought the dawn and Aeolus a sweet breeze and Helios brought the sun rising in the east and Morpheus granted a deep sleep to Daphne allowing me to rise and dress and take my defiled but pleasured body back down to the villa.'

Who was I to tell him she had been charged by Claudius to seduce him? Who was I to stain this memory he had just depicted with such passion, by relaying the level of amusement and satisfaction that had spread through the villa once the servant girl came down from the temple with the news? For perhaps it took place just as he described it. In the end, after all, the scorpion bite had not been staged, and though it had been she who engineered the sleeping arrangements, it was he who took the initiative by kissing her breasts. Surely a young woman so beautiful saw in him a worthy reflection. His tale, as he told it to me that night, when all of us, en route to Spain and Belerion, were thankful to be on land through such a storm, had a simplicity and authenticity to it that leads me to think he seduced her as much as she him.

Laura sat back in her chair. This last story, dictated so long ago, had moved her and even turned her on. As she saved the document before turning off the computer, she smiled at the thought that perhaps it had been Joseph of Arimathea who had made up or embellished the story, and that she might be dealing with an unreliable narrator, or at least one who, like the best storytellers, was not above altering or elaborating here and there, sacrificing objectivity when necessary for the greater good of a tale better rendered.

Chapter 18

She was so entranced by this last translation that she lost track of time. It allowed her to put aside the tensions that had come her way due to James and Carmensina's visit. Determined to avoid ruining the pleasant state she was in and not wishing to risk asking Camilla for permission to take the Land Rover into town, for fear she might try to change her mind, Laura went into the kitchen and asked Finn MacShane.

'Well of course you may. As far as Mrs Trevelyan is concerned, ever since we returned your rented car, the Land Rover is for your use for as long as you are here with us.'

Laura noted how the hawk-like man never used Camilla's full, married surname. She assumed it was just a bit too foreign for his taste.

'I'm going to have dinner with a friend at the local pub, so I won't be at table this evening.'

He gave her a look indicating that he saw through her blarney, 'And might, by any chance, the Missus know?'

'For that I was counting on you Finn, who knows just how and when to break such news.'

Doubtful, he aimed another stare at her.

'Would you mind terribly?' she added, giving him the most fetching and imploring look she could muster. 'I don't want to upset her, and I think everyone's dinner will go more smoothly this way.'

'All right, Miss.'

When she got to town around seven thirty, she decided to try the more traditional of the two pubs. The one where she had eaten lunch on the day before she was hired was a gastro-pub that boasted two large flat screen TVs showing rugby matches. It was a loud place that played to a younger crowd. The other had an older and darker look that appealed to her more that evening. All she wanted was a booth and a table where she could read and have some real pub food and a pint or two without getting hit on. The older one also had the advantage of being called The Wounded Hart. As she came inside and found a table, she saw there was no television and there were two auto-graphed photos of Tom Jones hung over the sticky wooden bar, one of the Welsh crooner, the other of Albert Finney as Fielding's protagonist.

During her meal she pored over a *New Yorker* brought with her from London, and before ordering some pudding she went outside to have a cigarette, justifying it with all that was going on around her. She was pleased to note it tasted awful and she put it out quickly. Before going back inside she toyed with the idea of phoning Fiona to gossip, and of phoning Nathan to check in, but neither notion was strong enough to spur her into action. By the time she finished a stale *tarte tatin* and a cup of decaf she asked for her bill, figuring it was late enough to return to Camilla's and go up to her room without having to see anyone. Then James walked in. He saw her, smiled, and came up to her.

'There you are.'

'Hello,' she said.

She truly hoped she was not blushing, or that if she were it would not be so apparent in the dimly lit space.

'I tried the other one first and just assumed I'd missed you or that you'd gone to some other village. Never expected to find you in here.'

'Is everything all right?'

'Fine. Carmensina and Noelma and the girls went back to the cottage after dinner and I stayed at the house to chat with Mother whereupon she promptly insisted I come and find you to apologize for this morning.'

'There was no need for that.'

'I'm not entirely sure that's true and, besides, I had the distinct impression there really was something you wanted to talk with me about. Can I buy you a brandy?'

'All right,' she said, removing her coat and sitting down again, agreeing to a drink she had never enjoyed. He raised a hand to the bartender and then realized he would have to go and order it himself.

'How was your meal?'

'Wonderful. Just what I wanted.'

He looked around. 'I haven't been in here for years. My father used to love this place. It hasn't changed at all.'

'How was your meal?'

'Fine. An immense Scottish salmon with béarnaise sauce, carrots, and a good Côtes du Rhône. You were missed.'

She let the remark go and her smiling silence cued him to approach the bar. Laura regretted the cigarette. After being so good to her throat these past weeks she had sent waves of burning smoke back against it and now there would be some firewater to boot. It also irked her, for some reason, that he might smell the smoke on her, although she realized that living with a woman who looked like she went through two packs a day had probably inured him to it. He returned holding two small snifters and handed her one.

'Something that has changed is the brandy selection,' he said. 'It's not what it used to be. This'll have to do I'm afraid.' She took a sip and looked at him. He seemed more relaxed, the Côtes du Rhône perhaps, and surely a drink or two before dinner, or maybe it was just being away from the estate.

'I did want to speak with you,' she said. 'Not to tell you anything I haven't already said to Camilla, but I'm a bit concerned that she has yet to take what I've been telling her seriously enough.'

'I'm all yours,' he said.

'Has she told you what it is I'm working on? In any detail, I mean.'

'No. I mean the damn things have been around forever, so I know they're very old.'

'I hope she won't mind my telling you. I suspect she wants me to. But you must promise me that, for now and during the near future, you'll not tell anyone.' She leaned forward, '*Anyone.*'

'What the deuce is it? And yes, I can promise you that.'

'They are three, very beautiful, very valuable, and very explosive documents. Camilla seems focused on their potential monetary value, while I'm more concerned about the explosive part.'

'Explosive in what way?'

'The scroll – and the codices that are Greek and medieval French translations of it – if authentic, is a memoir written by Joseph of Arimathea who was the uncle of Jesus Christ. In it he tells the tale of a trip they took together when Christ was seventeen years old, from Nazareth all the way here to Cornwall. Joseph of Arimathea *was* a wealthy tin merchant and did business with Cornwall tin miners. So far, and I'm about three quarters of the way through it, they have reached Sicily on the voyage out. At one point, Christ has been sold into slavery and rescued. And this afternoon I translated a passage in which he is seduced by a beautiful maiden, a high-end call girl perhaps, who kept a private temple dedicated to the Roman goddess Minerva.'

'My God.'

'Well, exactly.'

'And *are* they authentic?'

'It was you who brought the samples to Oxford, wasn't it?'

'Yes. They seemed quite convinced of their findings.'

'So, there's an excellent chance they are authentic, in which case, once they go up for sale, if that is what you decide to do with them, and word gets out about what they contain, the reaction, worldwide, is going to be significant.'

'I suppose you're right.'

'I'm sure of it. Various religious communities will be up in arms and questioning the whole enterprise. The scrutiny brought to bear will be massive and the media attention unrelenting. I mean, I am actually worried that droves of angry people might come down here and picket the estate. That sort of thing. Not to mention random lunatics looking to shoot heretics. Camilla has heard me out on this, but I don't have the impression she's really thinking about it, which is why I'm telling you.'

He took a larger than usual sip of his brandy.

'I hear you,' he said in that British accent she enjoyed listening to. 'I'm glad you're telling me,' he said looking away. Then he looked at her again, 'I understand. And the first thing that occurs to me is that by the time word does get out, the scroll and the codices should be somewhere else, somewhere safe, like within a serious bank vault in London. I'll call Sotheby's and make a general inquiry about how things like this might be handled.'

'Thank you, James. That's the sort of suggestion I wanted to hear coming from someone other than myself. I think you and Camilla will also need someone to run interference. Your phones will be ringing off the hook. Your lives will be changed, for a while anyway. Do your daughters attend a religious school in Barcelona?'

'Hmm. Hadn't thought of that. They do, as a matter of fact.'

'I'm just trying to think of everything. This will be on the cover of every magazine and newspaper around the world. Hopefully it will all blow over after a while.'

'They'll be coming after you the most, surely?'

'Probably.'

'Are you ready for that?'

'No. Not yet.'

'Did you have any idea what you were getting yourself into?'

'None. But I'm thrilled. Don't get me wrong, this is the best thing, professionally, that could ever happen to me. The work itself is very moving, and I'm doing my best to get it right. I'm trying to make the translation as contemporary as possible. But no matter how it comes out, or how long I might have to work on it, people will be criticizing it, some of them viciously, until the day I die. I've no doubt about that at all.'

'You're brave.'

'Not really. Not yet anyhow. Anyone I know in my field would have killed to get this opportunity.'

He finished his drink.

'You can have the rest of mine if you'd like,' she said, moving her glass over to his side of the table. 'I'm actually not much of a brandy drinker.'

He smiled and took it into his hand, 'Thank you for this Laura, for bringing this to my attention. Let me give it all some serious thought.'

'You'll find it does need to sink in a bit. It's been that way for me. And I do worry about your mother. I've come to care for her a great deal, and I'm concerned this whole thing may end up making her unhappy. The publicity might be overwhelming, and your family will be looked at through a microscope. Or maybe I'm just being an alarmist and it will go much more smoothly than I fear.'

'No, I think it's wise to prepare for the worst. You're quite right about that. She cares for you too by the way. She was furious about this morning – something I only did to please Carmensina who gets a bit insecure sometimes and it comes out as hostility, I'm afraid.'

She decided not to say anything negative or positive about Carmensina and it led them into a brief and awkward silence.

'We should be getting back I suppose,' she said, 'I mean, for your sake.'

He sat back and sighed and did take a sip from her glass. Then they looked at each other.

'I'm glad we could talk like this,' he said.

'Me too.'

'I understand you're a pal of Fiona Phillips.'

'It was she who put your mother onto me. Here I've been slaving away in the academic world all these years and it ends up being Fiona of all people who sets me up with the best job I'll ever have.'

'Say hello to her for me next time you see her. I've known her all my life it seems.'

'So I understand.'

'She's a force of nature.'

'That she is. Why not call her yourself? I have her mobile.'

He took another sip of the brandy and shifted about in his chair. 'Don't know about that.'

'She's over you if that's what you're concerned about.'

'Ah. She told you.'

'We're old friends.'

'Of course. And you say she's well.'

'Very well – madly in love with some fellow – still going out every night. I get exhausted sometimes just hearing about it.'

He downed the rest of her brandy.

'Have you ever been married?' he said.

'No.'

'It's a tricky business sometimes, I assure you.'

139

'I've noticed. I mean, not you ... Everyone I know is either divorced or just about to be.'

'Quite.'

It was clear to her he was closing up and she regretted going on about Fiona.

He walked her to the Land Rover. The night had turned foggy and the bonnet and windshield were covered in mist. With the exception of the gastro-pub where some light and motion still glimmered, the little village, all of two blocks long, was dark and abandoned. The air reeked of sea.

'How is this car holding up?' he said.

'Fine. I mean I know nothing about cars. Tonight is the first time I've used it. Makes me feel like Isak Dinesen.'

She unlocked it and he held the door open for her as she climbed up behind the wheel.

'You know, Laura, I'd love to read it – what you're working on – to have a look at it. If that would be all right.'

'It's still very much a work in progress.'

'Of course. Well, when you're ready ...'

'No, but I would like you to read it. It would do me good to share it. Funnily enough, Camilla has never asked to see anything yet. I tell her what I've read in bits and pieces and she seems to be fine with that.'

'She's very respectful of your expertise and doesn't want to disturb you, I think. Perhaps I should do likewise.'

'I'd like you to read it. Thing is, I don't want to print it out yet or send it to anyone by email. But you could read it from my computer screen in the library.'

'Understood. We're off tomorrow morning before lunch but if I can find a way to finagle it ...'

'I'll be in the library all morning.'

They drove back to the estate together, him leading the way. There were no other vehicles on the road. He waved to her as he went on toward the cottage and she blinked the lights of the Land Rover at him before parking. She went into the kitchen to hang the keys back in their place and found Camilla in a bathrobe and slippers standing at the stove warming some milk.

'Hello there,' Laura said.

Camilla turned and smiled, 'Hello dear. You caught me.'

'At what?'

'Making myself some Spanish cocoa. It's one of my favourite things, since childhood. Would you care for some?'

'No thank you. I think I'll just have a glass of water.'

'It helps me sleep; though it really shouldn't, but such is the force of habit.'

'I just had the nicest meeting with James thanks to you.'

'Good. He improves considerably one on one, don't you think?'

'I do.'

James let himself into the cottage like a burglar and was relieved to find everyone sound asleep. He undressed and brushed his teeth in the dark and stealthily slipped into bed next to Carmensina. He felt a tug at his heart at the thought of having to leave the following day. Each time they came for a visit he inevitably resolved to spend more time there, to take a good portion of their summer holiday there for example, but it never seemed to happen. Something always got in the way. The pull of Carmensina's family who always insisted they stay with them near the Costa Brava, the children's desire to be close to their cousins, or having to oversee some badly needed repair job of one sort or another at Camilla's house in Mallorca. But this was where he felt best, this house and its surrounding countryside that never failed him.

He also realized part of him was excited by his encounter with Laura. It had felt on some level like an illicit date, at The Wounded Hart of all places. Being alone with her and speaking about such extraordinary things so alien to his normal life had ignited something inside him. She was stylish in a particular New York way he had always found intimidating and appealing in equal measure. He'd always felt that Manhattan women saw right through you. A man's old-world European manners, the stratagems established for getting along and for impressing people, though viewed as charming at first, were processed rapidly by these women, and if you did not have something more substantial to say or show for yourself, they generally moved on without a second thought. But Laura had something European about her as well; she was at ease in new surroundings, and seemed free from any compulsion to talk about herself or to draw unsolicited comparisons between where she was and where she came from. And there she was in flesh and blood back at the house, immersed in bringing his peculiar family heirloom to light, thanks to his mother's sudden resolve.

Chapter 19

Deciding it would be rude not to, Laura joined the communal breakfast table and was rewarded by an unexpectedly affable Carmensina. She presented a calm demeanour, had her hair pulled back into a youthful pony-tail and was making an effort, noticed by all with approval, to interact with her daughters. Her interventions in the conversation were sparing and low key. Camilla wondered whether there might be some medication at work within her daughter-in-law's system, while it crossed Laura's mind that perhaps it was an aftereffect of early-morning sex. Both factors were in play, plus the circumstance that Carmensina was relieved to be returning to London that day, and then back to Barcelona the morning after.

While Camilla joined her son at Laura's computer screen to read what they could of the ongoing transla-tion, Laura and Carmensina went for a walk with the girls down to the beach. It was a clear but windy day and the four of them wore windbreakers and wellingtons and spoke in English.

'What is it you are translating exactly?' Carmensina asked.

'It's a very old story,' said Laura. 'A history of the Mediterranean world with some bits about ancient Cornwall as well, although I haven't got that far yet.'

'Do you think it really is valuable?'

'I do. I've never seen anything like it. Camilla is quite keen to sell it at auction once I'm done.'

'I can't imagine why,' Carmensina said. 'She is very well off. She reminds me of an aunt I had who was the same way, who lived very frugally and then after she died, it turned out she had been sitting like a hen upon a pile of golden eggs.'

'It happens.'

The girls, walking ahead of them, were having an animated conversation, the sense of which was lost to the wind. Observing them brought back a sadness Laura sometimes felt at being an only child.

'What is her house like in Mallorca?'

'It is in a very beautiful place,' Carmensina said, 'with gardens and views of the sea, and it has a lovely pool. But the house itself is droughty and hard to organize, for me anyway. The girls love it and Camilla loves it. It is kind of like a hippie house on the inside, if you know what I mean. Maybe I've been too spoiled by modern conveniences, but I like a house that is easy to keep.'

They went the rest of the way in silence. The wind and the occasional difficulty of negotiating the terrain

146

were sufficient distractions. The tide had gone out leaving exposed, rust-coloured rock formations that ran diagonally to the strand with numerous pools, and the girls walked along them looking for crabs while the two women stayed back on the sand.

'Have you ever been married?' Carmensina asked.

'No,' Laura said, taking note that everyone in this family had now asked her this question. 'I guess I've come close a few times, but, no, it hasn't happened yet.'

'Wouldn't you like to have children?'

'I'm not sure. I like spending time with the children of my friends. But the idea of having my own feels daunting. Then, sometimes, I get a craving, so it's confusing.'

'It's biology.'

'Like almost everything else about us, right? Your girls are very beautiful.'

'They are very different from each other, even though they are being raised the same way. They are our treasure. But I still want a boy.'

'Ah ha. And James?'

'He says he does, but I am not so sure. He may just say it to please me.'

'But you're trying.'

'Oh yes. All the time.'

Though she said it almost offhandedly she employed a particular inflection that revealed a smidgen of the other evening's Carmensina. It was an intonation proclaiming that though she and James were on the verge of middle age, though her breasts and cheekbones might not technically be her own, though Laura might be entertaining fantasies that James was taking a fancy to her, the truth was that the married couple were still screwing like jack-rabbits. On the other hand, Laura had to admit that Carmensina was making a genuine effort to be civil.

'I was an only child,' Laura said.

'Not me,' Carmensina replied. 'We were five and I was the only girl. My mother and father worshipped my brothers, and I sometimes felt unwanted. Being an only child can have some advantages.'

'That makes sense.'

'Sometimes I feel I am mean to the girls. It is a terrible thing. It comes out of nowhere. It comes from my mother. It's like I am repeating a pattern. It's why I wanted boys really.'

'Families are complicated by definition, don't you think?'

'Yes. Yes, I do.'

They walked on in peace with each other and joined the girls.

This excursion gave Camilla and James almost an hour to read the first draft of Laura's translated text. Camilla was the quicker of the two and was forced to wait at the bottom of each page for her son to catch up. When they finished the enslavement and rescue episode they read on through the following instalment as well which allowed them to turn the computer off without such a lurid taste in their mouths.

'My word,' Camilla said, folding her reading glasses into her right hand.

'It's astonishing,' he said. 'Astonishing.'

'Do you think perhaps the teller of the tale, the uncle, might be a bit of an exaggerator?'

'I hadn't thought of it,' he said. 'We can ask Laura's opinion. But in terms of the effect this will have on the public's reaction and that of, say, the Vatican, I doubt such a thing will make much of a difference. Exaggerated or not they'll be screaming for blood – our blood.'

'Don't be absurd, James. They'll do nothing of the sort. They'll try and refute the whole business and take it under study and that will be that.'

'What an extraordinary thing this is. And here it's been, all these centuries.'

By the time Laura returned to the house and as Carmensina helped Noelma pack up the girls' things, there was only time to give James one of her cards that he had asked for, and to answer a few of their questions, one of which was whether anything else particularly scandalous had been revealed thus far. She quickly mentioned the Daphne seduction chapter she had alluded to with James the night before. What she wished to know was their opinion about the translation's style.

'I think it's wonderful,' James said, looking into her eyes. 'Really.'

'Camilla?' Laura asked, turning to her.

'It's not Matthew, Mark, Luke or John, that's for sure. But it reads very well, dear, very well indeed. Carry on.'

After James and his family left, Laura found it difficult to work. The house felt more isolated and abandoned than before. She killed time reading until lunch, which she took with Camilla who was in a chatty and animated frame of mind and that cheered her up. After having their coffees, Camilla retired to her room for a nap and Laura decided to take another walk. She could not get James out of her mind. She set a brisk pace and headed back toward the cottage, which took almost an hour to reach walking along the edge of the paved drive.

The wind had subsided considerably making for a glorious afternoon. Small clumps of clouds moved slowly off to the east, and all of the pastures, lawns, and leas presented a vivid variety of greens. When she reached the cottage, she found the kitchen door unlocked and was pleased to discover the maids had yet to appear to set things right. She realized it might be a day or so before anyone got around to it. It was only when she was satisfied she was alone that she could admit she had come to snoop.

There were some dirty dishes in the sink, but the refrigerator was empty save for a bottle of Pol Roger that had possibly been there for years. In the living room in front of the hearth she found the remains of a fire, an unfinished Monopoly game, and a quite finished glass of what smelled like whiskey, next to an ashtray filled with Marlboro Light butts whose filters were stained with lipstick. Upstairs she looked into all of the bedrooms and baths, saving the master suite until the end. It was easy to determine who had slept where. The girls' room was a mess, the nanny's room much less so. Letting herself into the master suite she inspected the bathroom first. She gazed at the large shower stall where some spigots were still dripping and where the tiles were still damp. On the floor next to the bathtub was the requisite bottle of Aqua di Parma. Its top was missing. She looked for it, found it, and screwed it back on. She looked at the bidet that had obviously been used and at all of the towels that had been tossed upon the floor. She opened the medicine cabinet and found nothing of interest. When she closed it, she stared at herself in the mirror.

Then she walked into the bedroom and looked out of the windows, down to the swath of forest she had crossed the day she spoke with Fiona about James. But all she could think of was how James and Carmensina had been in that room only hours earlier. The bed was unmade but the covers had been brusquely drawn up. She drew them back down and saw stains of sex drying on the light blue bottom sheet. She laid herself down and smelled the four pillows, finding the pair that had been his. Then she rolled over onto her back and slipped her jeans and panties down to her knees.

Chapter 20

That evening after dinner, she translated the next segment.

We anchored off a cove at the island known as Insula Maior where the ship's captain had the profitable custom of trading for salt. An expedition led by the lead mate and a group of slaves headed inland, embarking on a journey that kept us there for two days.

This captain, a descendant from authentic Phoenician stock, or so he claimed, treated his crew and his slaves with a level of dignity unusual in my experience. During a walk in the nearby countryside I spoke to him about it. He believed the practice of enslavement to be barbaric and, in the end, counterproductive for the Empire. Yeshua stated his agreement. I, who had profited thanks to the labour of slaves over the years, made no comment, once again allowing the Romans to speak for me. 'Any nation, any leader foolish enough to challenge the spread of Roman law and justice must know he is putting at risk the treasure he hordes, the freedom of his subjects, and the virtue of his women,' said Lucca. 'And as you know,' added Octavius, 'the condition is not irreversible, and most slave owners are like yourself, just and well-intentioned men.'

'I disagree,' said the captain. 'The number of slaves who regain their freedom is very small and from what I have seen abuse is more common than kindness. Resentment spreads among a not inconsiderate portion of the Empire's population, a portion that will not rally to the Emperor's or to the Senate's defence in times of difficulty.'

'And yet your own slaves are not free,' said Octavius.

'If they were mine, they would be,' the captain answered, 'but they belong to the man I work for, my father-in-law, who thinks as you do.'

We walked through groves of almond trees planted in grassy recesses above the sea. Before turning around, we gained a vantage point up a rocky bluff from which one could look far out to sea and down at the ship afloat in the transparent water. The sun shimmered upon the rocks, upon the furled sails, upon the white sand. It was a sight I made an effort to memorize and hold onto. On the following day we would be off again, en route to Iberia, but then and there, in that moment, all was peaceful and calm, and all of nature that surrounded us was pure and benign. I knew that life was a chain of moments, some of them painful, some fearsome and dangerous, too many of them listless, repetitive and dull. But then there were moments like these, when being alive and the small corner of the world one is in blend together in wondrous harmony. These moments, always fleeting, constitute my true religion.

My reverie was broken when Octavius informed our small party that certain inhabitants of that island were prized in the Roman legions for their skill with the sling-shot. Lucca, who claimed to be born, like Moses, upon the banks of a river, in his case the Tiberis, pretended to take offense and promptly produced a sling with which to prove his own prowess. The walk, now downhill, back toward the beach where the ship rested, had all of us in single file along a steep slope where wild olive trees grew, some of them askew with their branches hanging over the abyss. A falcon flew overhead, and Octavius demanded that Lucca hit it. It took him five attempts accompanied with much cursing that made the last part of the walk amusing for some, including Yeshua, and unpleasant for the captain and myself. And then he hit the elegant creature and it fell like a stone into the Mediterranean just off the side of the ship. As Lucca cheered at the top of his lungs, I watched it struggle in the salt water before it drowned.

Chapter 21

Laura made an exception to her rule and printed this section to give to her hostess, knowing she would enjoy reading the reference to Mallorca. Camilla appreciated the gesture and after she read it at breakfast, she went along with Laura and James's words of caution and had Bidelia burn it in an oil drum used for waste paper that was next to the compost heap behind the stables. At dinner the following evening, both of them were content to have the house to themselves again. Camilla, for the first time, expressed genuine interest in the contents of her heirloom.

Afterward, Laura took her customary evening stroll and then went up to her room. Before undressing she checked her email. Among the usual assortment of uncaught spam, university notices, some queries from colleagues wondering what had become of her, and three articles from *Foreign Affairs* sent by Nathan that she would never read, there were two emails that jumped off the screen. One, which she opened second, was from a colleague in Paris who she had written to who specialized in medieval French literature. The other, which she opened right away, was from James:

Dear Laura – Just a brief note to reiterate (or is it simply 'iterate'? I've never got that one clear in English) my gratitude for what you are doing, the skill and the discretion you are demonstrating, and for bringing all we spoke of the other evening to my attention. I am confident that, between the two of us (plus Mother!) we shall devise the best way of navigating the shoals you are justifiably wary of. I spoke in the most general terms with a good barrister in London and he has promised to look into things. As a plus, his wife's sister has been with Sotheby's for years. I have to travel to New York the day after tomorrow on business; the media firm I work for, still too linked to the Spanish economy, is hunting for outside investors. Upon our arrival at the hotel in London on the day we left you, Carmensina had a bad headache and I took the girls to Kensington Gardens, to the Peter Pan statue I have loved since early childhood. I don't know why I am telling you this. I am currently at a bar in Barcelona, enjoying a solitary brandy, a good one this time, fondly remembering our encounter at The Wounded Hart. I hope this finds you well and not working too hard. Yours, James

She read it twice. Then she opened the message from her colleague:

Dear Laura,

What a pleasant surprise to hear from you after all this time, and how nice to hear you have not abandoned your interest in Medieval France! Believe it or not I know two people who specialize in Gerard of Amiens who might be helpful to you. Both of them work in the States of course where scholars still get paid. Isabelle Diderot at UCLA is one of the most cutting-edge investigators around today. She is a former student of mine. Then, and this would be my first choice because he is such a personage, *there is Jean-Paul Bonnerive who is retired and lives in your very own New York where he is a professor emeritus at Columbia. I think you might remember I stayed with him once during a visit to New York when I last saw you. He claims to have actual correspondence of Gerard of Amiens but has never published it. Here are their email addresses. I wish you* bonne chance *and if you do not come and see me when you next pass through Paris, I shall never speak to you again. Pierre*

Laura decided a quick trip home was in order.

After some reluctance at breakfast the next day, Camilla supported the idea. James reacted better still, something she endeavoured, with little success, to keep out of her mind. It took her another day to make travel arrangements, pack, and get to London. Once her plane took off from Heathrow she relaxed and pulled down the shade of her window seat, pleased with the willpower it had required to resist advising either Fiona or Nathan of her travel plans. Fiona she could see on her way back to Cornwall, and Nathan she was mad at. They had ceased phoning each other and his responses to her emails of last week had been unusually sparse and hurried.

After lunch was served and cleared, she abandoned herself to the wonder of flight despite its discomforts. Then, while many of the other passengers watched a film or attempted to sleep, she opened her laptop and continued with her work.

Chapter 22

After leaving the Mediterranean for the Atlantic we arrived at Gades for repairs and fresh provisions. Octavius and I explained to Lucca and Yeshua how the ancient city that juts out into the sea had been founded by Hercules after the completion of his Tenth Labour, the slaying of Geryon. When we described what Geryon looked like, a monster with three heads and three torsos standing upon a single pair of sturdy legs, Lucca's eyes widened and Yeshua scoffed. A burial mound near the site of the city was believed to be the monster's resting place.

The four of us went to visit the temple dedicated to Melqart, a Phoenician deity associated with Tyrian Hercules. It rests on high ground from which one can see the ocean and the estuary on the other side, where flocks of exotic birds gather to rest on their way to and from Africa. A statue of the bearded god stood by an olive tree and a small fountain surrounded by columns from antiquity. That this god was primarily known as a protector of Tyre, the city from where we started on our journey, imbued it with special significance for me.

Yeshua picked an olive from the tree and guarded it in the pocket of his tunic. The Romans offered prayers. Then the three of them wandered down a goat path to a stony ledge where they began a competition to see who could cast stones the greatest distance. As I listened to their cheering and yelling carried off by a gentle breeze moving through a grove of towering umbrella pines, I realized that I had stood there upon that very spot on nine occasions. I thought about how the temple had been there long before I was born. After I left Gades it would remain there. As my life proceeded, moving from place to place, and even at the moment of my death, that temple shall be there, just as it is. While we slept that night in the city, this temple and its statue and the olive tree would be here, silent, in the dark. One would be hard put to call attention to a more ordinary observation, but the sensations these thoughts provoked could not be disparaged. What is time? What is home? Why do we wander so?

Chapter 23

Once again Laura found herself astonished by the naturalistic realism of her ancient author, overturning her beloved Erich Auerbach's theory which claimed that authors from this period were incapable of introspection. According to him they could only keep events front and centre, their use of dialog limited to expressions of rhetoric, their views of the world two-dimensional, far from an individual's inner thoughts. And yet the feelings that Joseph of Arimathea was describing were as human as language itself. It was one seized upon in modern times by the likes of Proust, Thomas Wolfe ('a stone, a leaf, an unfound door ...'), and found in the final pages of *Finnegan's Wake*. That it had been transcribed two thousand years ago and that it was she of all the people in the world who was bringing it to light, brought her to tears. She put on a pair of sunglasses. To her relief the man sitting in the aisle seat to her left, absorbed in an action film, did not pick up on her state. She shut down and closed her laptop. Bright light shone upon her right wrist through a sliver of window not covered by the shade. She closed it fully, removed the sunglasses, and dried her eyes with some tissue.

Sleep took hold of her above the North Atlantic and by the time it released her she could see the eastern tip of Long Island below. She recognized towns and bays and beaches and saw the stretch of shore between Water Mill and the Shinnecock Canal where the Beach Club and her stepfather's summerhouse stood. Soon after the plane descended and swung out to sea, making a long slow turn that put it onto its final approach into Kennedy. As it came to a stop at the British Airways gate it felt like she had been out of New York for a year rather than the three weeks it had actually been.

She took a taxi into town and thought to warn Nathan, feeling sheepish about what had been her plan as she entered Manhattan through the Midtown Tunnel. But then she got an email from James telling her he was at The Bowery Hotel and might they meet for a drink before a dinner he had to attend? She did her best to answer him typing against the frantic driving style of the man at the wheel. Before she knew it, the cab came to a stop by her building's awning near the corner of Tenth Street and Fifth Avenue.

The doormen were glad to see her, and she suddenly felt happy to be back, amazed at how easily she had allowed herself to adapt to Camilla's world in Cornwall. But when she got out of the elevator on the top floor and stepped into her apartment, a woman's voice called out, called out a single word as Laura closed the door. The word was 'Nathan?'

As her heart began to sink and anger rose, she found a waif-like girl in her own bed. The sheets were wrinkled into a messy bundle at the foot of it. The girl, wearing one of Nathan's white T-shirts and a black thong, was startled. She made no attempt to cover herself.

'Who are you?' she asked.

Her accent was strong.

'This is my home,' Laura replied. 'The better question is, who are you?'

'I am Oksana. You are Laura?'

'Yes.'

'You're not supposed to be here.'

'Neither are you.'

Less than two hours later Oksana was preparing the dinner shift at Veselka's and Laura had already had the locks changed. Movers had been alerted to remove certain items of furniture belonging to Nathan, along with his clothing and books to be put into temporary storage, all of it tagged by Laura with Post-its. She also called the painters she had used when she was first given the apartment. She asked them to repaint the entire place starting the following week. Then she watered her plants out on the terrace, collected some favourite clothes, shoes, and mail, and reserved herself a room at the Bowery Hotel.

Her greatest relief was that Nathan did not return to the apartment while she was there. The girl had probably warned him away. Mixed with her anger and sadness was a less recognized portion of relief. Oksana's presence in her bed had solved a significant conundrum. She even felt sorry for the girl. Her fury was only marginally connected to Nathan's betrayal. More of it derived from the fact that he had not brought the girl to his own apartment, the one NYU had given him – a drab but perfectly adequate two-bedroom in a Village high-rise with vast views of lower Manhattan. A young woman like the Eastern European waitress would have been just as impressed with it as she was no doubt by Laura's penthouse, but Nathan's ego apparently knew no bounds. She did not want to see him or speak with him. Alarmed with herself for having wasted four years of her life, she finally sent him a text message from the safety of her room at the Bowery:

Met Oksana in my bedroom. Very cute. I've changed the locks and the doormen have been instructed to accompany you only once back into the apartment. The movers come on Thursday for your things, either to put them into storage or wherever you like. Don't ever want to hear from you again you dumb pompous bastard.

Only then did she allow herself a mega shower. She was in the bar in the hotel lobby by seven thirty, ordering a Ketel One on the rocks when James arrived.

'Laura.'

'James.'

He was dressed in a dark suit and a white shirt open at the collar. She thought he looked very good.

'Sorry I'm late,' he said. 'I've been glued to the phone with Spain where, clearly, people need to learn to go to sleep.'

'That's OK. I've been happy here,' she said. 'It's a lovely spot. I've walked by this place many times and had no idea it was so nice inside.'

'It's totally fake and totally authentic.'

'Something like that.'

'The English gentleman's club motif. You'd think I'd run from it, but it gets me every time. Not quite sure what that means. But of course, it's also very "downtown". Lots of film and rock stars stay here.'

'Your kind of people.'

'My true family, as it were.'

This was a playful, far from home, wife, and children side of him she had not seen before.

'Speaking of which,' she said. 'Camilla asked me if I was going to see you here – and I didn't know what to say.'

'But you said something.'

'I said "yes, of course, if our schedules permitted".'

'And here we are. She's off to her house in Mallorca for a few days anyway, taking advantage of your absence, so she's pleasantly distracted.'

'She mentioned she might do that. I'm glad.'

The bartender appeared.

'I'll have what she's having,' James said to him. Laura smiled.

'Isn't that the famous line from *When Harry Met Sally*?'

'If it's a film you are referring to – I've never seen it.'

'Amazing.'

'What's amazing is this. A few nights ago, we were in The Wounded Hart for God's sake.'

'It *is* strange. I promise I'm not stalking you. I wanted to see this man up at Columbia University while he's still alive – and I needed to deal with some personal stuff too.'

'As disappointed as I am to hear that, I don't doubt it for a second. But still, this is like kismet, isn't it?'

'It is.'

'Whatever kismet actually means.'

'It's from a Persian word, referring to fate or chance.'

He was seized by a sudden urge to kiss her. His drink arrived. She raised her glass.

'Cheers.'

He did the same, before taking a good sip, 'God that's good.'

'I can't live without it these days,' she said.

This reminded him of Carmensina, a thought he did his best to push away. 'So, how was your flight?'

'Fine. How was yours?'

'Fine.'

'Well I'm glad we got that out of the way.'

They both laughed nervously.

'Where's your dinner?' she asked.

'Here – at the Italian place they have on the corner. It's lively, the food is perfectly good and it's perfect for jet-lagged pseudo-executives.'

'Would that be you or your clients?'

'That would be me. The clients, fortunately and unfortunately, are the real thing.'

'But not you, not even in that gorgeous, executive suit.'

She could not believe she had just said that. She blamed the vodka.

'No.'

'Don't you like what you do?'

'Not really.'

'That's too bad.'

'I don't believe anyone has ever asked me that question.'

'Here you are in a foreign country, and me a virtual stranger – it's a golden opportunity to let it all hang out.'

'What does that incredibly vulgar sounding expression actually mean? Can't be Persian.'

She laughed. 'You're right.'

'Anyway,' he said, 'it's fine what I do. It's respectable and pays many of the bills and gives me sharp looking business cards and a corner office in a renovated, beaux-arts building in Barcelona.'

'The media company,' she said. 'The one Carmensina's family owns.'

'Precisely. She gets a failed Bohemian aristocrat with land and a title. I get a well-paying job and two beautiful children. Not a bad deal as things go these days.'

His frankness was startling.

'Are you on something?'

He downed the rest of his drink.

'No. It's you. I don't know what it is, but you have this effect on me.'

She smiled, flattered, and began to feel an inner glow of her own.

'Do you really have a title?'

'Yes, which, as you New Yorkers used to say, along with a token, or I guess these days, a Metro Card, will get one on the subway. But for Carmensina and her family it's worth a lot.'

She finished her drink too. The bartender arrived like a shark and they went for another round.

'Tell me more about this failed Bohemian aspect,' she said. 'That interests me.'

'Are you seeing someone?' He asked it very quickly. 'Mother mentioned something about a beau.'

'That's very Celtic,' she said, 'answering a question with another one.'

'Guilty as charged.'

'Not the sort of behaviour toward a lady one would expect from an aristocrat in a gentleman's club.'

'Quite right. I'll go first then. Let's just say that had I been a successful Bohemian I would not have this job.'

'What would you be doing instead?'

'I'd be rising early in a little villa nestled in some Mediterranean hillside writing a novel – based on my childhood for example. This just came into my mind.'

170

'I would love to read that.'

'Really?'

'Really. On the other hand, if you didn't have your current job, we wouldn't be here having this conversation.'

'Like I said – kismet.'

'Do you really need to work? I mean, work-work.'

'Pretty much. What I collect each month in – call it inheritance – isn't enough to keep a family of four.'

'But if it was just you?'

The new drinks arrived along with some salted almonds.

'If it was just me, I could probably swing it. But that's not the case. But enough about me. It's your turn.'

She ate an almond and took a sip, considering distinct levels of disclosure.

'I've had a "beau" as you call it, these past four years.'

'Aha.'

'Aha. I've had a beau these past four years, until today.'

He actually blushed. 'I didn't realize this suit was quite that compelling.'

She looked down and in a second, he felt the truth seeping in. 'Today,' he said. 'Good Lord. What happened?'

She took in another mouthful of the vodka.

'I got off the plane from London, went to my apartment, and found a twenty-year-old waitress in my bed.'

'No.'

'Yes.'

'What did you do?'

'I kindly asked her to leave, told her she'd been

misinformed about the "open" nature of my relationship with Nathan – that was his name – then I changed the locks, hired movers to get his stuff out, and then I came here.'

'This just happened.'

'That's right. I got myself a room here too. The idea of spending the night at my place tonight is just too upsetting.'

He put his hand on her shoulder. 'Laura. I'm so sorry. What a cad.'

'Things have not been great for a while between us actually, and a big part of me *was* looking for a way out, and "boom" he handed it to me on the proverbial silver platter.'

'But still.'

'It's not what I needed today – and what I can't forgive was that he brought her to my place when he has a perfectly decent apartment of his own.'

'Of course. So, you're staying *here*. I can't believe it.'

'You put the idea in my head and I'm glad you did because it's very nice and cosy. The only other place I know of in the neighbourhood is a depressing dive on Washington Square that NYU uses for visitors.'

'God. What a day you've had. Come and join us for dinner.'

'I don't much feel like dinner.'

'As my guest. It's right here, right through that door.'

'That's very kind but I don't think I'd be very good company. What I really want to do is get into that white robe up in the room, turn on the TV, and fall asleep. It's my idea of heaven right now.'

172

Later on, she discovered that staying in a hotel in her own city, four blocks east and three blocks south from her own empty apartment, was harder to do than she had imagined. She had so much trouble falling asleep, even with the jetlag, the vodka, and an Ambien, that she almost got dressed and went back to Tenth Street. She even came close to calling Nathan at one point. But then she remembered James was there, somewhere in the hotel, and her favourite shops and local stores were nearby, and out of the window, down below, the elegant frenzy that defined her town flowed on its honking way, just as it had before she was born and just as it would after she was gone.

She came to the conclusion that she had done a healthy thing coming to the hotel and she was grateful for having the resources to do it without worrying about it. That she was finally in the thick of breaking up with someone she should never have got so deep into to begin with was progress. Tomorrow would be another day and, after all, she was on the verge of a professional breakthrough. With a little perusing of Shopbop on her phone and an extra pillow, she soon fell sound asleep.

She woke at dawn, famished and refreshed, took a quick shower, and got dressed. In the dark wood-panelled lobby there were two crisp piles of the day's *New York Times* and *New York Post* she helped herself to. The young hotel doormen in their red vests and black derbies were cute and friendly, and it felt familiar and reassuring to be out on the street at that hour. Garbage trucks were finishing their rounds and some homeless were still asleep in doorways lending a note of realism to the otherwise gentrified avenue. She turned west at Cooper Union going toward Broadway, avoiding the entire Veselka area as best she could. It was going to be another clear, warm, and fresh autumn day. At her bagel shop on University Place, the Moroccans and Latinos who worked there greeted her like she had never left. The morning doorman at her building, one of the last standing Irishmen in the union who was already alerted no doubt to yesterday's drama, tipped his cap with an appreciated mixture of warmth and reserve.

The apartment felt better at that hour. She enjoyed the coffee and the buttered bialy out at the table on her terrace. Most of the plants had miraculously survived the stingy ministrations of Nathan. The birch tree and the small fir trees planted in half barrels were doing well, and some pansies and geraniums were thriving. A robin was perched on the edge of the birdbath when she came out. Looking down Fifth Avenue toward the arch, the plantain trees were still green-leafed even with the late September nip in the air.

She went back inside, got a trash bag, and went through the medicine cabinets tossing every item that was Nathan's. Then she tied it off and placed it in a bin by the service elevator before leaving and walking back to the hotel. There had yet to be a single message from him. She imagined that his hurt pride had trumped anything resembling remorse.

She thought to try and schedule a session with her therapist while she was there, but knew too well what they would talk about – how Nathan had been an awkward fit for her still unresolved and ambivalent Oedipal strivings blah-blah-blah and so what had she expected? Was any of that true, or had it just been a mess of chance, hormones, and stubbornness?

Back in her room at The Bowery she read the papers she had been carrying around all morning. Instead of visiting her favourite bookstore on Prince Street or walking down to the new Whitney where there was an exhibit she'd been meaning to see, she put in a call to her favourite day spa, booking treatments that would take her right up to the time she would have to head uptown to meet Jean-Paul Bonnerive. A text message from James appeared:

Dinner tonight?

She smiled and replied:

Yes.

Chapter 24

It stormed during the final days of our outbound journey. The mainsail ripped in two and perilous amounts of seawater were taken aboard. Much of the food was soaked and ruined and our supply of drinking water was contaminated. Luckily all of my containers of the oils I needed for trade were safe. Then, one day, all was calm. The crew set about repairing the sail, the oars were manned, and just before dusk the skies opened and the setting sun appeared bringing great relief to all. Then we sighted land.

We sailed into a bay familiar to me the following morning. By the time we came ashore a delegation from the nearby village, all of them men I knew and traded with – Athain, Casdarth, Phenbir and Kraugh – were gathered on the strand. Out of respect for the local population and for their emperor, Octavius and Lucca came off the ship in full battle gear, including breastplates, capes, and plumed helmets. I introduced them as my friends. The local men had heard of the Romans from the time of Caesar's invasion, and they were more alarmed than pleased. But I was able to explain our relationship and our hosts were impressed. Then they enquired about Yeshua who stood just behind me. Try as I might, I could not make it clear he was my nephew, and in the end, it was left that, in their eyes, he was my son.

We walked to the village, passing over streams of clear fresh water. This and the sighting of cows and sheep grazing in meadows, and then fields of wheat blowing in the morning breeze, filled our captain with great consolation. It made the Romans hungry.

What I remembered as a simple village from just a few years earlier was now a proper town – still primitive in many ways – but comfortably supporting numerous families and tin streamers come to work and settle there from other regions of the isle. Our arrival caused considerable excitement and we were shown to our accommodations straight away. The news that went from mouth to mouth, along with the fact that I had two Roman soldiers in my employ, was that I had brought my most handsome son to walk among them. After a repast of mutton, meal, and goblets of mead that left us all well sated, we were taken on a tour of the nearby mines. It gave me pleasure to show Yeshua the large ragged veins of tin mixed with rock and soil, and the small deposits of lead, copper, and gold that burst forth upon the surface of those coastal territories the way palms and date trees sprout near our deserts.

As the days passed, the captain went about repairing the ship and refilling his barrels and amphorae with fresh food and water. After a week he bid us farewell promising to return in a month's time to collect us and to load in my ingots. We adapted to life in the new town. Lucca found himself a companion, a rugged tin man from afar. Octavius found himself a comely widow with two small children he was not averse to entertaining. And Athain, the chieftain and town leader, invited Yeshua and me to a special supper.

The general conversation during the meal centred on the lands and cultures we came from. Each of us ventured guesses as to what an accurate map of the world might look like. The Roman Empire, its reach and power, was also discussed, as was the topic of religion. To my relief, and for the first time that I could remember since our departure from Nazareth, Yeshua said nothing. Perhaps this reticence, that I was hoping to ascribe to maturity, had more to do with what was clearly the main reason for this special repast. For all the while we were waited on by Athain's two beautiful daughters. Though not hidden from view during the course of a normal day in the town, they were always dressed from head to toe in dark vestments. That evening they wore white gowns that clung to them and their heads were uncovered revealing long tresses of golden hair. To our host's obvious pleasure, it was difficult for us to keep our eyes off of them. As the evening drew to a close, he escorted us out of his home. Thousands of stars bore down through gaps in the low-lying clouds, and with the scent of ripening wheat wafting through the air, he made it clear that he would be honoured were we to take his daughters as our brides. I told him I was far too old, even for the elder of the two, the one called Canlia, who was probably eighteen. Venusha, the younger one, was all of fifteen. But he brushed this qualm aside. I imagine he saw it as an advantage to him and to his future. He had no sons. By marrying them off to us he would have my business guaranteed for many years, and he would avoid igniting rivalries among other leading families with eligible sons. We promised to consider his offer and bade him goodnight.

Chapter 25

Over a year had passed since Laura had taken the IRT line uptown. During her stint at NYU the Upper West Side fell off her normal itinerary, and Nathan was claustrophobic, so even trips to and from Lincoln Center were always by taxi. She remembered how often they used to fight over the meagre tips he gave the drivers, and his small-town indignation with respect to tipping, period. The last time she had taken the local train this far up Broadway was to see Pierre when he was on his way back to Paris from California. Pierre had wanted some real New York Jewish food, Pierre who flirted with her so openly and innocently that it never bothered her. She took him to Barney Greengrass on Amsterdam and 87th Street, the famous Jewish deli, the 'appetizing' store renowned for its sturgeon, whitefish, and Nova Scotia. They had scrambled eggs with kippered salmon and strong coffee, and he had kidded her about her heritage, being half Palestinian and mad for Jewish food.

She got off at 116th Street and came up onto the

pavement by the main entrance to Columbia University. The day was so lovely and romantic, smelling of fall and the river, and the foot traffic of students and professors so appealing, she was tempted to stroll through the campus. But she was running late. She had tarried at the spa and fallen asleep on the massage table and then she had stopped at Astor Place Liquors to get a bottle of wine. She crossed Broadway and headed down the hill to reach Bonnerive's building at 448 Riverside Drive. It was the sort of solid, elegant, pre-war campus housing that was unlike anything at NYU, and unlike anything Columbia would probably ever have again. The graceful, granite, ten-storey apartment building, one of two that were identical, faced Riverside Park and the Hudson.

Bonnerive buzzed her in. The man she saw standing in the doorway of his eighth-floor apartment was close to ninety. He was trim and dapper, with horn-rimmed glasses, liver spots on well-manicured hands, and thinning grey hair that was a bit too long. He wore a herringbone jacket in need of mending over a classic work shirt with an ascot, in short – *un jeune premier*. She greeted him in French.

'Now I see why Pierre is so in love with you,' he said, 'why he has kept you from me all this time.'

She handed him the bottle of wine, 'Pierre is a married man.'

'You can qualify the noun with whatever modifier you wish,' he said, 'but the noun is what counts.'

182

He took the bottle with both hands and admired it, holding it up to her, 'Shall we?'

'It's a bit early in the day for me.'

'Nonsense,' he said, showing her into the main hallway that was lined with abstract paintings that looked to have been done by students. He took her coat. 'If I can handle it, you certainly can.'

'What was it that Audrey Hepburn once said?' Laura declared. 'It must be cocktail hour somewhere in the world.'

'Precisely,' he replied, 'and in fact it's coming up on five here in New York.'

He gave the bottle back to her, 'There are glasses and a corkscrew in the kitchen.'

She decided not to be offended and surmised that at his age he might find pulling the cork embarrassingly difficult. The apartment at first glance appeared neat and orderly, but on closer inspection she saw it was simply frozen in time and in need of a thorough cleaning. She wondered if he had anyone who came in to help, but she was not going to rain on his parade by asking. The only thing visible in the huge yellowy-beige kitchen that might accompany the wine were some Ritz crackers she arranged on a beautiful chipped plate from Schoelcher et Fils.

She found him in an immense living room lined with floor-to-ceiling bookshelves where three wide windows, chipped paint on their sills, looked out over the Hudson and at New Jersey across the way. It was an afternoon that cried out for them to be opened but she was not there to rattle the man's routines. The wine, highly recommended to her by a store employee, was delicious, and they sat across from each other in easy chairs that still wore summer slipcovers adorned with a faded flowery print.

'How long have you been here?' she asked.

'Here in this apartment? Probably since the day you were born.'

'It's a magnificent space. Maybe I should try to come here and teach. Do you think they'd give me one of these if I did?'

'Very doubtful. But you could live here with me. There's lots of room.'

'Is that a proposal Jean-Paul?'

'Yes.'

'We've hardly met.'

'I still have eyes my dear, and nothing would please me more – just imagine how green with envy Pierre would be.'

She took another sip.

'You've not been tempted to return to France, to retire there? New York can be such a tough place.'

'When my wife was alive, we mostly lived in France. I only had to teach one semester here per year. It was a wonderful and generous arrangement. But she was from New York and wished to be buried here and when she died, I brought her back here, up to the Catholic cemetery in Westchester where Lorca's father is buried. And – this must sound very silly – I've been unable to leave her, to put an ocean between us, ever since – and that was fifteen years ago.'

Laura swallowed and, maddeningly, tears came into her eyes. She did all she could to stop it. 'You loved her very much.'

'I did. I do. And she loved me. We were very fortunate.'

'Yes, you were.'

'Do you love anyone like that?'

'You're a direct young man, aren't you?'

'When time is short one goes to the grain, my dear.'

'No. I don't think that I do.'

'You're young still.'

'Not that young.'

'Let's just say you are younger than Mary was when she met me.'

'So, there is still hope.'

'Absolutely.'

A shiver of displacement passed through her, akin to the sensation one is said to feel when an angel steps over your future grave. What and where was home? Joseph of Arimathea had asked the question too. She assumed the answer had less to do with place and more to do with being part of a large family – a sensation she had no experience with.

'Did you say Lorca's father? Federico García Lorca?'

'That's right. This used to be their apartment.'

'My maternal grandparents and my mother were born in Granada.'

'You don't say.'

'My grandparents were very right wing I'm afraid.'

'It happens in the best of families, in fact, mostly in the best of families.'

She raised her glass to him.

'After Lorca was killed,' he said, 'his family fled to New York. I collaborated with his brother Francisco who taught Spanish literature here and when he retired in 1975 the family moved back to Spain and I inherited the apartment.'

'That's quite something.'

'Yes, but they left the patriarch here in his grave in American soil, because when he escaped from Spain in 1939, with what was left of his children, just before their ship left Bilbao he said, 'I never want to come back to this fucking country ever again.'

'I'd no idea. And yet Spain is OK now.'

'History is fate and timing. We've no choice about the era we're born into.'

As he said this, she noticed that his right hand, the one holding the wine, began to quiver so he grabbed the glass with his left. He held forth for at least half an hour on the topics of history and the Spanish Civil War until he realized her interest was flagging.

'But you've not come here to see me about Spain,' he said.

'No. But it is fascinating.'

'Gerard of Amiens – what possessed you?'

She laughed, 'What possessed *you*?'

'For me he was a local hero. I was born in Abbeville. My family has been there for centuries. One of my ancestors worked for one of the Counts of Ponthieu.'

186

'It was the part of France that Eleanor of Castile inherited.'

'That's right.'

'And did Gerard of Amiens write a story for her?'

'He did.'

'I'd like to show you something.'

'By all means.'

She took out her mobile phone and accessed a photo she'd taken before leaving Cornwall. It was of one of the vellum sheets from the French codex. She made it as large as possible and came over to where Bonnerive was seated, getting down on her knees next to his chair to show him the screen.

'I'm sorry I don't have anything larger for you to look at. I'm not supposed to show any of this to anyone yet. Do you recognize the handwriting at all?'

He looked at it carefully, 'Where did you find this?'

'Is it his writing?'

'Yes.'

'Are you sure?'

'Yes. For what it is worth, I am the world expert in this kind of trivia. But where did you see this?'

'In a private house in the southwest of England. It's part of a project I'm working on. But I've been sworn to secrecy at the moment so I can't tell you all that much.'

'Why?'

'It's an eighty-page codex that's a translation of another from the fourth century written in Greek, which in turn is a translation from a completely dilapidated scroll from the first century.'

She rose to her feet and returned to her chair.

'You are in possession of an eighty-page codex written by Gerard of Amiens?'

'Translated and written down by him. And I think he did it for Eleanor of Castile.'

'Why?'

'Because the family that owns these objects are descendants of Eleanor of Castile and Edward I.'

He sat there, still, then took a bit of wine and began to sway one of his legs back and forth. 'What I would give to see such a document,' he finally said.

'When the sale goes through – the owners are going to put it up for auction – I can send you a facsimile of it, in its entirety.'

His hand began to quiver again. To dissimulate he removed a handkerchief from his breast pocket and took off his glasses and cleaned the lenses. 'Well I hope I shall live that long.'

'Of course you will,' she said. 'Do you know anything about what sort of relationship Gerard had with Eleanor?'

'I have an idea, yes, perhaps.'

'Pierre mentioned you had some correspondence of Gerard's, but that you've never published it.'

'Pierre believes one has to publish everything. I am long past that phase in my life. What people do with what I have, after I'm gone, shall be up to them. But for now, I still keep myself alive by working on this correspondence. It amuses me.'

'And perhaps you have something that might shed some light on all of this?'

He smiled at her, 'Perhaps.'

'Let me tell you one more thing,' she said. 'The text of the scroll, from what I can judge, was faithfully translated into Greek, but the version Gerard did from the Greek into Old French is different.'

'How so?'

'Names were changed, and, well all I can say is that his version is a censored version of the original – the original tells a very startling tale, especially in light of who the personages are. His version transforms it into a romantic saga with fictional characters. In everything I have read about Eleanor of Castile it says she was a devout woman and that she had a special affinity for the Dominican order, due perhaps to the friendship she nurtured while in Sicily with Thomas of Aquinas. But Gerard, correct me please if I'm wrong, was known as a bit of a heretic, right? As a man irritated with religious orders, and someone who had a large library of classic texts, some of which were banned by the Church. Eleanor was also a great lover of books. I'm trying to find some kind of bridge between the two positions.'

'I may be able to help you with that. But not today.'

'I'd be so grateful.'

'You are a most fortunate young woman, Laura.'

'I know.'

'Be careful. The academic world is as venal and nasty as it's always been.'

'I know.'

'Good. And I promise to send you something that might help.'

'Thank you, and I promise to send you a copy of the codex.'

She didn't finish her glass of wine. By the time she got up to leave Bonnerive had downed two. As they left the living room, she was taken aback by the golden light reflecting off the river streaming through the windows. He noticed her expression. 'As you can see, in exchanging the Somme for the Hudson, I've not done too badly.'

'No, you haven't.'

Laura put on her coat. He kissed her on both cheeks, giving her forearms a brief squeeze. She could smell the wine on him plus a dab of cologne, all of it mixed with a faint scent of moth balls.

Chapter 26

She took a taxi back down to the hotel and texted James en route:

> Could you bear another Italian meal this evening and might I make the reservation? I have my reasons. Laura

He answered within the minute:

> Of course.

Unable to think of a single uptown restaurant that was appealing or cosy, and knowing Nathan's preferred downtown haunts, she got them a table at the insanely expensive Cipriani's on West Broadway – inside – knowing it would be the last sort of place he would go. She met James once more in the hotel bar at seven.

'Ahoy there,' he said as she came in. He got off the bar stool and gave her two kisses.

'*Bonsoir*,' she said. 'What's that you're drinking?'

'I believe it's referred to as white wine.'

'I mean, what kind?'

'Something dry – a Macon Villages I think.'

'I'll have what he's having,' she said to the bartender. 'And can we get some of those almonds?'

'You look ravishing,' said James, 'Very French,' referring no doubt to her blue and white Breton stripes. 'How was your day?'

'Very French,' she said. 'Yours?'

'*Un grand* pain in the ass.'

'Sorry.'

'It was entirely expected. No one here gives a shit about Spain really. It's amazing to me how far off everyone's radar it continues to be, the misconceptions, the hackneyed clichés – you know, bull fighting and flamenco and perhaps a mention of Almodóvar or Zara, but that's it.'

'Maybe that's not a bad thing.'

'It's bad when you're trying to sell yourself to boring investors like these gents have been. But now they're gone and you're here. It sounds like your day was far more interesting.'

'It was. I fell in love.'

'That was fast.'

'But he's ninety.'

They went by taxi at her request.

'I've never heard of this Cipriani,' he said.

'The good one is uptown, at the old Sherry Netherland, where my stepfather used to take me.'

'That's the one I know.'

'Then there's a cheesy one on 42nd Street, across from Grand Central Station that's like a mausoleum. And there's one way downtown that's also unappealing.'

'You're an expert.'

'But the SoHo one is fine, and I know we won't run into Nathan there.'

'Have you been to Harry's Bar in Venice?'

'I've never been to Venice.'

'That's got to change.'

'I know,' she said. 'But you know what? Clichés and all, I think it's a place you should only go to when those scary cruise ships aren't there and when you're in love with someone.'

'Have you heard from him – this Nathan chap?'

'No.'

'Isn't that a bit odd?'

'Yes and no. I expect he's too furious to apologize or to say anything nice or remorseful.'

'Has this sort of thing happened with him before?'

The taxi had one of those screens jammed onto the back of the front seat intruding into the narrow passenger space with local news and weather reports. She kept on trying to shut it off, but it didn't respond.

'You mean has he cheated on me before? Probably. He,

and his mother who is still very much alive, think he's God's gift to mankind, and he entertains *droit du seigneur* fantasies, I think, that I was supposed to good-naturedly ignore and find alluring. You aren't like that, are you?'

'Do I seem like I am?'

'No. But men, heterosexual men, can be very sneaky.'

'Women can be sneaky too.'

'True.'

'We're both being sneaky this evening,' he said.

'I'm not being sneaky. I've nothing to hide. What are you being sneaky about?'

Moving west on Prince she noticed a restaurant she'd always enjoyed on the corner of Crosby Street that was now something else.

'Do you actually think I've told Carmensina we're going out to dinner together? Do you think I've even told her you're here in New York?'

'I guess not. Well then you better hope Camilla doesn't say anything.'

'She won't.'

'Does she know about all of your indiscretions?'

'There haven't been any others.'

'What about Fiona?'

'That was just a flirtation. Nothing ever came of it, or did she tell you something different?'

'She told me she thought you chickened out at the last minute because of Carmensina.'

'What a nice way of putting it.'

'Do you mean to tell me you've been married for twelve years and that you've never been unfaithful?'

'Is that so strange? I've been tempted a few times, one of which you know about, but no, I've never done it.'

'Because you're in love with her?'

'Can we get another drink before continuing this discussion?'

'I'm sorry. I'm being awful. It's none of my business.'

'It may be none of your business, but now I feel like some sort of wimpy freak.'

The crowd that filled the tables in front of the restaurant, clusters of euro air kissers, was exactly as she remembered from the last time she had been there. They went inside and had to wait at the bar for the table she'd reserved. They both ordered vodkas and James asked for the wine list.

'I'm really sorry,' she said. 'I've let my rage at Nathan spill over onto poor you. Please forgive me.'

'I forgive you.'

'I think it's quite something you've never cheated on your wife. I don't think it makes you a wimpy freak at all.'

He downed his vodka and closed the wine list. 'Look. This is a very tricky topic for me, tonight especially.'

'I'm really sorry.'

'Especially because it had been my intention to do all I could to cheat on her tonight.'

'My goodness.'

'There you have it.'

'Tonight. With me?'

'With you.'

'"Had been" – so you don't want to anymore?'

'I can't think of anything else. Ever since our drink at the pub last week I've been obsessing about you like a sixteen-year-old. I can't get you out of my mind and when I heard you were coming to New York I couldn't believe my luck; when you told me last night you'd split up with your ego-maniacal boyfriend I was thrilled.'

She put her drink down on the bar – glad she had put in so much time at the day spa. Then she looked at him, 'I think you need to kiss me,' she said.

He did – slowly – and it was as if someone had handed him a key to a room he'd all but forgotten. She liked the way it felt and kissed him back. The maître d' appeared, 'Right this way please.'

They were half way through a Brunello di Montalcino and two baskets of breadsticks before the food arrived. Neither of them made further mention of the kiss or of anything preceding it.

'The barrister in London was intrigued and encouraging,' he said. 'He got me the name of his favourite Sotheby appraiser, who I've already spoken with and who is going to come and see the scroll and the codices.'

'When?'

His mobile phone rang. It was Carmensina tracking him down and he took the call. He got up and walked out onto the street. For all the ill will she felt for the woman, Laura was glad not to be in her place that night, and it made her feel bad. Betrayal was in the air. As she sat there waiting, she was forced to admit for the first time that the main reason she had chosen to come to New York was because James would be there too. When he returned to the table, they ordered another bottle of wine.

'I'm so sorry,' he said.

'Don't be silly. It's normal.'

'Yes. Yes and no.'

'It's two in the morning there.'

'It's two in the morning and she's weepy and has had too much to drink and is a mess.'

'I'm here following in her footsteps.'

'But you're not drunk and weepy almost every night.'

'No.'

'Well she is. And it's got worse. And she refuses to deal with it, in any way.'

'And the girls?'

'The girls notice, obviously. I feel guilty as hell when I have to leave them. It's not a good situation.'

'Do you want to just call it a night?'

'No. I'm starving and getting tipsy myself. We should both eat something.'

They shared a salad, and each had a bowl of pasta and avoided any intimate topics by talking about his family history and her family history and about Sotheby's and the project. They both skipped dessert and ordered decaf espressos.

'I feel I should confess something to you,' she said, dissolving half a cube of sugar into the coffee.

'Be my guest.'

'My friend Pierre, the fellow in Paris, suggested two people for me to speak with about the French translation. I chose the one here in New York primarily because you were going to be here.'

'Really?'

'Really. I'd no idea about what Nathan was up to and I came here pretty much resolved to end it anyway.'

'I see.'

'I just wanted you to know that, and I needed to hear myself say it out loud.'

He smiled at her, somewhat ruefully she thought.

'So, what do you think?' she said.

'How do you mean?'

'This,' she said, gesturing at him and then back at herself.

He took another sip of wine and looked at her, 'I'm not sure. I think it's something good, I hope. Though I find the more I think about it, the obstacles just grow and grow.'

'So, you try not to think about it.'

'That's right.'

'And how is that going?'

He laughed, 'Terribly.'

She laughed in kind. They both looked away.

'I've been wanting you to kiss me like that ever since the pub,' she said, 'when you walked me to the Land Rover.'

On the way up to his floor in the hotel elevator he took her in his arms. But shortly after they entered his room, she fell asleep on the bed while he showered. When he emerged wrapped in a hotel robe, he found her there, boots off but overcoat still on. He helped her out of it as gently as he could, and it reminded him of how often he had performed a similar task with his daughters. Laura awakened and apologized and mechanically stripped down to her bra and panties and crawled under the covers as he opened them up for her. He kept the robe on and got in beside her, and as he did, without warning, an unexplainable dread took hold of him from nowhere. It persuaded him to shy off trying to seduce her just yet, and he was relieved when she fell asleep again in his arms.

He lay there for a while, praying the phones would stay silent, enchanted by the presence of this beautiful, brilliant woman asleep beside him. They lay there in the darkness of the large anonymous room overlooking the western frontier of the East Village. He pictured Manhattan as it was – the rivers at either side joining at its tip and flowing out to sea. He thought about his daughters in Barcelona. He thought about Carmensina. He thought about the possible consequences of his actions. He worried about the guilt he would feel. The guilt and his performance anxiety joined forces and sniggered at him while his hand gently grazed the small of Laura's naked back. Then he fell asleep.

She awakened in the dark around three and got her bearings. James was turned away from her and still. She liked the way he smelled. Apart from the freshly laundered scent of the bathrobe still wrapped around him there were no traces of cologne or deodorant or sweat – just a human odour somewhat akin to dry wood, or warm cereal. She rose silently from the bed and looked out of the large latticed window, peering down at the streets still filled with traffic impervious to the hour.

She peed and washed out her mouth with toothpaste and slipped back into bed and began to kiss the back of his neck. She kept her lips there, grazing his skin and smelling his hair until he stirred and rolled over onto his back.

'Sorry I fell asleep,' she said to him in a whisper.

He rolled onto his side towards her, beginning to harden.

'I did too. Do you realize we've been saying sorry to each other all night?' he said.

He kissed her and continued doing so as he unfastened her bra and slipped down her panties. He could feel her reacting. Then his hand drifted down her torso and found her wet. She reached for him too. He grabbed her by the shoulders and pressed her down on her back and climbed between her legs. They kissed again. 'Shouldn't we do something?' she asked him. 'I mean, I'm still on the pill, but even so.'

'Of course,' he said, feeling like a fool, regretting the ambivalence that had hounded him since leaving Barcelona and that had prevented him from overcoming his stupid shyness about buying some protection. 'What an ass,' he said. 'I've got nothing to offer.'

She grabbed him with one of her hands and kissed him again, 'It doesn't feel that way to me.' Then she moved out from under him, 'I may have something in my purse somewhere.'

He watched her naked form look around the room for her things, like some sylvan nymph from one of those ancient isles she knew so much about. It took her less than a minute to locate what she was searching for. 'I can't even remember when this is from,' she said. But by the time she came back to him he had lost it and judging by the misery and low-grade panic slowly possessing him, he sensed it was gone for good.

'We'll get him back,' she said, kissing his shoulder.

'I know,' he said, 'but it may not be this time around. I'm so sorry, so embarrassed.'

'Well,' she said, 'I'm hoping you had more in mind than just this time around.'

'I most certainly did. Though to tell you the truth I've thought absolutely none of this through.'

He kissed her again and put his hand between her legs. But she gently moved it away. 'I'd prefer to wait,' she said, 'until you manage to stop thinking so much.'

He was grateful to her but unsure about trusting it. Even though their professional arrangement would maintain them in some proximity, there was no guarantee this would happen again. She might have been definitively turned off by what had transpired, and he worried it could happen again, precisely because it would be what he most feared.

'People are complicated,' he said.

'Some more than others,' she replied.

He wondered if she meant it as a reproach.

'Could you just hold me?' she said.

He spooned in behind her and they fell asleep again like that, facing the windows until he woke at dawn. Pink light filled the room. He felt her shaking against him, quietly sobbing.

'Laura. What is it?'

She didn't reply. He asked her again, as quietly as he could. She got up and went into the bathroom and he feared the whole encounter, so desired these past few days, had reached a ghastly end. He could hear her blowing her nose. He lay there, in limbo, contemplating getting up to close the first layer of curtains so as to keep the approaching morning light in check, but he couldn't bring himself to move. And then she returned and got back into bed with him and put her arms around him and hugged him tight, and he realized that in his spree of self-involvement and internal moaning over his wounded vanity, he had under-estimated her. She was an adult, perhaps more than he in some ways. She had her own life and problems, and his wounded pride was already behind her. He hugged her back, tenderly, and didn't say a word.

She turned away from him, lying on her side once more, facing the window. She pulled him back against her so that they regained the position they were in when he woke up. She spoke in low but very clear tones.

'I don't know why I'm crying.'

He kissed her between her shoulder blades.

'I feel so good with you,' she said. 'I knew I would. But I don't want to mess up your life. My own has been such a disaster.'

He continued to kiss her. She started to cry again but kept on speaking. 'I keep picking overbearing men who don't even know who I am.'

He remained silent a bit longer before saying to her as carefully as he could, 'Do you think I know who you are?'

'Maybe,' she said, 'someday.' They both started to laugh.

She turned to face him. The room by then was filled with light. A slight wind noise hummed through an invisible fault in one of the window fittings. She kissed him and he kissed her back.

'You've had a hard time of it,' he said.

'Sort of. But I've no right to complain.'

'Everybody has a right to complain.'

'Both my parents have been very strange. My mother was a hysteric and half demented, and my father may have been a very sweet and decent man, but I never got to know him.'

'I was thinking about my father this morning,' he said. 'How Mother never speaks of him. The older she gets the more ashamed of him she becomes. It's like she looks at her marriage now the way her own mother did. I imagine she's never mentioned to you how he died.'

'No.'

'He took up flying, a macho activity he and his rich friends got into. He wasn't a crack pilot. He insisted on taking my little sister for a joyride one day; she had been at him about it and Mother gave in. They crashed off the coast near a village called Tamariu. People watching said he had been getting too close to the water, showing off. They found three people in the wreckage. My father, my sister, and another woman, a mistress no one had known about and who had obviously been the true reason for the outing.'

'My God.'

'She's never forgiven him for it.'

'No wonder you're so frightened of betraying your wife,' she said.

'I never thought of that,' he said. 'It certainly has nothing to do with being in love with her. I was once. I think. But I'm miserable now and have been for a long time.'

'I know.'

They lay still for a while, until he leaned over and kissed her once more. They began to caress each other. Nature took care of the rest. Just before six, with the full curtains closed, they fell asleep, sated and smiling in the dark. Then his phone rang again. He saw it was coming from Spain, but it wasn't Carmensina.

Chapter 27

Late September through June were Camilla's favourite times of the year in Mallorca. James and Carmensina took the house in July sometimes and she rented it each August to a Danish gentleman who appreciated it and took good care of it. The crowded Mediterranean summer was not to her taste anymore, and it was then when the estate in Cornwall was at its peak.

Not computer savvy, without a travel agent, and not wanting to bother James in the States, she had Finn drive her all the way to Heathrow. She went to a British Airways counter as if she were at Victoria Station and purchased a ticket. The only remaining flight available that day left in the late afternoon. By the time she landed in Palma, night had fallen, and she had little desire to open the house in the dark, so she hired a taxi to take her to La Residencia Hotel in Deià where she checked-in in time for dinner. It was too chilly to sit outside, and the hotel restaurant was too fancy for her to bother with, so she took a small table in the bar where she ordered white wine and some olives while waiting for a simple omelette. She ate slowly and read a crumpled copy of the day's *La Vanguardia* newspaper feeling about as content as she could remember.

Her room, as beautiful as any bedroom in her own house, but cleaner and more orderly, faced the Serra de Tramuntana mountains. She fell asleep around the time that Laura and James were meeting at the Bowery Hotel bar that second night. When she awakened the following dawn, she opened the windows and looked for a good long while at the terraced landscape, bathed in salmon and violet hues, while smelling the air and giving thanks to whomever might be responsible for such a plethora of riches. After a bath and breakfast, she checked out and left her suitcase with reception. She walked to the local *florestería* and then continued on to the cemetery next to the church up on a hill where Robert and Beryl Graves and her daughter were buried.

The day was clear and ideal. The trek up to the church was arduous and she was soon too warm for the cardigan she wore. She rested on a stone bench in the shade and looked north. The village and the whole island had that off-season, cleaned-out, after-a-storm feeling that she cherished. It was the island as she had known it in her youth and much as she had imagined it when reading the scroll excerpt Laura had printed out for her.

She visited the tombstones of Graves and his wife first. Beryl's was covered with dead leaves and the poet's had a sad-looking bouquet of plastic roses resting on it that she tossed into the nearest trash receptacle. Then she distributed some of the flowers she brought with her and said a little prayer. Though she had stayed in touch with Graves in his waning years and visited them whenever she could, he had barely recognized her during his last decade. That, she thought, was something she must never allow herself to live through, or to put anyone caring for her through.

Then she made her way to Inmaculada's tomb. Her husband's family had pushed hard to have father and daughter buried together in their family plot near Barcelona. But she had not allowed it. She wanted her daughter there where she herself would be buried. Camilla's mother and all their line were in cemeteries in Cornwall, and her father was in the Trevelyan pantheon in Ireland. This was her spot, a place for her and her little girl, protected from the Tramuntana winds by the green mountains, looking toward the Mediterranean, near palm trees, vineyards, and shaded earthen paths between stone houses she knew so well.

As she cleared the dust and bits of dried plants off the tombstone, and then laid new flowers about its perimeter, she recalled how she had looked at herself in the bath that morning. The air and the light entering through the window had been as radiant as always. The hotel towels folded nearby were thick and newly laundered. The soap had been organically made and unwrapped only minutes before. But the body in the water, this current version of herself, was old and grey. She remembered getting her first period and her mother being uncharacteristically gentle, and later that day realizing that Graves had been informed as well when he presented her with a crown made from honeysuckle vines. She remembered how exciting it had been to be naked in a shower or tub in her twenties, and how sexy and arousing her romantic life had occasionally been throughout her thirties, forties and fifties. But once the narcissistic disappointments began, they had continued unabated.

She did not miss sex. She did not miss her husband. She had enjoyed the play of flirtation when she was young and she had gone on about it with friends at school and at university as much as anyone, but trying to be honest with herself there at her daughter's grave, she had to admit that she had not known a lot of passion nor the degree of sexual hunger that often went with it. Some of her friends had. Even her mother had. Perhaps it skipped a generation, for Inmaculada would have had it – for better or worse. It had been there already in the way the little girl had seduced her father into taking her on that damned little airplane. The closest thing to passion Camilla had ever felt was what she had felt for her daughter, who did not live long enough to get her period. When they fished her from the Mediterranean she had been as white as snow. She'd had no visible wounds nor broken bones. It was as if she had merely fallen asleep.

And James, she wondered, walking back down toward the village; was James a passionate boy – or man? To her he was always a boy. In the beginning with Carmensina the sparks had flown, but maybe most of the heat had come from her. She really did not know. Now he seemed anxious and elusive and saddled with the marriage – damned if he did and damned if he didn't – all for the sake of his little girls, something no one could understand better than she. When Anna and Montse first came into the world Camilla had toyed for a while with a belief in reincarnation, hoping one or the other might prove to be Inmaculada come back for another try at life. But as they grew and began to reflect Carmensina's vanities and her son's equanimity, she had let that notion go.

The walk from the church to her house took almost an hour and by the time she reached it the excitement she felt at arriving was somewhat diluted by pangs of hunger and sharp pains in her right hip – an age-related lesion she had been ignoring for years. A good number of her contemporaries had had replacement surgeries performed as a matter of course, but she remained staunchly opposed to it. The keys were in their customary spot and though the house had been cleaned a week earlier, it had a cosy but slightly sorry feel to it. One really had to live in a place, she thought, and this was where she should be. Everything within her attested to it, and as she opened various pairs of shutters and windows filling the house with light and fresh air tinged with sea and blossoms – lemon trees, avocado trees, grapevines, boxwood, geraniums – the estate in Cornwall felt lugubrious to her in comparison.

She said another prayer, there and then, begging – and the irony was not lost upon her – that Laura's work might bring forth the sort of sum required so that she might come to James's aide, while continuing to maintain the estate in a dignified fashion, and to still have this house, her sanctuary, for herself.

Neither the pain in her hip nor this stream of agitated thoughts dampened the pleasure she derived from opening the house. The only good thing about not living there permanently was the now decades-old thrill of returning to it like this, and especially at this time of the year. The closed-up smells did a slow, familiar and intoxicating dance – the old well-waxed floor tiles in the *zaguán*, the wicker patio furniture piled up in the ground floor guest bedroom that was never used anymore, her collection of summer hats hanging on pegs near the beautiful medieval wooden chest, the *barqueño* Graves had given her as a wedding gift. The bookshelves in the living room and the study lined with hundreds of fading Penguin editions arranged in no particular order, mixed with airport novels left behind by years of visitors. Two signed prints by Miró and some good family paintings. The coffee and tea canisters in the kitchen pantry, the packs of sugar and rice and flour and pasta, the liquor closet, the maid's bathroom, the laundry room with its detergents and containers of bleach, the wooden basket filled with half-used, years old, suntan lotions.

She went outside and walked down to the swimming pool, pleased to see it had been properly emptied and covered. The state of the gardens and of the trees and shrubbery in general dismayed her, but this too formed part of the ritual. She went up to her bedroom to use the toilet and remembered she had still to collect her suitcase from the hotel and if she was going to stay for a few days she might as well go and do a bit of food shopping too. There were friends she could call for a touch of social life and she would have to phone the maid to make sure she would come the following day, but none of this appealed to her then. Wearier than she would like to be, she stepped out onto her bedroom terrace to survey her domain once again before going back inside for a nap. Naps had never really been her custom there as they were in Cornwall, and she hoped as she drifted off, that she was not coming down with something.

She awakened half an hour later, hungry and stiff and existentially challenged – mildly depressed – and then got angry with herself for feeling that way in a place she loved so much and which she had made such an effort to get to. As James and Laura were making love for the first time in New York she brushed her teeth with an old toothbrush, squeezing the last remnants from a twisted tube of dried toothpaste and then went down to the garage. Her old beige diesel-powered Santana started up on the first try, and she was feeling better already being back in her favourite vehicle that smelled of oil and summer sand and cracked leather.

Backing out onto the street without looking behind

her with any degree of thoroughness, she was hit by a speeding Mercedes SUV driven by a thick-set, air charter executive from Dresden talking on his mobile phone. His attempt to brake and swerve out of her way came too late. The powerful, engine-heavy prow of his vehicle hit the passenger-side door of Camilla's with brutal force. It propelled her halfway through the driver's-side window, breaking her neck, and initiating a chain of biological events that, some five minutes later, stilled her heart. In her final moments of consciousness, oblivious to pain and to the hysterical man's ranting in German, she saw her little girl again. She went to her, clasped her and smelled her, crying tears of joy.

Chapter 28

Red-eyed and numb, James got himself on a morning flight to London. Exhausted and distraught, he had to run to the departure gate at JFK for fear of missing the plane. He was booked on a connecting flight from Heathrow to Barcelona where he would pick up his family and then on another flight with them to Palma de Mallorca.

Halfway over the ocean he locked himself in one of the aircraft's bathrooms and broke down. He'd been fifteen and far from Spain when his father and baby sister died, fifteen and already a rebellious teenager. He'd been too self-involved then to let it get to him too deeply. But Camilla was his life. Camilla was there always, like the sun coming up each morning. The various hits he'd taken thus far in his life had all been bearable knowing she was close by. They spoke on the phone at least once a day and only fought when one of them, for whatever reason, was in one of their moods. They'd had the great luxury of being able to take each other for granted. And though he knew she would surely pre-decease him someday, it was a day, even as she'd grown frailer these past few years, he'd kept way out in some undefined future. He looked at himself in the mirror, drying his eyes with a paper hand towel, thirty-six thousand feet over the Atlantic, trying to connect with the person staring back at him.

Laura had seen him off in the hotel corridor by the elevators, wrapped in a robe from his bathroom, her clothing gathered in her arms. Her flight back was not until the following afternoon. After she returned to her room, drew the curtains and got into her own bed, she tried to make sense of the news. She took a pill and slept another few hours. When she woke and ordered breakfast there were five messages, finally, from Nathan, begging at first for forgiveness before turning increasingly hostile. She ignored them.

She ate breakfast in the room, looking down at the noisy two-way street and across to a classic hodge-podge of Manhattan buildings, short and tall, old and new. Camilla, with all of her peculiarities, had come to be a kind of mother figure for her. Midway through her bowl of oatmeal she was finally able to cry. She took a bath in the dark until she was all cried out, trying to make some sense of it.

She dressed and went out for a walk, first to her apartment to water the plants on her terrace. The doorman told her that Nathan had been by on two occasions and that, as requested, was not allowed entry the second time, and that he had stalked off furious. This dissuaded her from meandering any further in the surrounding NYU neighbourhood, and so she headed north along Fifth Avenue until it met with Broadway at 23rd Street where she veered east and sat down on a bench in what was for her the unfamiliar Madison Square Park.

She was overwhelmed. Nathan's betrayal. The shock of Camilla's death. What had happened between her and James only hours before. The growing, explosive translation. What would happen now? What would happen with James? What would happen with the project? The project Camilla had hired her to bring to fruition. Camilla, with whom she had been out riding less than a week ago. Camilla with whom she had begun to feel such a special kinship, and who never would have gone to Mallorca if she hadn't gone to New York.

Of one thing she was almost certain: the translation should remain a secret. Though it frustrated her to admit it, she knew deep down it was too volatile. It would provoke scandal and upheaval. And for what? Well, perhaps for the power of truth. She was not a believer in anything supernatural, and was convinced that Christ, Allah, the God of the Old Testament, and all of the gods and goddesses of all religions throughout time were human inventions, human myths created to control and to explain and to help people get through life's difficulties. So why not expose the contents of the scroll and the codex? Would that not be a service and a lesson to everyone? Didn't she owe it to her own belief in physics, chemistry, and reason? Didn't she owe it to the testimony that Joseph of Arimathea had dictated to his scribe? And yet, she knew as well that the world was still a primitive place, that she pertained to a privileged minority, and that it would probably be just plain foolish to tempt the fates, to tempt the irrational fury of so many by releasing such a thing. She was overwhelmed.

While ordering an early dinner in the hotel lobby she got a text from James telling her she was in his thoughts. She answered in kind and then went up to her room and translated the next segment that overwhelmed her even more.

Chapter 29

Yeshua felt a strong attraction to Venusha, the younger of Athain's two daughters. Canlia, to my surprise and gratitude, took a liking to me, and the four of us were married in a seaside ceremony followed by great amounts of food and drink.

Let it be known that Yeshua was a man like any other, with the good fortune of finding love in all its forms. They embraced each other with an energy only youth can know. They took long walks together and swam together. Yeshua worked with the tin streamers, and he worked the fields, he worked in the sea hauling fish, and he worked in the woods, stacking logs for winter. He became a rugged young man, a devoted son-in-law, and a beloved member of the community. He spoke no more of his Heavenly Father. Already advanced in age, I was too set in my ways to embrace this other culture so wholeheartedly.

We remained there a year, and then another, until the chaos of my business accounts demanded a voyage back home – home at that point being a relative term in everyone's heart, save for Lucca and Octavius who never wavered in their allegiance to Tiberius and the Empire.

And then, as if ordained by one of the great Greek dramatists, it was this voyage back home, looming out ahead, that seemed to precipitate all the other events I am about to describe.

Yeshua became a father a year after marrying Venusha and shortly after she found herself with child a second time. Canlia had yet to conceive and they invited her into their bed. I was the only one that knew. Blessed with Yeshua's seed she too found herself with child. Though piqued at first, I accepted it, for it improved my standing in the eyes of my business partners. I was not a very energetic man by then and Canlia never failed to attend to me when I wished it, so in truth I had little cause for complaint.

Then Lucca slipped and fell one day, wounding his leg. A man inured to all manner of physical suffering he paid it little mind. But the wound festered. Applications of local herbs and potions seemed to make it worse. He became feverish and Octavius decided to sever the limb. Yeshua took part in all of this and suffered – for he loved Lucca – and Lucca suffered greatly. Once the limb was cut and the stump cauterized with hot tar – a procedure I could not bear to watch but had no choice in hearing – the fever continued and the dear fellow, so beloved to all of us, died a raging death. It was the first time I had ever seen Octavius weep. I remember Canlia proclaiming this tragic event to be an omen of troubles to come. But Yeshua told her to hold her tongue. Both women were nervous about the journey awaiting them, one that would take them so far away from their land.

We decided to send Lucca off in a traditional manner and with help from some of the tin men including Lucca's burly mate, we carried his body into the woods on a two-day journey north. There we felled some trees, constructed a proper pyre, piled a great mass of brush beneath it, and set it ablaze. We remained until it collapsed in an explosion of sparks. Through the stench and smoke and flame we could see the gleaming bones of our comrade. Both Yeshua and Octavius were very affected by it. I, who was older, and who am now so much older still, took it as yet another lesson in life's fragility and fleetness. We built him a shrine of stones.

Upon our return we found the town in ruins. All of the dwellings had been put to the torch. Perhaps fifteen or twenty inhabitants remained alive, among them my dearest Canlia who had managed to run and hide. We found Venusha dead and disrobed with her unborn child cut from her womb. The other child, Yeshua's baby daughter, had been run through with a wooden stake. Athain and many of the town's leading men had been crudely hacked to pieces. It was, in brief, a vision of hell I shall waste no further ink describing. Yeshua cut locks of his daughter's and of Venusha's hair, and kept them with him until, fifteen years later he was stripped of his garments. He also found one of the marauders, wounded, trying to crawl away from this orgy of sin. He caught up to him and stabbed the fellow over and over, as I had once done to the man who slit my father's throat. Octavius had to pull him away.

We found him later, stained with blood and sitting alone by the sea, where he remained for two weeks until our ship arrived. He refused to return to what remained of the town and would not even speak with Canlia who still carried his third child. There were just enough men available to load the ingots aboard. The marauders, who had come from the sea, had not touched any of the tin. It was as if they cared little for it or knew not what to do with it and had landed only to wreak pain and death.

I offered to take the townsmen with us, but they refused. Canlia, at my insistence, did come aboard with us, and one summer's morning after what had been two years of bliss concluded by the death of a beloved comrade and a sudden intrusion of Armageddon, we raised anchor and began the journey home.

Chapter 30

After some initial moments of crying and hugs at the airport in Barcelona, a bad mood began to take hold of Carmensina. This ill humour, and the bottle of wine she consumed at lunch egging it on, was primarily, albeit unconsciously, a camouflage for her excitement at being so suddenly close to attaining a genuine aristocratic title. It expressed itself as irritation, at the disruption Camilla's death was causing – so much to organize, the sudden journey, having to remove the children from their normal routines. James, in the grip of strong emotions, was insisting they stay at Camilla's house in Mallorca, even though the five-star hotel close by was one where they were known and welcomed. To comply with his wishes, Carmensina would have to get food and supplies, to deal with maids and a gardener, do the cooking, deal with the house's antiquated heating system, its mismatching sheets and towels, all of this in addition to the funeral arrangements.

During the flight to Palma she kept at him on all these points. By the time he wrangled them into a red rental car he hated, his level of buried fury was threatening to explode. To be bothering him with these kinds of complaints, given the reason for the journey, seemed unforgiveable. It also granted him permission to absolve himself from the fast disappearing guilt he'd been feeling for having slept with Laura. 'How is it possible to be so insensitive?' was the mantra he repeated to himself over and over. But with the girls and Noelma present he didn't say anything aloud.

When they reached Deià he left them at the house, promised to do the shopping himself, collected Camilla's suitcase at the hotel, and drove alone to the town of Soller where, at his request, her body had been taken. The erstwhile beautiful village, overrun for twenty years by droves of tourists fleeing northern Europe, had at least some resemblance to its former self that day. He parked in front of the Gran Hotel and, filled with mounting dread, walked to the funeral parlour on the Plaza de la Constitución.

He found his mother covered with a sheet on a metal gurney in a neon-lit room. The police and local medical authorities had already finished their paperwork and he was brought there by a young woman in a white lab coat. She folded the sheet down exposing Camilla's head and shoulders. Apart from a large hematoma colouring the left side of her face she looked peaceful. After he confirmed her identity he was left alone. He stood there, paralyzed by the absurdity of it, by the insane-making reality of it. As he leaned over and kissed her cold forehead the sound of little children playing outside reached his ears and it made him cry. He remained there for half an hour until the young woman returned to see if he was all right. He gave her a dress Camilla had packed in the suitcase, picked a casket, paid the bill, made final arrangements for the following day, and walked away. Coming back out into the light of day he observed the village absolutely oblivious to his tragedy. Shopping at a supermarket at that point was beyond him, and he drove instead to a cove below Llucalcari where, as a boy, Camilla had sometimes taken him to swim.

Access to the cove was difficult and he was glad to find only one other car parked by the stand of pines up top where the dirt road ended and a largely eroded path down to the beach commenced. He turned off the engine, got out, and listened to the breeze whispering through the boughs. He took a deep breath and closed his eyes. It was difficult to imagine, but he did so nevertheless, trying to push away the image of his mother's corpse, that he had been in bed with Laura in New York the day before.

He made his way down to the aqua-green sea that was visible through the branches. Though late in the day, the temperature was unseasonably mild. He pulled off his Shetland sweater and tied it about his waist, becoming aware once more of the new girth and softness awarded him for many dinners out, too little exercise, and a sedentary professional life. The path was steep and arbitrary in places, and he had to hold onto tree trunks sometimes to keep from sliding. Pinesap stuck to his fingers. Thirty years earlier, lean and sure-footed, he had raced down through this grove nimble as a goat, Camilla taking her stately time behind him carrying too much paraphernalia. He would swim there all day and she would feed him and make him nap under an umbrella and only join him in the water when they first arrived and just before they returned home. He remembered how slowly she got into the sea and always with a bathing cap, immersing herself by degrees, gingerly splashing herself until she would finally launch herself forward with a grand swoosh. But once in she stayed in for a long while, often swimming a steady, graceful crawl far out until, frightened, he would call her back. Now she was dead in that ghastly room.

Just before he emerged from the trees onto the beach he saw and then heard a couple having sex. It was impossible not to stare even as it annoyed him. He had hoped for a less adventuresome pair of occupants belonging to the other car. He wanted to sit on the sand undisturbed, to gather his thoughts and feelings and perhaps go for an autumnal dip. It was a young boy and girl splayed upon a large faded towel. They seemed to be in too much of a hurry he thought, as if they had come there to perform the act for its sheer theatricality rather than responding to an urge nudged awake by an afternoon of naked sunbathing. Such was youth he thought, youth looked upon from the perspective of his softening middle.

When they finished, the girl got up quickly, laughing and exhilarated, running to the water, diving in and swimming out. The skinny boy leaned up on his elbows and watched her for a while before joining her. James remained hidden at the edge of the wood and only stepped onto the beach once they were out of the water and collapsed back onto their towel. He nodded at them briefly and then found a spot by the water's edge as far away from them as possible. The girl said something to her mate and giggled. James sat on his sweater looking out to sea, ignoring them and rejecting two calls from Carmensina. He sent a text to Laura:

Am alone on a familiar beach, missing you. What a horrible day in such a beautiful place.

Twenty minutes later the young couple stood and dressed, gathered their things and left. Though he had not found their encounter erotic, it did fill him with envy. As an enormous weight of loss crushed down on him, he vowed to change his life while there was still time. He thanked his mother for her departing gift, her insisting that he go and find Laura at The Wounded Hart the other night, something that felt like it had happened months ago. As he rose and stripped down to swim, he swore upon Camilla's departed soul that he would not go on like this.

As soon as she saw him return to the house empty-handed Carmensina resumed her recriminations. 'Where have you been all this time? Why didn't you answer the phone? What are we supposed to eat? What about the girls? The swimming pool is empty. They took one look at it and burst into tears.'

'Show me,' he said.

'What? You think I am lying?'

'Show me.'

He put up with it as they walked down through the garden because he wanted to move her out of earshot from Noelma and his daughters.

'Look,' she said, pointing to the navy canvas tarpaulin covering the empty pool. There was a puddle of rain-water suspended in the middle of it where dead leaves had gathered.

'You look,' he said, turning to her, furious. 'This has got to stop. Right now. What is wrong with you? My mother is dead, and we have come here to bury her. This is a terrible thing for me.'

'It is a terrible thing for me too,' she said, refusing to cede protagonism.

'Then stop your whining. Stop your drinking. Stop your complaining. Just stop. Show some compassion for God's sake. I can't stand to hear your voice anymore.'

'*You* wanted to stay here,' she said, ignoring the insults, holding on like a terrier. 'If we stay here, we need food and drink. Is that being so demanding? We've only one car. You volunteered to do the shopping and I thought I was doing you a favour by sending you on your way.'

'What I shopped for was my mother's coffin.'

'I'm sorry James, I truly am. But—'

'I don't want to hear anymore 'buts' from you. I don't want to hear you anymore.'

226

'What are you saying? What do you mean by that?'

Tears came into her eyes. He looked at her and then looked at the puddle in the tarpaulin and damned everything to hell. He felt terrible, for her and for everyone.

'We'll go stay at the hotel,' he said, deciding in an instant. 'Come. Get Noelma and the girls.'

'You don't want to hear my voice? I'm your wife. I am the mother of your children.'

They took a suite at La Residencia, plus an additional room with three beds, and had a family dinner in their room, and when they finished eating the girls zoned out on a sofa watching cartoons on a massive flat-screen television. The marital spat devolved into a soul crushing, simmering silence they both knew by heart. Finally, James stood and wheeled the room service table into the hallway outside their door and announced he was going for a walk. Neither of them was looking forward to the moment they would get into bed together.

He strolled down to the large hotel pool, illuminated and solitary in the damp night. A layer of mist hovered over the surface of the heated water. He had to admit that moving to the hotel had been smart, and the proper thing to do. He would throw her that bone later in the hope it might be enough to allow them both to sleep. Tomorrow would be another day, the day of Camilla's funeral, something – his visit to the funeral home notwithstanding – that still felt absolutely and brutally surreal. He dialled Laura.

Chapter 31

She was in London by then dining with Fiona at La Famiglia in Chelsea.

'Mummy's in shock,' Fiona said, digging into a risotto with asparagus.

'Me too.'

'She said Camilla had always been a disaster behind the wheel.'

'I don't know what to do, say, or think.'

'Oh God, that's right. What about the job?'

'I wasn't referring to that, but there's that too.'

'Have you spoken to James about it?'

'It's not the right moment. Best to let some time go by.'

'He must be devastated. He really relied on her.'

Laura had not said anything to her friend about meeting James in New York. Part of her wanted to, just to have someone to talk to about it, but she had decided to hold back for a while. Fiona, in the midst of her own adulterous affair would have too many opinions and she felt her own news would lose its patina somehow, even in her own eyes perhaps, getting pulled as it inevitably would, into Fiona's relationship vortex. Worse still, she had got into bed almost immediately with James, something Fiona had failed to do after trying all manner of tactics. Even though that was a story from years ago, her intuition counselled silence for a while. But she did tell her about Nathan and the Veselka waitress.

'You've certainly had a freaky time of it,' Fiona said.

'I keep thinking that if I had just stayed in Cornwall none of this would have happened. Camilla would still be alive, and Nathan would be happily screwing his teenager ...'

'In your bed, the sod. Don't go down that road.'

'I can't help it.'

'Fate is fate Laura. Shit just happens. You know that. Just one thing after another.'

'I know. But even so.'

'Even so my ass.'

This made Laura laugh.

'How are things with Giles?' Laura asked, looking to change the subject. 'Good I hope – I couldn't take any more bad news.'

'I'm meeting him in Amsterdam next week, for two nights. I'm so looking forward to it.'

'And the wife still suspects nothing.'

'Who knows?' Fiona said. 'The key is that she doesn't ask him any questions, no email or text message snooping. She deserves an Oscar.'

'Or another husband.'

'I've brought this up with Giles and he doesn't think so. He says he can't imagine her going out with anyone, doing all one has to, to make that sort of thing happen. That she's complacent by nature. And you know. He's there most of the time. They go to the school plays, they take their summer holiday together – most of it anyhow.'

'How about sex?'

'That too, every other Christmas.'

They both laughed at this. Then Laura thought about James and it brought her up short. Fiona noticed.

They walked past the Chelsea and Westminster Hospital and crossed the Fulham Road and made their way to Fiona's house on Redcliffe Road. It was three storeys tall and very grand for one person and Fiona had friends staying with her often. Laura was exhausted from the flight and everything else and wanted to go upstairs to take a bath and write to James before going to sleep. But Fiona was still wired and insisted they have some green tea in the kitchen. Another hour passed before Laura got into the tub in the bathroom adjacent to her room. It had a pergola over it laced with green ivy and it was there the call from James reached her.

'We're all here – and fighting as usual,' he said.

'How awful.'

'I miss you.'

'I miss you too. Where are you?'

'Out by the hotel swimming pool.'

'I feel like I should come. I feel bad not being there.'

'It would just be too confusing.'

'I know. But I will go, afterwards, sometime soon I hope. I've promised myself that.'

'She would have liked to know that. Maybe I can come with you.'

'Are you going to be OK?'

'I'm in an altered state. My mother and best friend is dead. But thanks to you I've never felt more alive. But then I think of Carmensina and the girls and I feel terrible.'

'I know.'

For both of them the evening's end was an occasion for further mourning. Lying in bed in the dark at Fiona's house, exhausted from travel and emotional upheaval, Laura's tears turned into tears for the loss of Nathan as well, and for the hurt his anger had inflicted on her. Try as she might to hold on to all of the bad things, things that had been so easy to access the past few weeks, she lost her footing and was swept into a flood of tender memories. They had first made love in that very same bed at Fiona's four years earlier. She had thought him an exciting catch then and he had played his role – the charming intellectual satyr – to perfection. She remembered their trips, to Paris and to Berlin, to St Petersburg and to Washington, when things were still good between them. New York and NYU had done them in. Both of them had been burned by the city's voracious appetite for celebrity, and the university's rampant competitiveness. It had gone to his head and pummelled hers. But was he so self-involved and so narcissistic that he was unable to offer her the slightest indication of common courtesy? Perhaps she had been too harsh with him these last few days, but wasn't it up to him to respond with something other than texted vitriol? What was it in these angry men that caused them to close up like molluscs? James at least spoke. He recognized demons. He was not afraid to admit to being afraid.

When James returned to the hotel room a thousand miles south of London, Carmensina was in bed looking at a photo album she had taken from Camilla's house. Going through it together, delving into the past, fostered a kind of truce between them. They looked at pictures from when Camilla had been young, lithe, smooth, tanned and coquettish, when James's father had been thin and tanned, in espadrilles and always with a cigarette in hand, and often holding little Inmaculada aloft on his shoulders. The cocktail parties, the birthday parties, the costume balls, the beach picnics, the tennis games, and always with the Mediterranean present and the same plants and shrubs, the same bougainvillea and palm trees he and Carmensina had argued by that afternoon near the covered swimming pool.

There were pictures of himself as a boy, wrapped in a big towel after too much swimming, as an adolescent with bad skin and ridiculous hair, with an adored teenage girlfriend he had lost track of completely. And then it was him and Carmensina at the beginning – in one she looked alluring in a bikini, in another one the two of them were in formal summer dress posing at an Andratx regatta dinner next to one of the Spanish Infantas and Queen Sofia. Then there was a picture of Carmensina pregnant with Anna, tanned in a T-shirt and panties playing solitaire, radiating sensuality and satisfaction.

'We were happy back then, weren't we?' she said.

'Yes,' he said. 'We were.'

As Camilla's funeral mass came to an end the following day, Laura reached the estate in Cornwall. She had taken a taxi from the Truro train station. Finn came to the door wearing a black armband about the sleeve of his jacket. With a grave and embarrassed face, he told her she would have to leave.

'I don't understand.'

'Neither do we, Miss. But Mrs Figueras was very adamant about it.'

'What did she say exactly?'

'She called this morning and said that your position with Mrs Trevelyan ended with Mrs Trevelyan' demise, and that you were not to stay here any longer.'

'I have things of mine here.'

'I know, Miss. Please, come in and we can help you with that.'

She was furious.

'I can't believe this.'

'I'm so sorry miss. We're not even sure how much longer our services will be required.'

'That's absurd,' she said angrily. 'I'd call James about it right now if it wasn't such a terrible time for him.'

She made an effort to calm herself while cursing Carmensina.

'You two will be fine,' she said.

'I certainly hope so, Miss.'

The house felt different to her. The week before she had been treated like a daughter. Her meals had been served, her laundry taken care of, her bed was made for her and her bathroom tidied by the time she came back to her room each afternoon. After what had been an initial, standoffish period, she and Camilla had bonded. Now Camilla was dead and Laura was being cast out like a hired consultant who had made the mistake of taking too much for granted. The week before, the estate had been absolutely Camilla's. She had dominated the scene with confidence and naturalism. One had the sense of a woman who genetically belonged there. Now it felt unmoored and adrift and it was hard for Laura to imagine it being run with the same sort of elegant ease by anyone else. On the train heading south from London that morning she had been looking forward to her arrival, to getting back to her magnificent room, and to working with the actual artefacts nearby. She had looked forward to feeling grounded again, if only for a while. It had been her hope that she would continue to be looked after there and be left alone, with occasional visits from James.

Consumed with frustration at not being able to call him she sent Fiona a text:

The wife is booting me out of the house!

Fiona called right away but only managed to plant further worries, about the validity of Laura's contract and possible new powers Carmensina might have, now that the head of the house was gone.

She reviewed her original list of bed and breakfasts in the area and reserved a room in a place that was just a block away from The Wounded Hart. Having that settled and packing her things made her feel marginally better. She realized she was going to have to have a serious conversation with James, on a professional level, one she would rather not have now that they were getting involved.

After a kind but awkward lunch in the kitchen with Finn and Bidelia, Finn drove her into town and made sure she got good treatment at the B&B. The room was neither as nice as she had hoped, nor as dreadful as she had feared, and after a fitful nap she fired up her computer and resumed work.

Chapter 32

Yeshua did not speak again until we returned to Gades. Our ship put in there for two days. I was gripped by a strong desire to revisit the Temple of Melqart, an inclination neither Octavius nor Yeshua shared. I took Canlia with me. Though she carried his child, though her loved ones and her community had been slain, so that there was no further need for pretence, and though her sister no longer dominated the affections of Yeshua, she had nevertheless grown closer to me. With her mother, father and sister gone, and the father of her child turned away from her, my own value had increased.

We reached the temple within an hour. I introduced her to this foreign god, and she knelt down before the statue with such awe and longing it moved me to see it. She walked among a vast grove of olive trees adjacent to the temple – trees as old as her abandoned homeland and that were exotically new to her. The red soil, the tufts of grass, the gentle sun and the sparkling sea spread out below us, in such contrast to her natural environ – induced a sense of wonder in her and a possibility of hope.

She walked down a path and sat on the low thick wall of stone from where, years earlier, Yeshua and Octavius and Lucca had enjoyed their rock-throwing contest. I sat beside her and put my arm around her. She looked at me and, without bothering to stand, disrobed. By then she was three months away from reaching fruition. She placed her garments upon the wall and lay back on them. It was an invitation so bold, so tender, so unexpected, that I felt myself responding, and as I lay with her, she cried out and wrapped her arms around me – that young girl, so bereft and far from her jagged shores, accepting this aging merchant from the Levantine desert. Never had I been so grateful to Melqart, and I thought to myself, not without some degree of shame, that, for me, my nephew could remain silent and in mourning for as long as he wished.

And as if by intuition, that very same evening as Canlia slept and Octavius roamed the city, Yeshua finally broke his silence.

'I had grown accustomed uncle.' He said it just like that, staring into space.

'To what Yeshua?

'To wellbeing.'

'Ah.'

'To falling asleep and waking by her. To the sound of the little girl breathing. To the view from the wood down to the bay. To the days and the nights and the seasons running into each other. To the winter fires and the spring rains. I had grown accustomed uncle. It was my life. Not my mother's or my father's, not even yours who brought me there and showed me the way, but mine, my own life. I had grown accustomed to it in my own way.'

I felt obliged to say to him, 'Of all those things to which you became accustomed, all those things that took you from your past, two cling still.'

'No,' he said. 'All is lost.'

'Two cling still,' I insisted, 'Venusha's sister and the child she carries that comes from you.'

'Canlia is Venusha's ghost,' he said. 'Each time I see her I am only reminded of what I have lost – and of how.'

'Canlia is not a ghost,' I said. 'I assure you. But a fair young woman of flesh and blood, and within that flesh and blood, swimming in it, curled within it, growing from it, is your own living child.'

'No,' he said, for the third, and for me, final time. 'My children are no longer of this world.'

It was the one thing he kept within him, always, that was there the day we left Nazareth and there the day he died. It was as if the world spun round him, so that much of the love he gave out to the world was a mirror reflecting back upon him.

Chapter 33

Laura put her coat on, grabbed a notebook, and walked into town, past The Wounded Hart, on to the livelier gastro-pub for a drink and an early dinner. The word used in the codices had been 'ὕβρις'. 'Altier' or 'hautain', 'arrogant' or 'proud' were the adjectives that came to mind when trying to translate what Joseph of Arimathea was saying about his nephew. It was a harsh criticism she thought – certainly with its grain of truth – one applicable to all megalomaniacs. How else could you describe a person who came to believe they were God come down to earth in the form of a man? But she also considered the possibility that it was too harsh an assessment – in this case at least.

She wondered how old Joseph of Arimathea had been when he dictated this. She imagined he must have been in his early forties when they began their journey, forty-three or forty-four then in Gades which was modern day Cádiz, and in his sixties when recounting it for the scribe. He seemed to have been a confirmed bachelor when Miryam asked him to take her oldest son away from the Holy Land. How odd was that in those times and in that culture? And when he did marry it was in a cavalier fashion to a young pagan girl thousands of kilometres from Jerusalem. She considered the possibility that Joseph might have been gay. Perhaps, she thought, when he speaks of the courtesans and servant girls he bedded down, he is in a Proustian mode substituting Albertines for Alberts. Then again, his lust for Canlia at the Temple of Melqart, and his reluctance to cede her to his nephew felt genuine. In any event, his sexual preferences were beside the point. What she perceived within his harsh view of Yeshua – or maybe she was just being too influenced by recent events in her own life – was a certain coldness, a numbness to his nephew's suffering. When Yeshua was kidnapped by the Arab slave traders the uncle's main concern was how the news would reflect upon him with respect to Miryam, not for his nephew's fate per se. When he encouraged Yeshua to buck-up after a trauma of catastrophic proportions in Cornwall, he seemed insensitive to what a person, young and in love and equipped with a more normal sensibility, might be going through not a month after witnessing the brutalized remains of his wife and children. Then again, the adolescent Joseph of Arimathea had seen his own father's throat slit before avenging it. If such an experience did not harden one to life's precariousness, what would?

Fathers and sons, she thought, entering the bar. Though

Yeshua worked with his father as a boy – the commoner, the carpenter – the parent he bonded with and stood by was his patrician mother. The only father he refers to ninety-eight percent of the time is a heavenly one, not the joiner who shed tears for him when saying goodbye.

Although it was the evening of the day Camilla had been laid to rest, the loud and jolly atmosphere prevailing at the gastro-pub, the local youths ordering pints at the bar, the blaring Irish rap music, and a range of passable French wines by the glass, were just the things Laura needed. She convinced herself that Camilla of all people would understand, and she decided that if things did not improve with respect to her status at the estate, she would cancel the painters and return to her apartment in New York straight away. James, she knew, was in a tough spot at the moment and cutting him some slack would not only be smart but also the most appropriate thing to do. He might not be the strongest fellow she had ever met, but she was fairly certain he was not a liar. The intimacy they had shared felt real.

An additional advantage to the gastro-pub was that it had a row of battered computer consoles in the back, set up for violent video games catering to teenagers with raging hormones, and that could also be rented to send and retrieve email. Using her New York based mobile phone was stupidly expensive and there was no Wi-Fi at the inn. Before sitting down to dinner, she ordered a glass of wine and went online and was immediately

rewarded with an email from Jean-Paul Bonnerive that
included an attachment.

> *Dear Laura,*
>
> *It was a pleasure to meet you the other day and how
> very exciting it was to engage with a fellow researcher
> in possession of such valuable documents. Just when I
> had given up all hope of encountering anything new
> you have come along and surprised me.*
>
> *Please find attached a scanned copy (I believe that is
> how it is called – I asked an assistant to do it for me)
> of a piece of correspondence from Gerard of Amiens
> addressed to Eleanor of Castile that in all likelihood
> refers to the document you are working on. As you
> will see, the notion that people during the Middle Ages
> were a bunch of dark and irrational religious fanatics
> is grossly exaggerated. I look forward to your response
> and commentary.*
>
> *Yours, JPB*

She opened the attachment and what appeared on the
screen was an elegant image of two sheets of yellowed
parchment covered with script written in old French in
a hand now familiar to her. The irony of her contemplating this document in the room she was seated in,
with the music of Black 47 vibrating from large corner
speakers, and the computer screen just to the right of hers

displaying muscle-bound commandoes shooting the heads off bearded terrorists, was not lost on her.

Your Highness,

I trust this finds You and His Majesty comfortably at Your leisure in Paris. I am now more than halfway through my work transcribing the manuscript You so graciously left in my keeping and I hope that when we next meet, I shall have two copies finished. I also hope You will agree that I have managed to chart a course that preserves the narrative flow and the lyrical tenor while enabling me to preserve my head. I continue to marvel at this most extraordinary text, just as I continue to scold my own cowardice. Woe to all of us who live in such intolerant times, and yet, thanks to Your great generosity and counsel, I know the path I have chosen is the correct one. I remain your most humble and grateful servant.

Gerard

She answered Bonnerive and then moved back into the dining room to order some food. All of the day's setbacks were erasing themselves from her mind. Here was the first bit of outside, corroborating evidence, supporting the validity and provenance of the scroll and codices. It was proof as well, as Jean-Paul had indicated, of a future Queen already skilled at showing her public the face of a devout monarch while hiding a free spirit, someone receptive to the intellectual rewards that can come from keeping an open mind. The idea of writing a book someday about this ignored and fascinating woman suddenly felt like an obligation. Halfway through the meal her phone rang, and it was James. She took it outside onto the much quieter street.

'Laura,' he said – she loved the way he pronounced her name, 'I just got off the phone with Finn and he told me what's happened.'

'It's OK,' she said.

'No. It is not OK. And I told him to go and get you right away and to bring you back to the house. I am livid.'

'James,' she said, 'There's no need to rush. We can wait a day or two.'

'That's my point. Not today of all days. This does it for me. It is unconscionable. She is out of control. Finn and Bidelia work for me. The house is mine. The estate is mine. The project is now mine, and you shall have all you need to finish it properly, and you shall be my guest for as long as you wish.'

'James.'

'I can't speak any longer I'm afraid, but I just needed to reach you and to tell you this and to hear your voice. I am so sorry.'

'Do you think one day we'll be able to stop telling each other that?'

'Yes,' he said, 'one day very soon, I hope. I'll call you

tomorrow from Barcelona and I'll get up there as soon as I can.'

'All right. Good.'

'I miss you terribly.'

'Me too. And I'm sad you've had to deal with this.'

'I've got to run.'

'Bye James.'

'Ciao Laura.'

She called the Bed & Breakfast to ask them to tell Finn where she was and to say she would be checking out. Finn, all smiles, walked into the gastro-pub twenty minutes later.

'Top of the morning to you, Mr MacShane,' she said.

'And to you, Miss.'

'Have a seat.'

He sat opposite her, looking about.

'What will it be?' she said. 'I'm inviting.'

'It's a lively place isn't it? You've heard then from Mr Figueras?'

'I have.'

'He called us – imagine, on a day like this – called to see how we were doing, and to make sure you had all you needed to be comfortable – so of course I was forced to tell him about his missus.'

'He's a good man Finn.'

'That he is.'

The waitress appeared and he ordered a glass of stout and a shot of Jameson's.

'Now there's a healthy combination,' Laura said. 'Perhaps I should take the wheel on the way back.'

'There'll be none of that.'

'How long have you known James?'

'He was barely twenty when we first came to work for Mrs Trevelyan.'

'My goodness. He's like fifty now. How old were the two of you back then?'

'We were in our twenties as well, Miss.'

'Do you and Bidelia have any children?'

'No, Miss. Which is fine by me, though it's been Bidelia's great tragedy.'

'Right. So, you must have known Camilla's mother too.'

'Oh yes, Miss, for many years.'

'What was she like?'

His drinks arrived and they toasted.

'Thank you for coming to get me Finn.'

He had a sip of the stout and then downed half the shot of whiskey.

'My pleasure, Miss. I expect we're all feeling a slight better than we were a few hours ago.'

'I'm glad.'

'Mrs Trevelyan's mother was a lady of the old ways, and she was a grand dresser, with a healthy appetite for food and wine. She'd often tell us how when she was a girl the norm was to eat five full meals a day. Meat and fish courses at breakfast – that sort of thing.'

'But she wasn't overweight.'

'Far from it.'

'And how did they get along do you think, she and Camilla?

'Badly. If I may be so bold, I'd say she was jealous of her daughter's youth and never forgave her for it, and she was very disapproving of the husband, the Spanish gentleman.'

'How long ago did she die?'

'It will be five years this winter, Miss, though during the last year of her life she hardly knew who or where she was.'

'Camilla's youth,' Laura said, almost to herself. 'She seemed young to me even though she was seventy.'

'She was a very active person. And she'd become very fond of you, Miss.'

'Thank you, Finn.'

'It's true. We could tell.'

'And now there's the Carmensina situation.'

'We're not looking forward to it, I can tell you that. I'm sure we'll retire as soon as we can.'

'You think she is that bad?'

'Look at today, Miss.'

'Why do you think James married her in the first place?'

'That's not for me to say. Why does any man marry? Mrs Trevelyan was well off of course and owned lots of property but she lacked liquidity I fear, relatively speaking, and I think Mr Figueras was eager to find himself a good paying position, and then Miss Carmensina came along.'

He had more stout and finished the whiskey. It suddenly dawned on Laura why Camilla had been so eager to auction off the scroll and the codices – she was probably worried about James and his overdependence on the resources of Carmensina's family.

'Do you and Bidelia have any idea what I've been doing here?'

'Yes, Miss. Mrs Trevelyan told us before you came to see her, that you were going to make sense of the old scroll in the library chamber.'

'She told you that before I arrived?'

'That she did.'

Laura recalled the two Oxford dons she had been warned with and smiled.

'Do you have any idea what's in it?'

He paused, considering his answer.

'A little,' he said. 'According to Bidelia who heard it discussed in the dining room. She's upset by it.'

'Ah.'

'We're Catholics you see.'

'Well,' she said, slightly embarrassed, 'that's understandable.'

Back at the house that night in her high wide bed, with the vast and wild countryside around her, and the thick dark sea in front of her, she relished her reprieve. She woke at dawn between linen sheets and worked on the translation.

Chapter 34

As we neared Sicily again, I wondered if Yeshua might regain a hold on life. It was my hope to try and reunite him with Daphne. But upon our arrival at the villa we learned that the Emperor Tiberius had recalled Claudius, Octavius's father, to Rome, and Claudius had taken his entire household with him, including Daphne. Six servants of local origin were left behind to maintain and protect the property, plus a Roman associate who informed Octavius that his father had put the villa and all its land up for sale. Four days later, after cashing in my tin at a new market, one that produced a massive profit, the villa was mine.

I decided to make my home here. I would never find a more beautiful place, one immeasurably closer to the mines, a place from which I could trade more profitably. I knew that Canlia would never adapt well to life in Jerusalem, and I hoped I might dissuade or at least delay Yeshua's return as well. Octavius was pleased when I told him that he and his family would forever have a place here. I kept the servants but made few improvements. There was something about the old-fashioned style of the villa's construction, its cracked tiles and fading murals, the black and white patio design dedicated to Neptune with his trident standing upon a dolphin that appealed to me and seemed appropriate for a man my age.

Octavius maintained his battle-ready exercise regime and sought the company of other Romans in the area, and even found himself a young woman among them he thought to marry. Canlia, who was now the mistress of a fine house and estate, relaxed in the safety of my company. That was proof enough that I had made a wise decision. And at first, Yeshua seemed to make peace with his grief. Though he remained quiet and withdrawn, his physical appearance improved, and he took once again to wearing clean garments. A tranquil rhythm of living took hold of our lives as the horrors of the Belerion raid seemed finally behind us.

Then, one evening, at the dinner hour, Yeshua was nowhere to be found, and recalling how he had gone missing here once before, I made my way up to the shrine to Minerva and there I discovered him looking out to sea.

'Yeshua,' I said to him. He turned and smiled at me.

'Uncle,' he replied.

'The evening meal is served.'

'I apologize uncle, but I am fasting.'

'Ah,' I said, as a bad feeling entered my spirit, 'that is something I should try more often. Giving one's entrails a rest is a practice they appreciate.'

'I am fasting for my Father, not my entrails.'

He was seated on the edge of a low wall from where there was a commanding view. I settled myself beside him. 'Your father is a Nazarene carpenter and as much as any man he values the sustenance to be had from a well-prepared meal.'

'My Father is everywhere and only values what I am prepared to renounce.'

Then he smiled at me again and put his hand on my shoulder. 'I know,' he said, 'this is not what you enjoy hearing from me. I know you had hoped to draw me away from this. And for a time, you succeeded. It started here.'

'What started here?'

'The straying from my path, my weakness, my capitulation to the life of the flesh.'

'The flesh, entrails, and the rest, is all we have nephew. It is sad perhaps, but true.'

'I know that is what you believe,' he said. 'I know you are angry with those who promise redemption in a world where terrible events take place each day. I know you think your view is stronger, that it reflects the heavens as they are and not as I know them to be. I know you think my beliefs are a weakness that proposes invisible explanations for earthly disappointments. Thus the fasting you see – to toughen me up.'

I covered the hand he had placed on my shoulder with one of my own and said to him, 'I only seek, for myself and for my loved ones – you among them Yeshua – peace and pleasure, escape from pain, acceptance of disappointment

– to work as one must but to spend as much time as possible contemplating the sea like you are doing now, enjoying the scent of wild flowers, the curve and swell of a woman's breast.'

'I know,' he said, looking away. 'I know you uncle. I know you well, and I have tried your way, and I pray for you so that God can make room for your admirable stubbornness. My path is different. I strayed onto yours and lost my own and the terrible sign my Father sent to me, his rage at my abandonment of his will, has sent me back to Him to beg His forgiveness, and now a calm invades me as I see what I am meant to do. As I see who and why I am.'

'Who are you Yeshua?'

'I am who I am uncle, and I promise you, here and now – regardless of your thoughts and deeds – I promise you everlasting love in Heaven. I promise that to you and to Canlia and to the child she bears for you.'

'You can promise such a thing?'

He nodded his head. It was as if he was once again the proud and sullen adolescent I had led away from Nazareth.

'And Octavius?' I asked him. 'Can you promise that to him?'

'We shall have to see.'

'These things you say dismay me,' I said to him. 'The whole purpose for this journey from its beginning was to show you a way out from these things that you say again now. I was so pleased when you married, and so wished your mother had been there.'

'To savour your victory.'

'To savour yours.'

'And yet, had she been there and stayed on, she would have been violated and murdered.'

'And resting no doubt with your Heavenly Father.'

'You mock me,' he said.

'I am disappointed.'

'You are angry with me.'

'Because I love you, like you are my own son.'

'You are a good man, uncle.'

'And a sinner, according to you.'

'As fine a sinner as ever there was. And far less than I myself have been.'

And so it came about that he left me, left us. I had failed him and failed his mother and father. And to my great surprise and further woe, Octavius decided to go with him. In order to properly retire from his legion so that he night return and marry and settle nearby to us, he would have to return to Jerusalem. He also wished to communicate the news of Lucca's death to their comrades still in service to the Emperor. But what most touched me with respect to his motives for returning, were the words he spoke to me the night before they departed.

'Though grown into a man, Yeshua is still young in many ways,' he said. 'And he is not a fighter. I feel bound to complete our original agreement and would not feel right were he to sail off alone.'

Canlia and I slept fitfully that night and many tears

were shed the following morning. Yeshua placed his hand upon Canlia's swollen abdomen, blessing the fruit of her womb. It was hard for me to let go of him after so much time together. It would have been far harder still had I known that the next time I would see him – thirteen years later, on the day of my arrival to Jerusalem – he would be hanging from a cross.

Chapter 35

She closed her laptop. The only noises she could hear came from the breaking waves of the Celtic Sea and a dripping faucet in her bathroom. A week earlier it would have been much the same, except Camilla would have been in her room down the hall. It seemed inconceivable to her that in only a single week, Camilla had died and been buried on the island of Mallorca, she had been to New York and back, had broken up with Nathan and started an affair with James.

She remembered her promise to James to go and visit his mother's grave. Though the elegant dowager was interred where she wished, next to her daughter in the town where she was born, the idea of it felt foreign and lonely to Laura. But she'd never had the opportunity to observe Camilla in the context of Deià. She had only known her, and briefly, there in Cornwall from whose soil the woman seemed to have sprung fully formed. Laura thought Camilla would have preferred to be buried along with 'her line' as she called it. But such perhaps had been the degree of misery the woman had gone through with her mother.

She recalled the story Jean-Paul Bonnerive told her about Lorca's father being buried in Westchester. She thought of her own mother buried in the Sacred Heart Cemetery, close to Gary Cooper's grave in Southampton, Long Island. Where would Jean-Paul end up? For it would be soon. She had not been bold enough to ask. Where would she like to be buried, if at all? Against her will she imagined what those buried corpses would look like at that moment – the older ones reduced to bone and sagging clothing darkly stained, sealed within pitch-black, satin-lined coffins under the ground. Camilla's body would still be relatively fresh, but soon it would begin to putrefy. The whole thing was brutal and ghastly. Cremation made more sense to her. But of course, sense had nothing to do with it, and she knew that to the dead the whereabouts or state of their remains had no meaning whatsoever. Once you were dead, one place or method was as good as another. The significance of one's homeland or tribe lost all importance. It was only important to the living.

The more she thought about this business of living and dying the crueller it seemed. Philosophers and psychiatrists, wise women and men, tended to emphasize its naturalness, its inevitability best met with acceptance and equanimity. Few spoke of the terror, of Kurtz's 'the horror'. Few expressed rage at the unfairness of it. Dylan Thomas perhaps when he wrote,

'Do not go gentle into that good night,
Old age should burn and rave at close of day;
Rage, rage against the dying of the light.'

A scene from a film she saw years before had stuck in her mind, the Clint Eastwood western *Unforgiven*, when, at the end, the Eastwood character is about to kill the nasty sheriff played by Gene Hackman. Hackman says, 'I don't deserve to die like this,' and Eastwood replies, 'Deserving's got nothing to do with it.'

She knew that death was as natural as being born, or chewing on the meat of other animals, or defecating, or having sex, that it was part and parcel of the frenzied, gene-driven instincts that swept up all living creatures despite human attempts to deny or rationalize it, to translate or pray one's way out of it. She too would die. Her day would come. Just as sure as she was lying there awake and alive and comfortable that autumn morning – her life would someday end, and once it did all that she had done and experienced would lose meaning in an instant and forever, because when we die the universe dies with us. Those left behind cease to exist or matter. When insects and fish and most animals are born, they separate from their parents quickly. But for humans it was different. How were you supposed to love someone, and then lose them? How were you supposed to do that and survive without always mistrusting any further moments of grace?

With thoughts such as these coursing through her it

became impossible to sleep again. She rolled over on her side and remembered how it felt waking up next to James at the Bowery Hotel before the phone call had upset everything. Holding onto that memory, using it to shoo the others away, she got up, brushed her teeth, and ran herself a bath.

Half an hour later, she was in the kitchen eating a raft of toast with a soft-boiled egg and a cup of tea. Both of the MacShanes were there, Finn in an upbeat mood despite the black armband and what it stood for, Bidelia quiet and distant.

'How did you sleep, Miss?' He asked her, pouring the tea into the porcelain mug that had the estate's coat of arms on it.

'Very well thanks,' she answered, 'but the house feels very different without her, don't you think?'

'If it feels different for you,' he said, 'imagine how it is for us. Thank goodness for routines is all I can say. Otherwise we'd be just moping about not knowing what to do.'

Bidelia's silence and the serious, preoccupied demeanour on her ruddy face lent an awkward note to the ambiance in the room. Laura imagined the woman was still upset, both for the loss of the employer they had been so faithful to for so many years, as well as from a lingering reaction to what had been Carmensina's attempt to oust them.

'Do you think it would be all right if I were to go for a ride on one of the horses?'

'For sure, Miss,' he said. 'With Mrs Trevelyan gone who knows what will become of them all.'

'Are the two women here today?'

'Yes, Miss. They come every day, including Sundays, from eight until one p.m.'

Laura left the house through the rear kitchen door and crossed the gravelled square to the stables. When she came in, Gin and Jen were spreading fresh hay in the paddocks with pitchforks. Laura commiserated with them for a bit and then Gen saddled Daisy while Laura sat in the tack room pulling on the same boots she had worn when riding with Camilla. Before mounting the horse, she looked into the office and studied the painting of Camilla's mother. The young girl arranged upon her side-saddle stared back at her with an imperious intensity.

Rather than head off in the direction of the cottage and the dolmen and the lake, she rode around the walls of the massive house and left through a small gate that put her on the shoulder of the main road. After a while she crossed the road and took an earthen path that led down to a bay with a curving strand of beach she had not noticed before. Upon arriving there she dismounted and read a small plaque affixed to a post that said the bay had been used centuries earlier for ships loading tin from the nearby mines. It pleased her to think this may have been the place where Joseph of Arimathea, Yeshua and the Romans had landed, and where Yeshua had mourned, stricken with grief, after the village massacre. It spurred her on to return to the library and her computer to continue her work.

Chapter 36

Canlia's child was born at night on the thirtieth day of October, a boy we named Dawid, or David, the beloved, after the ancient King of Judea from whose line, it was said, the Messiah would come. I thought Yeshua would appreciate that. And in deference to Venusha and Canlia's father we gave him the second name of Arto-Uiros, or Arthur.

Anyone who has witnessed the birth of an animal can see that we are animals too. Anyone who has seen up close the innards of animals and humans must know, as Yeshua himself once observed, that none of us reflects the image of God. The tubes and the blood, the bones and the sinew, the nerves and the muscles are all too densely packed, too preposterously configured. Surely God would have put his creatures together in a simpler fashion.

I was alone with Canlia when the child came out of her and I watched her awaken it and clean it and take it to her breast and I watched her bite through the cord that kept them together and then toss the afterbirth out for the dogs. My fierce and holy pagan girl – braver than I hope I shall ever have to be.

I was humbled. When the women servants arrived to tend to her and the child, I left them and walked out to the reflecting pool, tranquil under half a moon, the autumn's clear skies a riot of stars. Some leaves floated in the water. Leaves with little veins in them like the ones seen through the child's thin new skin. Leaves that had been blown from branches that sprouted from trees like the nerves within the child's tiny muscles. Trees that grow and come from seed, like that which fertilized Canlia's small, blood filled womb. All life is wondrous.

David Arturious grew into a beautiful boy with good friends, some of them Roman children, some of them local islanders. They filled the villa with life and kept me young. After a time, I gave up dealing in tin. The journeys grew more tiresome, took me far away from the villa, and it was not a vocation I wished for my son to learn, for it would take him far away from us as well someday. Once upon a time all I wished for was to be able to travel as far afield as possible from Judea and the small world surrounding me there. But now I was a settled man with my own wife and child, a condition I had never aspired to and that took me pleasantly by surprise. It came about through marrying a pagan and having someone else's child, but still it came about.

I looked around and asked my neighbours and all agreed that in addition to the wheat and fruit trees already produced there, the villa's lands would also be ideal for viniculture. I had numerous hectares cleared and I imported vines from the mainland – for I did not fancy the sweet wines common to the island – and within a few years the business prospered and instead of being an importer I became an exporter.

But a final journey awaited me. When David turned thirteen, I told him we should go and visit his real father's homeland.

'You are my real father,' he said to me, kissing my cheek. And in truth I did not wish for us to leave.

'I know,' I said to him, 'but later you will thank me for having shown you this other part of the world, and you have family there who will rejoice at seeing you. And is it not true you have always wished to sail across the Great Sea? And the sooner we do this the sooner we can return and now is a good time for leaving the vines behind.'

Canlia wished to stay put and there were trustworthy men and women keeping the villa and the grounds and working the vineyards. Before we departed, she asked me to leave her once again with child and as her charms were still considerable and my own body not yet buried, we tried and managed to plant seed within her in the hope it might bear fruit. I think in truth she feared we might not return.

Chapter 37

As real as his anger had been after speaking with Finn and discovering what had happened when Laura returned to the estate, James was reluctant to speak with Carmensina about it. The funeral had been draining, and throughout that day and afternoon Carmensina had comported herself in an exemplary fashion. She handled the girls beautifully, answering their difficult questions with frankness, grace, and tenderness. She treated the odd assortment of guests with charm and patience. Thinking about it that evening, James had little doubt that part of her serenity derived from the satisfaction she felt from exercising a new-found authority, from having lowered the boom on Laura and threatened to do so on poor Finn and Bidelia. He sensed that, linked to her outrageously brutal timing, was an eagerness to take over Provence House in Cornwall, to make some changes, and probably to hire her own staff so as to make the transition, in her mind, complete.

After he got off the phone with Finn and Laura there was

still much to do. He had an important business meeting the following day in Barcelona. They managed to get themselves on the last flight off the island at ten p.m. It was not the best moment to provoke a confrontation. Back at the suite as they prepared to leave, he found Carmensina and Noelma efficiently packing. They were taking care of everything. All he had to do was drive everyone to the airport. After they got there and got rid of the car and waited to board the plane, the two women entertained the girls. During the flight Carmensina kept them busy until they fell asleep. He sat across from them and admired the innocent slumber of his daughters who were as exhausted as everyone from having buried their granny. Carmensina smiled at him and reached for his hand.

They were a family, he thought to himself, a married couple with problems of course, but what was unusual about that? Two startling things had occurred in rapid succession: his adulterous liaison with Laura, and the death of his mother; finding a young, compelling woman who admired him and who asked nothing from him, and the loss of the woman who had made and raised him. But there on the plane that evening returning to Catalunya, he was back with his own family, herding and protecting them.

Perhaps this was what Carmensina had needed all along to calm her down, for whatever reason. Perhaps the person she had been most jealous of, much more than the imagined mistresses, was Camilla and her unassailable position, and of his mother's hold over him and her. Perhaps now

268

that Camilla was gone, so suddenly, and as painful as that was, things could finally improve between them – or at least settle into a more relaxed rhythm of the sort middle-aged marriages often excelled at. Perhaps he could have his cake and eat it too.

Let her have what she wanted, let her fire Finn and Bidelia even – he would take care of them – let her redecorate the mansion a bit – his in-laws could afford it. Perhaps all he needed in return was the release and excitement Laura would provide. As Carmensina could start to call herself Lady Villar Polanc de Trevelyan-Figueras, inviting her friends and family to spend time at Provence House, he could recover the cottage for himself and stay there when and how he wished.

For, realistically thinking, he considered what might be the possible outcomes for him once Laura completed the project and had no further need to be so close by. If he divorced Carmensina he would lose his job. Would he be willing to move to New York to live with Laura there? What would he do? What about his girls? Carmensina would fight tooth and nail to keep them, and would Laura really want to take on the responsibilities involved in caring for two young girls anyway? If he were to find another position in Barcelona, something highly doubtful given the power and reach of his father-in-law, would Laura be willing to drop everything, just as her career would be taking a huge leap forward, to live with him there? Or could he live in Cornwall full-time on his inheritance, jetting back and forth each week to see his children? All of it was hard to imagine.

As he held his wife's familiar hand, he recognized that he and Laura were lovers just beginning an affair. What would be the point of seeking a divorce from Carmensina right now? Managing to repress the resolve he had sworn to himself only a day earlier on the beach, the idea suddenly felt absurd, amateur, like the behaviour of a man half his age. He even suspected Laura might prefer things the way they were anyway, at least for now, he with his cumbersome family baggage, and she as a free agent, both of them disposed to take advantage of any opportunity to enjoy each other, but without provoking a chain reaction of life-changing events.

For a moment he wondered if these second thoughts were just evidence of weakness, of cowardice, of him trying to justify inaction. He decided to cut himself some slack and concluded it was not the case, and that what some might call passivity, others would recognize as cunning realism, a worldly attitude that would allow the relationships in question to evolve and devolve at their own pace. What Laura wanted was to complete the project, and he wanted her. Surely it was too soon to tell if there might be something more profound than that going on between them.

He continued to review his options as the plane descended through the night, making its way toward the main runway at El Prat del Llobregat airport. He would be dealing with the details of Camilla's estate for the next few months at least. The thought of initiating divorce proceedings simultaneously was impossible to contemplate. His in-laws, his colleagues, and his daughters would look upon him as the primary culprit – especially if word of his involvement with Laura got out, and it would. Simply considering the logistics of what it would actually be like to move out of the apartment in Barcelona at that moment was more than he could handle. But Carmensina *would* have to be spoken to. He would have to tell her, and soon, of his decision to maintain the arrangement Laura had with Camilla. That conversation all by itself would be explosive, unless it came paired with an offering.

Chapter 38

Laura was eager to move on to the next and last section, to see what happened when they arrived in Jerusalem. She was also determined to finish the translation of the Greek codex for there were only a few pages left.

We journeyed east on a Greek ship. There were no storms or pirates. There was no illness. The crew was affable and kind to David. He spoke their language and learned much from them and by the time we landed in Acre he had become a good sailor. But the visit home, as I have already mentioned, was steeped in tragedy, bathed in blood and misery for all concerned. I regretted taking the boy into such a vile and brutal atmosphere at such an impressionable age.

We arrived in Jerusalem on the day of Yeshua's crucifixion. A carnival spirit prevailed in the streets. Those vehemently for and against this punishment were united by their morbid interest in the savagery on display. I left David with Joseph, his grandfather, who had refused to witness the agony of his son. The fierceness with which the

273

carpenter greeted and clung to David concerned me. But I put this worry aside when confronted with the horror taking place on Golgotha.

I found Yeshua atop that ghastly hill, nails driven through him, his head beset by a crown of thorns, Miryam standing beneath him, out of her wits, spattered with his blood. And there too stood a weeping Octavius, who even then was still in service, his Sicilian idyll long forgotten. It was to him I went without pausing. Fiercely I whispered into his ear, begging him to use the power of his office and the point of his spear to put our boy out of his misery. At least there was that.

After Octavius released Yeshua from this life we took him down. Miryam wrapped her arms around his bloodied corpse. Those of his followers brave enough to be present wept openly. I owned a proper tomb I had once purchased for myself, and it was there we carried him, wrapping him in linen after anointing his ravaged skin with herbs and oils. The tomb was sealed, and Octavius placed a guard before it.

I accompanied Miryam home and it was there she met David for the first time. Never have I seen a woman weep like that and never, I most fervently hope, shall I see anything like it again. Young David too, upset by so much turmoil swirling about, began to weep as well. I cursed Yeshua that day even though I had loved him dearly and treated him as if he were my own. For even in his death he continued to protagonize, ruining what should have been a joyous homecoming for his only son.

Late that night I met with Octavius. Both of us had aged. We had a long discussion and he confessed he had made a mistake by staying on in Judea. The pull of his former comrades had been strong, and the compensation offered him significant – but now he was eager to leave. The trial and martyrdom of Yeshua had shaken him profoundly. And it was then I made up my mind to bring them all back with me to the villa, and the sooner the better.

On the next day I visited a family of Egyptians who continued to maintain the knowledge and skills of embalmment. We came to an arrangement and within two days they had gathered together the necessary implements and solutions. Octavius and I went to the tomb at night and with help from the Roman guard on duty, rolled back the stone and carried Yeshua's body to where the Egyptians did their work. Two days after that his corpse had been emptied of its organs but preserved and a special container was made for him that was sealed tight with pitch and nails and loaded upon a wagon; we returned to Acre with it, David, Octavius and I, along with a complement of Roman soldiers. I invited Miryam and Joseph and their other children – all of them grown by then, but they refused. I am told that Yeshua's followers, upon finding the tomb empty, saw in it the handiwork of God and the fulfilment of Yeshua's own prophecy. Such is the extent of the madness and folly humans are capable of. The entire trip to Judea had been a nightmare of pain and disappointment. But I could not leave Yeshua there, even though he had freely chosen to go back. I wished to bring peace and sanity back into our lives.

I had to pay extra for bringing the coffin aboard, such was the fear and superstition it instilled in the crew. They believed it would begin to stink and bring misfortune. But after a week at sea no one paid it any mind, lashed tight to the deck by the prow. More than once we would sit upon it and hold forth, regaling young David with tales about the first trip we had taken, with Lucca along, sixteen years earlier. The ship was scheduled to bypass Sicily and go first to Rome before turning around to head for Siracusa, and Octavius insisted we visit once again with his family. In all of my travels I had never been to the Imperial City and I thought the idea a fine one.

The ship put in at Ostia and after securing Yeshua's coffin below deck and hiring a guard to watch over it we made the journey by sailing barge up the Tiber. Our stay there was most instructive. The city's architecture was magnificent but mixed with hovels where the less fortunate lived. There were too many people living there – and the stench on a warm morning was strong. Only in the hills above the river were the air and ambiance agreeable. Roman politics dominated everyone's waking thoughts and though one saw luxurious homes belonging to senators, men of property, and relations of the Emperor, a current of anxiety seemed to pervade even the loveliest gardens.

Octavius' family had done well for themselves. His father, Claudius, had aged considerably and they were greatly saddened by the news we brought about Yeshua and by the sad tale of what had occurred in Belerion. Daphne was still very beautiful and like Canlia she was in the midst of her third decade. She became fond of David and was especially glad to see Octavius, whom she had known since they were young. I was able to convince her to return with us to the villa in Sicily. She had grown weary of Rome. The temple they had there that she tended was luxurious, but small, and when I told her how beautiful her former outpost of worship still was, up the hill, back at the villa, she began to weep.

On the evening before our departure Claudius asked me to visit with him in his chamber. It had a spectacular view of the city. Torches lit the room and torches lit all of the buildings below lending a magical aura to the evening. A tone of burnt sienna illuminated the Tiber as it wended its way past palaces and courts, temples and amphitheatres.

'I wish I could return with you,' he said. He was reclined upon a pallet covered with silken cushions. His person still displayed great elegance despite the weakened state of his body.

'Perhaps you will someday, when you are feeling stronger.'

'Nonsense,' he said, but with a smile. 'You know, when I first learned you had bought the property, I had mixed feelings.'

'I can imagine.'

'A Jew from Judea, from the far provinces, taking the deed of such a fine estate from a Roman aristocrat like myself. I struggled with how to explain such a thing to my comrades.'

'Of course.'

'But I knew you, knew you to be a man of the world, an exceptional gentleman, a man not weighed down by his ancient culture and its punitive beliefs, a man at ease with Rome.'

'I understand,' I said. And I did. 'Though I must confess,' I added, 'I am more at ease with Romans, especially with those like yourself and your family, than I am with Rome, which I find too populous and frenzied, too obsessed with power.'

He reached for a goblet and took a drink of whatever was in it. The effort it demanded was considerable and we both waited for him to finish.

'In coming here,' he said, 'not that I had much choice, for it behoves one to say yes to Tiberius, but in coming here we gave up bucolic relaxation for official pomp and circumstance. We exchanged lazy afternoons for power and its trappings. We traded servant girls happy to sneak in to one's room at night with the scent of mimosa in their hair, for influence and the coin it brings. But it feels to me, because of when it happened, that I also exchanged my youth for old age. In a more natural scheme of things I would have spent my vigorous years here in Rome, and my waning years at the villa.'

'It feels to me,' I said to him, 'that wherever you are Claudius, that is the place to be.'

'What a flatterer you are.' I had to laugh. We both did.

'On two occasions,' he said, 'you have brought our beloved son back to us. For that we shall be forever grateful, and forever in your debt.'

'But I have taken him away as well.'

He waved his hand in the air. 'That is of no matter. He has been a man for a long time now and a good soldier and he knows his obligations. But you have brought him to us. He has told me all that happened with your nephew, from the beginning to the end.'

I only nodded and looked down at the ceaseless city.

'He showed such promise and was so handsome and spirited, and he seemed to be heading in a better direction when we last saw him. But then, I hear, he reverted.'

'He did indeed. It was the tragedy that did it.'

'I remember his seriousness, his cunning too, and his great charm.'

'He went mad when he saw what had befallen his wife and children and he took it as a sign, a punishment for straying away from his angry god.'

'Who knows how one will react to such terrible things?' he said.

'All I wish for now, for all of us, and most especially for David, is peace, gentle sunlight, the sea breeze, good wine, and laughter,' I said.

'And some passion.'

'That too.' He pushed himself up and swung his feet down upon the floor so that he was sitting beside me.

279

'I have two gifts for you, there on the table.' I rose and approached the table and found a small marble bust and a thin scroll.

'The bust is a likeness of Epicurus, my favourite philosopher. The scroll is a treatise by Titus Lucretius Carus – *De rerum natura*. I cannot imagine a more appropriate person than you to have them.'

'I am very grateful sir.'

'They have been with me for many years and once were kept at the villa – which is where they truly belong – with you and the boy, with Daphne and Octavius.'

'I am honoured. I understand,' I said.

'One needs to make love more and worry less,' he said in conclusion.

Laura paused and smiled. She remembered thinking in her hotel bed hardly a week ago, that she had inadvertently become a sort of modern day Poggio Bracciolini, the early fifteenth-century scholar and admirer of Epicurus, who had dedicated much of his colourful life to hunting down ancient manuscripts. She had discovered him by reading Stephen Grenblatt's book *The Swerve* that celebrates Bracciolini's discovery of Lucretius' *De Rerum Natura* in a German monastery. And here, in front of her, Joseph of Arimathea was referencing Epicurus and Lucretius both. Riveted by what she was learning in this section, she forged ahead.

Three weeks later David and I, Daphne and Octavius, stood on deck with Yeshua's coffin between us, watching Siracusa come into view. Upon our arrival at the villa Canlia was not with child but her joy at having us back more than made up for it. We buried my nephew up at the temple, sealing him within the marble chamber where Daphne had seduced him. Daphne married Octavius and they had two children. David is now the age his father was when Yeshua and I departed Nazareth together. He has a more generous nature than his father ever did. We make our wines together. I have added to our lands and the grapes grow nobly along the terraced hillsides.

Once again it is summer. Last week I found David lying with a girl from the village in the middle of the vineyard. It was a warm day, alive with bees. The grapes were green and growing, weeds flowered between the stalks, and a cool sea breeze whispered about. It was a day for an old man to rest in the shade. There he was, the son of God, according to some, lying with his girl, their limbs in motion just visible through the ripening vines, pollen, and wispy seeds floating in the full stillness, while a chorus of cicadas serenaded them. I looked a final time before sneaking away to let them be.

Chapter 39

James took Carmensina to dinner at their favourite restaurant, a carefully lit and cosy establishment where she would be reluctant to make a scene. Catalan to the core and located just off the Passeig de Gracia, it was nevertheless called Ondarreta. Half of the family who owned it were Basques from San Sebastian and the cuisine reflected the best of both regions.

As usual they were immediately served a rosé cava and he was intrigued to see her sipping at it sparingly. Every other time they had eaten there that he could recall, she had downed almost an entire bottle of it on her own while he chose the dinner wine. James was the foodie of the family and Carmensina indulged him because of the people who frequented these sorts of restaurants, people she either knew from family connections or wished to know, and about whom she could gossip with her friends the following day. She preferred more traditional fare.

Her main reason for favouring this restaurant, unbeknownst to James, had to do with an old flame. Just before she met James, she had been involved with a rugged factory worker she could never tell her family about, a young man named Patxi also from San Sebastian. He was a former *harri-jasotzaile* or stone thrower, who came from a family of dairy farmers. She met him at a bar one night, slumming it in the old quarter. The relationship, hidden from everyone except for her two closest girlfriends, had been intensely sexual, unlike anything she had experienced before or after, and it was only James's high-end suitability that convinced her to end it. Nevertheless, she thought about Patxi frequently – the tireless and handsome fellow she remembered, not the bald, overweight man he became in later years. When making love with James she would sometimes imagine she was once again in the back seat of Patxi's Seat sedan. The restaurant reminded her of this time in her life and the black and white photographs of old San Sebastian framed on the wall by the front door never failed to induce a dose of sexual nostalgia. But she had other things on her mind that evening, a revelation she wished to save for the end of the meal. James waded into what was on his mind as soon as their main courses were served.

'There's something I need to discuss with you,' he said.

'Something nice I hope.'

'I think so. But first I want to tell you I heard from Finn that you had told them to turn out the American woman.'

'Oh,' she said, as if just remembering it. 'That's right.'

'I don't want to argue about it because there's no point. I have reinstated her, but not to anger or contradict you.'

He paused for a second, searching her face for reaction. She remained unusually calm. It made him more nervous than he already was.

'Well then, why did you?' was all she said.

'Two reasons,' he said, putting his hands together. 'Out of respect for Mother, who was very involved with the project, and because I actually think the documents she is translating, and authenticating might be extremely valuable. The project needs to be finished.'

'How long will that take?'

'I'm not sure. I have to go up there next week to meet with an appraiser from Sotheby's who is coming by the house to look at it and I can ask her then.'

'All right,' she said, calmly eating her food. She did not look happy, but she was not on the verge of anger either.

'So ...' he said, momentarily derailed.

'So, what is the nice part?' she asked, smiling at him.

'The nice part,' he said, 'is that I am going to ask her to move into the cottage so that when you next arrive there we can stay at the main house, in whatever room you choose. I am also willing to have you hire your own staff if you wish. If you do, I'll have Finn and Bidelia move over to the cottage as well and work there for as long as they desire. I feel I owe them that. But what I am basically saying is that I am turning Provence House over to you, to us.'

She leaned across the table and kissed him on the lips, 'That is wonderful news.'

He reached into his pocket and brought out a small

package wrapped in ribbon. 'And I had these made up for you.'

She took it from him. 'What is it?' she asked.

'Open it and see.'

Tears actually came into her eyes as she read the calling cards that had her name embossed on them including her new title. Two addresses were featured, one in Barcelona, the other in Cornwall.

Throughout the miraculously civil meal that went so much better than he had dared to hope and that he had been dreading for days, his phone vibrated twice in his pocket. He did not risk looking at it until, after ordering a dessert for them to share, Carmensina got up to use the ladies' room. Both calls were from Laura. Before he had time to become alarmed, for she would never call him at that hour unless it was important, a text message from her came onto his screen as well:

Have made a remarkable discovery. Call when you can.

Laura had spent the entire day making calls and searching the Internet discovering all she could about first century Roman Villas in Sicily until, to her astonishment, she came across what she was almost certain was Joseph of Arimathea's villa near Akragas, now called Agrigento. It was in a JSTOR article entitled 'Archaeology in Sicily 1988-1995,' written in 1995 by R.J.A. Wilson in a journal called 'Archaeological Reports'. It made reference to a site called

Durrueli di Realmonte, where a professor from Tokyo had been excavating since 1980.

- A villa dating from the 1st Century A.D. on a more or less Roman plan was found near Camarona: M. Aoyagi, "Ripresa degli scavi nella villa Romana di Realmonte," *Kokalos* 26-27, 1980-1981.
- M. Aoyagi, "Il Mosaico di Posidone rinvenuto a Realmonte," in *QuadMess* III, 1988.

The article contained the following: '... but we do now have a publication of a much damaged black and white mosaic 6m square from the villa, depicting Neptune with trident standing on a dolphin, with an outer border of "city wall" type.' The description of the patio was almost verbatim to that described in the codex. The time frame was close enough and the location was the same. No mention was made of a shrine or temple dedicated to Minerva, but many Roman villas had such shrines and, from what she had been able to learn, the excavation at the site had not been completed. She knew from the codex that the Minerva Temple would be up a hill from the villa with a view to the sea. The idea that Christ's mummified remains might still be there had her wide awake.

When James managed to call late that night her news and excitement minimized the effect of what he had to report. She was fine about moving to the cottage, actually loved the idea. It was a paltry logistical detail compared with her possibly momentous discovery. She was excited to hear he would be coming to Cornwall in just a few days and that the Sotheby appraiser would be arriving as well. Her initial instinct to try and convince James to keep the documents secret, or to sell them privately, had changed at the prospect of actually being able to find Christ's remains. All she could really think about that night was Sicily, and how to go about getting permission and funds to excavate without having to say why. Even at breakfast the following morning, speaking with Finn and Bidelia about their move to the cottage, she fielded their complaints and worries by trying to put a positive spin on things. She was going to spend her day locating Masanori Aoyagi at the National Museum of Western Art in Tokyo.

What James had omitted to tell her, what he found himself unable to tell her that night, was what Carmensina, after ordering two more glasses of cava to toast with, had announced to him just before they left the restaurant.

'I have some news too James.'

'Something nice I hope.'

'Very nice,' she said, displaying a smile he had not seen for many years, 'We're going to have another child.'

Chapter 40

Finn and Bidelia moved into the apartment over the cottage garage. An Andalusian couple with a small child arrived and moved into the staff quarters at the mansion. Gin and Jen continued to tend to the horses and the stables. Laura installed herself in the cottage's master bedroom. Though she missed her views of the sea and the old-world luxury of the mansion, the cottage's more relaxed atmosphere was liberating, and its surrounding woodland ambiance paired well with the increasingly pronounced changes in the weather.

She located M. Aoyagi in Tokyo, telling him the villa he had begun to excavate had appeared in an ancient document. The Japanese archaeologist was excited but unable to return to Sicily anytime soon. He generously forwarded copies of his documentation and credentials to her. He copied everything to the Sicilian team he had worked with as well who then promised to secure the necessary permits and approvals. They would be prepared to open a new excavation area at the site within the next few weeks. She reached one of the Sicilian archaeologists by phone, confirming plans to visit the villa a few days after James was scheduled to return to Barcelona.

In the afternoon, after a long walk, she worked on the translation of Gerard of Amiens. This task was far less exciting than what had come before it but working in Old French was easier for her than Ancient Greek. As James's arrival neared, she had less to do and more time to consider her personal life.

It was clear to her that he had capitulated to Carmensina. But that was all right with her. On the night of the funeral when James had been so angry, she had worried about what he might set into motion. Even though she was comforted by his solidarity it concerned her that he might precipitate events too quickly. She thought it would have been too harsh for his daughters to lose the pillar in their life Camilla had been and then become enmeshed in a hostile divorce. It would have been criminal. Better to conduct their affair the old-fashioned way, as best they could, without dragging the rest of the world into it, until and unless it proved necessary.

In some ideal society, being able to tell everyone the truth in real time would doubtless be admirable, but she thought it rarely worked that way. James had little children. There was more at stake. That he should not be with Carmensina was evident to her. That it was prejudicial to the girls for him to continue in the marriage seemed probable as well. But timing was everything. And then, thinking about it more, she considered the extent of what he had ceded to Carmensina. That she, Laura, had been moved into the cottage was a crafty manoeuvre. But it was not the manoeuvre of the strong and outraged, the fed-up James who had called her at the gastro-pub that night. Providing Finn and Bidelia with an agreeable exit from a job they were about to begin disliking had been thoughtful as well. But it was not the action of a proud and indisputable owner of the estate. To placate Carmensina, the three of them had been demoted and exiled. The entire thing began to smell of appeasement. Camilla had only been buried a week. Camilla, she was fairly certain, would have been appalled.

She didn't press him on any of this and had accepted his explanations over the phone. In the end it was his business, not hers. All she wanted at that point was to see him again, and to continue with the project that had suddenly acquired a new level of excitement. She did wonder what manner of man he was underneath. But at the moment his positives still outnumbered the negatives by a considerable margin, and that was a lot after four years with Nathan.

On the night before he arrived, she went for a walk through the woods and down through the meadow once again to the dolmen by the lake. She noticed Venus and Jupiter in the night sky off to the east, appearing as two unusually bright stars. Turning, she found Mars, smaller, orange-reddish, in the west. The lake water was almost invisible, and the only noise came from what sounded like a large family of frogs. She had downed two shots of vodka before leaving the house and sitting on the bench at the water's edge, she felt awe at being able to touch the ancient stones next to her while regarding three planets of the Solar System. It underscored the relativity of time and the planetary-ness of the Earth. She contemplated the notion that all of her hopes and thoughts, all of her memories and feelings, were made from protein molecules that in turn were made of atoms and that each atom had its own micro solar system of electrons spinning about its nucleus. She knew this to be an absolute fact, a great and true miracle – and that the Earth she stood upon was a huge, heavy, slightly lopsided globe suspended in space with a molten core, and that it turned around its axis while moving about the sun, which was an orb as well, another star similar to all of those visible that night. It had been that way for millennia, godless, impersonal, unfathomable, and it would hopefully continue that way for millennia as well.

Forcing herself as she did when considering death a few nights earlier, she made herself remember that the human race and the Earth would go cold some day when the Sun began to expire, and that would be that. And when it happened the stories of Christ, Mohamed, the Buddha, and the history of her entire earthly world, the legacies of all its inhabitants, would be gone. It would be as if none of it had ever happened – like the way a day goes by, or a vacation, a love affair, or the lives of her grandparents and great-grandparents. And it would be that way for her life as well. Everything would disappear. The here and now really was all that mattered.

The vodka went on to inspire wonder and a bit of low-grade terror at the additional realization that after her conception in Granada, the molecules making up the cells in her body had been arranged in such a way so that the cells had differentiated and formed the myriad tissues that defined her, that held together and functioned for a time, mediated by millions of chemical events taking place each second of her fragile life. The clothes she wore were made from molecules too, and the bench she sat upon, the trees behind her and the water in front of her, the creatures crawling in the fields, the frogs croaking in the reeds, the clouds passing over her – all of it an energetic molecular humming – and all of it connected. That was just the way things were, as astonishing and impersonal as that. What was the rest really, the personal, mental life we carried about with us during our individual lifetimes? What was it but a distraction from what Captain Ahab had proclaimed from the foredeck of the *Pequod*, that 'the truth would drive thee mad'?

She was familiar with this state she was in, this mixture of inebriation and the cosmic. It never lasted very long. She knew her mundane problems, interests and concerns, would take centre stage again within a minute. But during the remaining seconds, looking up at the night sky and breathing in the night air of rural Cornwall, she availed herself to the universe she was part of, and embraced, however briefly, the ephemeral nature of everything biological.

James got his arms around her the following day. For decorum's sake he slept at the mansion, but the afternoons, while Finn and Bidelia trained their replacements from Southern Spain, were dedicated to making love at the cottage. Laura felt some degree of payback pleasure aimed at Nathan while making love with James in the bed that he and Carmensina, up until that week, had always slept in together. She told him about the day she had come there alone to snoop around the house, when she had masturbated thinking about him. He asked her to do it again and after she came, he got inside of her, crazed with desire.

Most of their conversation was dedicated to her excitement over the revelation concerning the Sicilian tomb and its implications, for her, for them, and for Christianity. Two days into his stay, on the day before the appraiser was to arrive from London, it rained the entire afternoon. Their lovemaking intensified. As the weather beat against the cottage windows, they went at each other with a ferocity that, afterwards, made them quiet. It was then he decided it was time to tell her.

'Congratulations,' she said in a neutral tone, staring up at the ceiling.

'Thank you,' he replied, trying to sound both ironic and slightly depressed.

'How long have you known?'

'Just a few days.'

She let that sit for a bit and, instinctively, covered herself up.

'Well you two have been trying, haven't you?'

'She's been trying.'

'On her own? I'd like to hear about that.'

'Laura.'

'What am I supposed to say? I mean, it is what it is.'

'It doesn't change anything,' he said. 'It complicates things for me right now, but it has no effect on my feelings about us.'

'Which "us" is that?'

'Both.' Why is life like this? he thought to himself.

'Well – we'll see,' she said. 'And you're pleased, right?'

'I'm confused. I'm many things. I'm pleased, on some level. But angry and depressed too. I mean what kind of a life is this child going to have? And I feel manipulated – yet again. Resentful. And I'm in love by the way, with you, very much.'

'That's nice.'

'Nice? Please Laura.'

'I'm sorry. Here we go again with the "sorries".'

He remained silent, feeling sorry for himself.

'So – what's the plan?' she asked.

'She'll be here for the weekend, going back to Barcelona on Sunday morning with the girls.'

'And with you.'

'Yes.'

She felt a sudden nostalgia for the weeks when it had

just been her and Camilla and the MacShanes at the estate, when things had been calm and fresh.

'You're going to punish me, aren't you?' he said.

'No,' she said. 'I'm not going to punish you. I'm the one who encouraged you not to tell her anything yet, remember?'

'I know.'

'You're the one who was all het up about levelling with her, and so, well I guess I thought it was really going to happen.'

'I was. And I'm still going to.'

'Anyway. I'm going to Sicily.'

'You don't believe me, do you?'

'About what?'

'My separating from Carmensina.'

'Oh, I'm sure you will – eventually – unless you are more of a masochist than I imagined. But who knows when? And that's none of my business really.'

'Of course it is.'

'James, we've been sleeping together for just a short amount of time. You've got two adorable daughters who rely on having two parents, and now you've got another child on the way. Then there's all this stuff with changing houses and what's happened to Finn and Bidelia. What should that tell me?'

'It should tell you that my life is complicated. Just as what's been going on in this bed the past three days should tell you something too.'

She successfully stifled an impulse to tell him what the intense sex might be about as well. But she knew she was angry and that it would just make them both feel worse.

'I know your life is complicated,' she said instead. 'Anyone over the age of twenty-three's life is complicated. I'm glad you told me. I appreciate it. And we'll just see how things work out. I'm happy with you, but not, obviously, with your situation. But that is part of you too. It's all very confusing. I want to be your mate. Do I want to be a step-something or other someday who has to deal with Carmensina every time something comes up about your kids? Maybe. I don't know. I don't think I can even see Carmensina at this point. Can you understand that?'

'Yes.'

'I should never have gone to New York.'

'Don't say that.'

She rolled over and hugged a pillow and looked out at the rain. He thought she looked beautiful lying there like that. But he was afraid to touch her or utter another word.

They both felt blue for the rest of the day. He felt trapped and weak and overly dependent on the contrasting affections of the two women in his life. If one threw in Camilla and his daughters, he saw himself surrounded by a sea of femininity, and what was that all about? Better in the end, he thought than being surrounded by a pack of men. He wondered if it might have been wiser, even taking Laura out of the equation, to have faced Carmensina head on, new baby and all, keeping her from Cornwall, being a hard ass, 'looking out for number one' as the Americans liked to say. But it just wasn't him, and that was all there was to it. Laura had brought up a point he hadn't considered until then. What was it going to be like for him to have both women there at the estate at the same time? Amazingly awkward.

They returned to the big house together. She claimed she needed to work and declined his invitation to go for a ride with him in the rain. Feeling listless, she sat at her table near the library, pretending to translate, gathering together the last of her things to bring back to the cottage. She could not believe that Carmensina was going to have another baby. And it would be a boy of course, the longed-for son, the heir to the squandered Plantagenet line. James would never leave her. European men of his calibre rarely left their wives. They came to arrangements. Laura was, after all, part of his outer world. Could she settle for that? Should she? She could keep her independence that way at least. If someone else came along she fancied she could allow that to happen too with a minimum of fuss. But was this how she wanted to live her life? Did she want to have kids of her own?

Just the other day Fiona, back in London from Amsterdam, told her a story over the phone. She and Giles had run into someone who knew him and his wife, at breakfast one morning at their chic little boutique hotel. The acquaintance sussed out the situation immediately and remained admirably hidden behind a newspaper. But

Giles felt he had no alternative but to greet the man on their way out, after the fastest and most unpleasant breakfast in Fiona's life, and he arranged to meet the fellow for a drink later in the day for a man-to-man, pleading for understanding and discretion. Fiona had put a humorous spin on the tale but the effect it had on Laura was anything but. Did she want to live like that? Not really, not for very long at least.

Chapter 41

She had, for some reason, on the following day expected that the appraiser from Sotheby's would be a man, a well-turned-out gent in a pinstriped suit with multiple degrees in Art History from Oxford and Cambridge. But just before lunch two women arrived, one was the appraiser, who was Laura's age, or less, the other a senior vice-president who, alerted to the possible star quality of the goods in question, wished to be present. After they reluctantly signed the NDAs James handed to them, Laura found them friendly and business-like, even as they grilled her, in what they hoped was an offhand manner, about her own credentials and qualifications. James, in no mood for Andalusian experiments when showing off his domain, had asked Finn and Bidelia to prepare and serve the meal, which they happily did while the Spaniards took their child for a picnic in the countryside.

'I understand,' said the senior vice president, a blond woman in her early fifties, well-dressed and accessorized and in whose presence the appraiser behaved in a suitably fawning fashion, 'that what we're about to see, apart from the value it might have due to its antiquity, has some possible historical importance as well?'

'That's correct,' James replied, realizing that, once again, he was the only male in the room. Though Bidelia stood in a corner, Finn had disappeared.

'Can I assume we have confidentiality here?' Laura asked, taking the reins.

'Oh yes,' the older woman said. 'Absolutely.'

'I don't mean to be melodramatic,' Laura added, 'but I think you'll agree the situation merits it.'

'What are we talking about exactly?'

'One scroll from the First Century AD,' said James, looking to maintain seniority, 'written in Aramaic, isn't that right Laura?'

'That's right,' she said. 'The scroll is in a very sorry state as you might imagine, but enough of it is there to show that the other two items, codices, one from the fourth century and the other from the thirteenth century, the former written in Ancient Greek, the latter in Old French, are translations of the scroll. All three items belonged to Eleanor of Castile, the first wife and Queen consort of King Edward I, a distant relative of James'.'

'It's been in our family for as long as anyone could remember. You've seen my documentation.'

'Why is it,' the older woman asked, 'that all of this is only coming to light now? It's very odd.'

'That is hard to explain to people outside the family,'

said James, somewhat toning up his accent Laura thought, 'but suffice it to say no one was ever that interested until my mother came along.'

Laura got to the point, 'The scroll was dictated to a scribe by Joseph of Arimathea, the uncle of Jesus Christ, and it is a convincing refutation of Christ's divinity.'

This caught the women's attention, including Bidelia's.

After the meal, James and Laura and the two Sotheby women spent over an hour in the chamber behind the bookshelf. As the veracity of the documents sank in, the excitement felt by the two visitors became palpable. Afterwards they sat in the library and Bidelia served them coffee.

'What you have in there,' said the older woman, 'is so astonishing it's rather hard to believe frankly, hard to fathom.'

'I know,' said Laura.

'But it all looks very kosher to me,' the appraiser said.

'I'd like to have it further insured,' James said, 'and moved somewhere safe, somewhere in London, so that when and if word seeps out, we won't be swamped with gawkers and religious fanatics.'

'I quite agree,' the blond woman said.

As the conversation made its way into the realm of legalities and financial estimates Laura excused herself and did not return until it was time to bid the two women farewell. Something the appraiser mentioned had struck her. The young woman, whose otherwise vapid personality had transformed into a laser-like observation machine when examining the artefacts, thought the central, tubular core the scroll was wrapped around unusual. She said it was thicker than most and that she had never seen anything quite like it, and that as an object, if separated from the scroll one day, might merit attention.

After they left, James was in excellent spirits and Laura went back to the cottage with him where they made love, napped, and took a bath together. In light of the fact that Carmensina and the girls were due to arrive the next day they decided in homage to themselves to have dinner at The Wounded Hart. Once seated at the pub however Laura began to find James's continued good cheer annoying. It took him a few minutes to notice her pique and decide he had no choice but to acknowledge it.

'Are you all right?' he asked her.

'Yes. Why?'

'You seem a tad distracted.'

The word tad increased her irritation, 'I'm not looking forward to your wife's arrival tomorrow. What can I say? I've had such a lovely time with you, and tomorrow it will feel bad and incredibly strange for me.'

'I know what you mean,' he replied.

'You seem fine. You seem very pleased, frankly.'

'I'm pleased with how things went today,' he said, trying not to sound too defensive, 'pleased to be here this evening in your company. I'm pleased to have had you in bed today. I love being with you. And I am looking forward to seeing my daughters tomorrow. I am not looking forward to seeing my wife.'

'I wonder,' she said.

'How can you say that?'

'Because people, as you like to say, are complicated. There's clearly something about this whole situation that works for you.'

'Laura, we've been over this. You told me yourself you thought it was too soon to do anything, for the sake of Anna and Montse.'

'I just wish you were feeling "a tad" more like I am right now.'

'I do.'

'Doesn't look that way. You look like the cat who swallowed the canary.'

'It's an English thing, compounded by a Spanish thing, geniuses at denial, at acting like nothing is amiss.'

'It's not an attractive feature.'

That pissed him off. His desire to comfort her was being challenged by her sudden fit of intransigence.

'I'm sorry,' he said, dryly.

'Me too.'

'I am mad about you,' he said.

'I know.'

'If you think I'm acting now, wait till you see me tomorrow.'

But it was too soon for him to try and utter something cute.

'You said you were acting, not me,' she said, 'and I have to say I'm going to do all I can not to see you tomorrow.'

He took a deep breath, praying this was going to resolve itself rather than worsen, 'I understand,' he said, placing his hand on top of hers.

'I mean objectively,' she said, starting down a road part of her was cautioning against, 'things are good for you. You've got a woman of independent means on the side, who you're having great sex with, and an attractive albeit scary wife pregnant with your third child, two beautiful loving daughters, this amazing estate here in England, a cool house in Barcelona, and a media-hip job – like, what's wrong with that picture?'

'What's going on here?' he asked, turning serious. 'This isn't like you. You know how I feel. You know how superficial this cartoon you're drawing is. And I'm still reeling, by the way, from my mother's death.'

It was her turn for a deep breath, and then a deep gulp of the almost rancid Rioja he had ordered.

'Who knows if it's like me or not?' she said. 'I'm unhappy James. Anyone in my position this evening with a shred of sensitivity would be.'

'And – like I've been telling you – I understand that.'

'It's just weird seeing you so bubbly.'

'Well I'm not anymore.'

'I'm sorry.'

'There we go again,' he said, smiling at her with what he hoped looked like tenderness.

'There we go,' she said, trying for a smile back at him. 'And I guess having those women from Sotheby's here today has got me down too.'

'How so? It went really well. You're on the verge of acquiring some high-octane celebrity.'

'Which maybe I don't really want or I'm not ready for. I like my anonymity basically. One thing I keep on repressing and that I know will happen is that the furies will drag out my Palestinian heritage and accuse me with it. But it's not that. More than anything it's the feeling that things are ending here. The Sotheby women's presence today marked a new phase. I've had such a wonderful time working here, when all of this endgame stuff was hanging out there, safely in the future. But now it's pretty much here. And now there's this Sicilian angle. It's a bit neurotic, I admit. I should be energized by all of this, and by what's going on between you and me, and hopefully, I will be again soon. Maybe I'm just getting my period or something.'

'Laura,' he said, touched by her honesty and relieved to see the storm passing, something that underlined a further contrast with how a similar confrontation with Carmensina would have evolved, 'we're both under a lot of pressure. We've both been going through a lot, some of it on our own and some of it together. But I'd like to think that in addition to having our health, we're pretty lucky; though things might feel shaky and topsy-turvy right now, they will lead to changes that will be for the good, good for both of us.'

He got out of his chair, came over to her, and kissed her.

'Careful,' she said quietly. 'Everyone knows who you are around here.'

He was going to drive them back to the cottage after dinner to spend some time with her before returning to the mansion for the night, but she asked him to stop at the big house first. She wanted to look at something. It was near ten when they came into the library together and turned on some lights. The new Spanish 'Finn' came in from the kitchen to see who was there and James put him at ease and sent him on his way. Laura opened the library shelf into the scroll chamber and turned on the lights and shut off the alarm.

'Are you going to tell me what this is all about?' he asked, coming up behind her and kissing the back of her neck.

'I want to check on something and I may need your help. Put these on,' she said, handing him a set of the latex gloves as she did the same.

'Is this going to get kinky?'

'No,' she said. 'I doubt it.'

She removed the top from the glass case and lifted out the scroll. As always, the scraggly papyrus looked as if it might disintegrate into dust at the slightest provocation. But the central, tubular core had handles as it were, at either end, resembling an ancient, metallic, ornate, rolling pin.

'That woman said something that intrigued me. She said this metal thing was unusual, unusually thick, and so I'm wondering whether it might have something inside of it.'

'Cool,' he said, trying to sound American.

'I thought it was worth a try to have a look, but super carefully, just to try and see whether either of the ends might be acting as a lid or a stopper.'

'Why not?'

'Screw fittings are a recent invention so it's either jammed in there, or it isn't.'

'The trick,' he said, 'is going to be how to get a good grip on it without touching the scroll.'

'Exactly.'

'Let me get the toolbox. I'll be right back.'

She smiled and nodded, and as she waited in the chamber, she recalled the first time she had visited it with Camilla, this hidden room where aristocratic Catholics long buried and forgotten had celebrated mass. She realized this might be one of the last occasions she would be alone there with her treasures. It also occurred to her that Nathan had probably never touched a toolbox in his life. James was regaining a number of recently lost points. He brought it back with him, metal and oblong and black, scratched and heavy, and set it upon the worktable, delving into it with boy-like relish.

'I never would have pegged you as the handyman type,' she said, placing a conciliatory hand on his shoulder.

'You can add frustrated plumber to the list,' he said.

'Frustrated Bohemian, frustrated plumber – a very frustrated man it seems.'

'Not as long as you're around.'

'See if you can hold that thought over the next few days.'

A flurry of images of Carmensina, drunk with triumph over the fruit of her womb, doing all she could to disarm and pleasure her handsome and all-too-pliable husband shot into her mind without warning, tempering Laura's regained affability.

Employing an adjustable spanner on one end that Laura held onto, and a mole wrench at the top that James controlled, they gingerly engaged in a fruitless struggle until Laura, too nervous, was about to give up. But James insisted they continue.

'It can probably be x-rayed,' she said, 'without doing any damage. This is just too dicey.'

'Laura, that will take weeks if not months to set up. Do you really want to wait that long?'

She had no idea where he was getting those time periods and correctly assumed he was simply making them up in order to continue. He was stubborn that way and she liked it. She gave him a look of scepticism.

'Let me try one more thing,' he said.

'Please be careful.'

'I will.'

But he took out a hammer, wrapping its head in the silk handkerchief that had been expertly stuffed into the breast pocket of his jacket.

'You can't be serious,' she said.

'Just a few taps. Hold on tight to your end and look the other way if you must.'

Two things happened. With the fourth and hardest tap applied to the top handle, he knocked it clear off. Laura almost screamed. James uttered a loud 'Damn!' But the second thing that occurred was that the hollow core of the tube was revealed and in it could be seen another, much smaller scroll, and a furled sheet of vellum.

'Holy shit,' said Laura, peering in while still gripping the spanner.

'You were right,' was all he said.

He leaned back and with one hand exchanged the hammer for a long-necked pair of pliers. The small scroll was wrapped about a crumbly wooden dowel. Gripping it with the pliers he drew it out, slowly, as if disarming a portable nuclear device. Once free of the core he set it down as gently as he could upon the towel laid out on the worktable next to the toolbox. Then, with the fingers of her free hand, Laura nudged out the sheet of vellum.

'The scroll looks hopeless,' she said, 'but I'm hoping the vellum might be a translation.'

It was in good enough condition so that it could be flattened sufficiently upon the towel.

'It's in Greek,' she said, pointing.

'It's all Greek to me,' he said.

'I recognize the scribe's handwriting. This is so exciting.'

James got a bottle of Pol Roger from the kitchen. After they clinked their glasses together and took a sip, she took up the vellum sheet and translated it aloud to him.

Chapter 42

After my true father died, we buried him as he wished, naked and covered with vineyard soil.

'Oh my God,' she said. 'This is the son speaking now, David.'
She went on.

My mother maintained her life and routines at the villa for almost two years. But in her widowhood she began to miss her family, her sister, her father and mother, her aunts and uncles. That almost all of them were long dead did not seem to affect her. With each passing month the intensity of her longing increased. And it came to pass that a woman averse to travel and afraid of the sea decided to return to the land of her birth.

She tried to persuade me to leave the villa and the vineyards as well. But I only agreed to accompany her and to see her settled. My life, my home, was here on the island, here at the villa, here among the vines, on the sunlit hills surrounded by the Great Sea.

A few days before the ship was to depart, she decided to bring the remains of Yeshua with her. Though not enthused, I nevertheless acceded to her wishes. Upon opening the chamber at the Minerva shrine there was no scent of decay. The space within was cool and clean. The wooden encasement about him was still well sealed.

The voyage north was a melancholy one. I had no Lucca or Octavius to accompany me. Octavius by then could only walk with a cane. I had two strong youths from the vineyard eager for adventure. After many days on the water with only a few ports of call in Hispania, the grey green cliffs appeared on the horizon. My mother wept tears of joy and tears of pain. She wished to bury Yeshua there because it was there, she said, he had been happiest and most fulfilled. Though I did not doubt it, I knew as well that she was also talking about herself. She had been happiest with him and her sister there and had only come to accept Yosef the tin merchant over time.

The village had grown again to at least half its previous size my mother said. Twenty years had passed since they fled its shores. She was treated like a queen and it was strange for me to see so many people who resembled her. And there were men who remembered Yeshua and who told me stories about him. A new burial site was prepared for him in a clearing back

*in the woods above the bay. None of the villagers
had ever seen a mummy's casing. They treated it as
a sacred object and buried it at the shore of a pond,
next to a –*

And here she came across a word she did not know the
meaning of: a 'something or other'.

All of this greatly pleased my mother.

*Leaving her was as painful a thing as I have ever
done. But after a few days back at sea I began to feel
whole again and free, and the idea of returning to the
villa where my true father was buried – whose only
shrine are the vines we make our wine from – was a
source of deep contentment. I have not seen my mother
again and doubt I ever shall.*

*I have sat with the elderly scribe and had him
write these things and entrusted him with the task of
taking these words and all that he has written down
for Yosef, back to Judea, just as Yosef asked of me.
He is to find Miryam or one of Yeshua's brothers or
sisters and give the scrolls to them. His ship departs
tomorrow.*

*I am soon to marry and make children of my own.
Daphne will perform the ceremony. The course of life
here mirrors the life of the vines. Seeds are planted and
cared for, year in and year out, then they blossom and
bear fruit before withering gently in the sun.*

Astonished, they left everything resting on the towel, went upstairs to what had been her old room, and finished the champagne before making love again. Neither of them felt very much during sex but they were happy. When he fell asleep, close to two a.m., she dressed and tiptoed out. As she contemplated the mind-boggling discovery that the remains of Christ might be buried somewhere in Cornwall, she used the powder room on the ground floor under the stairs to pee and wash her hands and face. The last and only other time she had been in that odd little space was on the day she first arrived. Much had happened since that windy afternoon, and it felt unfair to her that she could still be there, and that Camilla was not. Before leaving the house, she looked once again at her new discovery, reset the alarm and closed the shelf in the library. Outside she was quickly drenched in the mist, but she took time to breathe in the sea air before getting into the Land Rover and driving back to the cottage.

Not wanting to risk waking Finn and Bidelia by opening the garage doors to repark the Land Rover next to their Morris Mini Traveller, she left it out on the driveway. Only a single lamp was on in the vast living room and though she was the only person in the rambling house, with its warren of upstairs bedrooms, main and back stairways, old doors to the outside woods and fields that rattled with the merest gust of wind, she felt secure here. She went into the kitchen for a glass of filtered water. The light in that room she flicked on came from neon tubes hidden under the dish shelves and they aimed an ethereal glow at the yellow linoleum floor. As she searched in her bag for some Advil to take as a preventive measure after all the alcohol, her phone rang. Given the late hour, she assumed it would be James, awake and wondering where she had gone. But, finding the phone and the Advil simultaneously she saw that it was Nathan.

'Hello?'

'Laura.'

She could tell from his tone that he had been drinking.

'That's me.'

'Where are you?'

'England.'

'Oh my God. So sorry. Did I wake you?'

'Actually, I am still up,' she said.

'How's it going?'

'Fine. Good. It's going well.'

'That's great.'

'How are you?' she asked, taking the Advil.

'Good. You know. Same ole, same ole.'

'How's Oksana?'

'Oksana. God. How do you know her name?'

'It seemed a logical thing to ask considering how I met her.'

'Oh my God.'

'You've been drinking.'

317

'A little. Not too much. You know me so well. Better than anyone ever has, or ever will.'

She realized she did not have the strength or patience to deal with this now.

'What's up Nathan? Why the call, now, after all this time?'

'I was having dinner, alone, at the bar at Knickerbockers, and, you know, missed you. And I wanted to apologize for being such a selfish shit.'

'It's a little late for that, but fine. I hear you. Apology accepted. We were in bad shape.'

'You think?'

'I do.'

'So, are you seeing anyone?'

'That's not your concern anymore.'

'Just asking is all.'

'I'm just about to go to sleep. I've had a very long day.'

'OK. Well. Big kiss.'

'Goodnight Nathan.'

'*Bonsoir chérie.*'

She hit 'End Call' and stood there. She stood there appalled, appalled that a relationship that had taken such a heavy slice from the prime of her life could end with such a lame conversation. She went upstairs, showered, put on a fresh pair of pyjamas and got into bed. She decided to try and sleep for as long as she could. Tomorrow, Carmensina day, would be a sick day for her, a stay-in-bed day, with a walk down to the lake in the afternoon. There was no need to think ahead any further than that. In finding the smaller scroll she had just discovered something extraordinary, something earth-shaking. Life was good. Life was so good she did not notice that her computer was missing.

Chapter 43

Bidelia MacShane, née Clancy, was born and raised in Cork. When she was seven and attending St Columba's Primary School for girls, she won the Maynooth Catechism contest. She memorized the entire manual before receiving the sacrament of confession and then took her First Holy Communion in what the nuns declared was a state of absolute purity. Ever since she heard Laura speaking at dinner about the scroll and the codices, page ten of the Catechism flashed into her mind. And it stayed there, week after week, despite Finn's advice that she keep their employer and the American guest in her prayers and move on.

On page ten in the Catechism, a copy of which she conserved in the drawer next to her bed, there was the following exchange of questions and answers all good Catholics swore by.

Q. On what day did Christ rise from the dead?
A. On Easter Sunday, the third day after His death,

*Christ arose in body and soul glorious and immortal
from the dead.*

*Q. How long did Christ stay on earth after His resur-
rection?*

*A. Christ stayed on earth forty days after His resurrec-
tion, to show that He was truly risen from the dead,
and to instruct His apostles.*

*Q. After Christ had remained forty days on earth, where
did he go?*

*A. After forty days, Christ, on Ascension Day ascended
from Mount Olivet, with His body and soul, into
heaven.*

Q. Where is Christ in heaven?

*A. Christ sits at the right hand of God the Father
Almighty.*

That the scroll and the codices were hidden in what had
been a priest hole, a sacred place where mass had been
said for the faithful in fear for their lives, was, all by itself,
a blasphemy and a thorn in her side. But what boiled the
blood within Bidelia's Irish veins and shook her heart,
was what she learned to be in them. 'The Devil's work'
was how she referred to it in private with Finn. For her,
Camilla's death had been an act of God, a punishment and
a sign, a warning. It was followed with their banishment by
Carmensina, a woman who hardly spoke to them and who
had not been able to convert poor James to the true faith.
And when, at the lunch with the Sotheby women, Bidelia

heard the full extent of everything as Laura spelled it all out, while being simply taken for granted and ignored, and then hearing the price the devilry could be sold for, a sale that would give Carmensina millions of pounds, it was a call to action.

Finn protested. Finn reminded her of the eighth commandment: Thou Shalt not Steal. But the commandments were from the Old Testament. In Bidelia's mind the liturgy she'd learned so well from the New Testament, the one that kept her faith so strong and that had got her through all of life's unfairness thus far, superseded anything else. To steal the Devil's work was not a sin, but rather a mission to fulfil, a test of faith to respond to. Finn only gave in when he saw how determined she was, how she would do it with or without him. And, he then reasoned, it was time to leave anyway, time to go home to Ireland, and if they were pursued and charged, well to the Devil with them as well.

Though Camilla had shown them many years earlier how to access the priest hole, they did not know the alarm code. When less than a minute had passed and the alarm's persistent beeping began, the MacShanes, terrified of being caught, became exasperated. Bidelia had brought one of Camilla's Mallorcan straw shopping baskets, and as the alarm went off, she began to throw the two scrolls and the codices into it. Finn grabbed the towel and was attempting to stifle the noise, thrusting it against the tiny speaker. They left as fast as they could, not bothering to move the bookshelf back in place. The towel fell from the alarm speaker of its own accord and the noise it made was what finally penetrated the sleep of the Andalusian couple. It took them a few minutes to track its source for they had never seen the priest hole and then, going upstairs, they had to knock on many doors before finding James who was lost to the world in bed. It gave the MacShanes the time they needed to empty the contents of the straw basket into the oil drum where trash was burned. They doused it with a litre of kerosene and lit it ablaze.

James came downstairs, entered the priest hole and, horrified by what was missing, punched in the code to silence the alarm. Then he heard the MacShanes' Mini Morris Traveller leaving the estate. Entering the kitchen with the Spaniards, a rancid smell of burning leather, wood, parchment and papyrus drew them outside to behind the stables where the still sparking ashes were all that remained of his family treasure. Incensed and confused and unwilling to accept that the deed had been done by his faithful staff, he began to yell at the innocent pair gaping next to him, furious that they had not managed to awaken him earlier.

He took their little car and, filled with dread, drove to the cottage where he found Laura in tears. She was wrapped in a robe, sitting on the sofa in the living room, re-reading the note of apology Finn had written and placed in an envelope along with two thousand pounds for the loss of her laptop. Inconsolable and not wanting him to hold her, she cursed herself, over and over, for the paranoia that had prevented her from storing her work on the Cloud or keeping it backed up on a pen drive. The two photos still in her phone were useless.

By the time she and James were able to nibble on something for lunch, exhausted from anger and numb with shock, Bidelia was standing at the railing on the upper deck of a Holyhead Ferry. She made the sign of the cross, leaned over, and dropped Laura's laptop into the Irish Sea. As it disappeared under the water, briefly shimmering like a diving fish, she could almost feel Camilla's soul being released from the fires of Purgatory, rising up to heaven on the wings of angels.

Chapter 44

James swore the Spanish couple to secrecy. When Carmensina arrived that afternoon, he told her that Sotheby's, after careful inspection, had declared the documents inauthentic. Only vaguely aware of the tests James had commissioned at Oxford a year earlier, ignorant of the price Sotheby's had quoted, and more than pleased to have Laura's work discredited, she took the news with gracious stoicism. James also told her that on second thought and taking her wishes into account, he had dismissed Finn and Bidelia, who after all were well past the age of official retirement. This declaration gave her great satisfaction. In an email he informed Sotheby's that, after careful thought, the family had decided to withdraw the documents from auction.

He did not have the heart to go after the MacShanes. Though losing the imagined millions was hard to swallow and still made him angry, and though he felt terrible for Laura, part of him was secretly relieved to avoid what would have been relentless controversy. He tried to be philosophical about it and recognized that, in general terms, he was content with the money and property he had.

Laura was devastated. She left the estate that very evening during James and Carmensina's dinner hour. She caught a flight from London to Mallorca with the idea of driving to Deià to visit Camilla's grave. But then, en route, she thought better of it. She had also promised herself for years that she would one day visit her father's grave in Palestine, a promise she had yet to keep. It felt unseemly to give priority to Camilla. Suddenly Palestine and Camilla and the texts were linked in her mind and the whole thing was just too painful.

Instead she spent the night in Palma and drove the following day to Formentor where she spent a week on the beach reading mystery novels and venting her rage with long swims. In a calmer state she did go to Deià and found Camilla's grave, side by side with the tombstone of James's little sister. After that, saturated with the topic of tombs and burial, she flew to California to visit with her stepfather in Carmel. Though eighty he was still spry and eager to have her there with his new family. The thought of being housed and fed and far away from Cornwall appealed to her. But what she carried with her to each of these places, as a talisman, was a print-out of an email from James inviting her to spend a week with him in Venice at the end of January.

A week before Christmas, Carmensina felt ill at her gym in Barcelona while jogging on a treadmill. That evening she lost the baby. James took her and their two daughters to spend the holidays with Carmensina's parents and brothers at the family masia in the Empordá countryside.

Around the time Carmensina lost her child, Italian archaeologists at the villa in Sicily found what remained of the temple dedicated to Minerva. They reached Laura in California. Intrigued and desirous by then of recovering anything connected with what had been lost, she cancelled her direct flight to Venice scheduled for January and booked herself a ticket to Palermo instead, sending word to James that she would make her way to Venice from there.

She was more than ready to leave her stepfather's. When she first told him some of what had happened to her, professionally at least, his reaction was muted. His large McMansion, virtually bookless, was built on the edge of a fairway at the Pebble Beach golf course. Its blond wood floors were smothered with avocado-toned carpets that administered regular shocks of static electricity. Trophies from golf tournaments covered the surfaces of every table in the living room. His new wife and her grown-up children from a former marriage, glued to their phones all day, only talked about sports, diets, and exercise.

Laura found Gerald Cuddihy II considerably frailer than when she had last seen him. He was the man who had swept her mother off her feet, who had put Laura through school in New York, who was responsible for her financial independence, and who and given her the apartment on

Tenth Street when she obtained her PhD. At the Christmas Eve dinner, held not at the house but in the Golf Club's anodyne dining room, he publicly acknowledged Laura's discomfort. Giving a toast he leaned down and put his arm around her proclaiming, 'You must think us all terribly superficial.'

She decided to take leave of them a few days after that, bowing out of a New Year's Eve costume ball. On the morning of her departure, as she was packing her suitcase in the bedroom they'd given her that faced a fairway and took in a view of the Pacific, Gerald knocked on the opened door, came in, and sat in a corner chair.

'I've been thinking about what you told me when you got here,' he said, 'about what happened to you in England.'

This was a surprise. She'd become accustomed, all through her childhood and adolescence, to his New England reticence, his aversion to conflict and emotionality. She assumed some of that was a product of his former profession, diplomacy, though she also considered the possibility that perhaps he had exercised that profession so well due to his nature, a white Anglo-Saxon Protestantism instilled in him from generations of privileged male ancestors educated at elite prep schools and Ivy League colleges. Mentally, she fastened her seat-belt. Though he was not a man known for any sort of outspoken enthusiasm for his Presbyterian faith, who knew what dwelled under the surface? She could not remember them ever having any discussion about religion. Her mother had embraced the sect his family belonged to with her customary fervour, but he had remained a quiet man.

'It's been good for me to get away from it,' she said. 'I'm very grateful to you for that.'

'Perspective is rarely a bad thing,' he said.

An awkward silence ensued. He took one of the curtain cords in his hand and began to roll it back and forth between his fingers.

'So, what have you been thinking then?' she finally asked.

'That I admire you,' he said.

This was so unexpected it made her blush.

'Thank you,' she said. 'That means a lot to me.'

'I live out here, far from my roots, in this artificial, golfer's paradise,' he said. 'I try not to think about it too much because it's very comfortable. But when I do, I realize how withdrawn from the world I am now.'

'You don't seem unhappy.'

'No. No I'm not,' he said. 'But I've lost what little edge I had once upon a time, and you still have it. You are living *in* the world. You are doing interesting things. I admire you for it.'

She stopped her packing and looked at him.

'Much of what I do and how I've been able to get to do it, is thanks to you. I'm very aware of that too.'

He smiled, pleased, but waved her gratitude away. The gesture reminded her of Camilla.

'It sounds like you found something very extraordinary. Something that would have catapulted you into significant fame in your work. And then it was taken from you. And look at you. Still on your feet, working it through, thinking it through, figuring out what to do next. I'm very proud of you.'

His words caused her eyes to swell with tears.

'How I wish that were true,' she said.

'It is,' he said. 'Take it from an old hand. I can see it.'

Internally, she chided herself for having put this man into a box so quickly since her arrival there, a sterile container devoid of introspection. The overly manicured, dry-cleaned, almost Disney-fied surroundings, and the hyper-American quirks and style of his life there had blinded her, had let her off the hook from having to make an effort to engage with him. She realized that what she had said to him a minute earlier, trying to please him, that this time away from Cornwall had been good for her, was true. And that she had taken his protection for granted. As he stood and came over to her and embraced her, she caught a glimpse of the man her mother had fallen for. Though the hug he gave her was American as well, light, quick, keeping his body back from hers, it was heartfelt.

'Don't be a stranger,' he said.

She rang in the New Year back in New York on her terrace, sharing a bottle of champagne with a girlfriend and a grinning Jean-Paul Bonnerive who sat in one of her Adirondack chairs wrapped in a blanket. After the girlfriend left to attend a party, Laura told the French nonagenarian all that had happened, believing him to be one of the few people she knew who would believe her and appreciate the wonder of what she had translated. And he did. He comforted her and suggested that as a former graduate student at Columbia, she let him explore the possibility of having her hired there. He also told her to apply right away for a residency at the American Academy in Rome, something he could help her get admitted to as well.

A week later, on a sunny, wintry morning, a wave of relief swept through her as the Alitalia Airbus landed at the Falcone Borsellino Airport in Palermo. She rented a car and drove to the southern coast. She stopped to stretch her legs and have a coffee at a little bar on the shore where the beach was deserted. Finding the Pietro Griffo Archaeological Museum near the Valle del Templi was not difficult, and it was there she met the short, slim, and handsome head archaeologist, Nicola Carati.

'Would you like to go to your hotel first, or directly to the site?' he asked.

'What do *you* think?'

He drove a green Toyota jeep and she followed him. It took half an hour to reach the site. She had worried it might be unrecognizable or jammed up next to modern structures and was relieved when they left the highway and began to drive up into hills on a rural road made of dirt. They came to a stop next to three other vehicles and a large area cordoned off with plastic tape of the kind used at crime scenes.

She got out and breathed in the Mediterranean air. The sun felt good. A light breeze blew. Nicola watched her and didn't say anything. He just waited and smiled and then led the way up a narrow path until they reached what remained of the villa. There wasn't much to see, mostly broken columns, but there was the patio, the one described by Joseph of Arimathea in 34 AD and by Professor Aoyagi in 1988, the 'much damaged black and white mosaic depicting Neptune with a trident standing on a dolphin.'

'My goodness,' was all she could think to say. But what was pounding away inside her head was, 'They were here, they were actually *here*.' Of all the locations described in Joseph of Arimathea's text, this was the one she felt closest to. As she had translated the codex, it was Joseph of Arimathea she most identified with. The strength and humanity of his prose had reached across the centuries and bent her sympathies toward him and caused her to regard his nephew with the same ambivalence he had. And here, she thought, at this villa, is where *he* was buried, and where Daphne, Octavius, and David were probably buried as well.

'Come,' said Nicola, saying it gently. 'Come see the remains of the temple. It's going to please you.'

She had also formed her own mental picture of Daphne's temple, and had imagined the climb up to it from the villa as arduous and steep. She had imagined it far above, white and pristine, and commanding a spectacular view of the Mediterranean. But following Nicola she hardly broke a sweat. The hill was low and much closer to the main structures of the villa. She wondered, even hoped, that perhaps the ground had contracted or settled during the intervening centuries.

Where the hill levelled off the ruins were scant, but the view did not disappoint her. The sea, vast and glittering, was plainly visible below, and though she didn't say so, looking to the southwest in the clear January light, she would have sworn she was seeing some part of the Algerian coastline.

'I pictured it differently,' she said.

'The amazing thing is that it is here at all. We only found it thanks to you,' he replied.

She made a face.

'I was just the translator.'

'Nevertheless,' he said.

'Have you been able to find a statue of the goddess?'

'No. And I doubt we shall. Most likely that was stolen or taken away a long time ago. But come, look over here.'

She followed him into a ravine. Some of it had occurred naturally after two thousand years of erosion. Nicola's crew had dug out the rest. They walked along a long section of a white marble wall until they came to a narrow entranceway. She followed him inside.

'I'm fairly certain this is your Daphne's sleeping chamber.'

He turned on a small lantern. A mosaic of Minerva covered one of the walls and there was a raised slab right next to them. As she reached down and touched it, tears came into her eyes. She couldn't help it. She looked at him.

'I don't know why,' she said, 'but I'm very moved.'

'I understand,' he said, handing her the lantern. 'I'll let you be.'

'Grazie,' she said.

She did know why. Everything that she had been trying to repress and forget came back to her with full force. All of the work she had done. Its magical importance. The extent of the loss. She sat on the slab where Yeshua had ceded his virginity to Daphne's half-awake body. As far as she was concerned, this was where William Blake's 'arrows of desire' had worked their magic, not as arms for battle, but as slender darts awakening the pleasures of lust. It had happened right there, long ago, when they had been young and beautiful. And it was here that Christ's mummy had been stored for a decade at least before it was taken to England.

And it was then that she remembered the word written in Ancient Greek that was unknown to her, the one on the vellum sheet that was hidden inside the scroll core – 'μέγας'. She would have to look it up.

The archaeologists took her to lunch nearby and one of them, a woman from Turin, said she was so in love with the site that she had come close to buying a home there. But, married and with two young children in school, she knew she would hardly ever get to use it. 'Most of the land here is protected from development,' she said. 'It's against the law to build a house from scratch. But I found an abandoned shepherd's cottage on some property nearby, with the roof caved in, another ruin really, but it qualifies as a pre-existing structure that one could renovate.' After coffees and a shot of limoncello she took Laura to see it. It had a view of the villa and the sea and Laura was entranced by it. The woman, somewhat reluctantly at first, told her how much they were asking and who to call.

She dined alone at her hotel, The Villa Athena, texting James to work out a time they could speak later that night. Opening her new laptop, she looked up the word in Greek and saw that it meant 'megalith' or possibly 'trithillion', which is to say, a dolmen. They had buried the mummy case in Cornwall at the shore of a pond next to a dolmen. The word for pond could also signify a lake. An involuntary pressure slammed her solar plexus. Could it be? She quickly reviewed all of the dolmens listed in Cornwall, and though some overlooked the sea, not one of them appeared to have been placed near a body of still water.

She felt many things at once. She felt great excitement, the kind that had accompanied her during all the weeks of her translation. She felt a great temptation to shout it to the world, to justify her tale that no longer had any texts to back it up. Then she felt caution, and resignation, as she considered the wisdom of keeping such a discovery to herself. She knew that Finn and Bidelia's actions were but the tip of an iceberg. There was something to be said for leaving things as they were, for leaving the millions of believers with the comfort of their illusions, and, for what it was worth, leaving Christ's message of love intact and free from distraction. She went to the mini-bar and poured herself a glass of vodka, toasting herself in a mirror, content for the time being with the wonder of it all. When James called, she was in bed.

'I didn't wake you I hope.'

'I'm too excited to sleep.'

'About seeing me?'

'About that too.'

'What else then?'

She decided, suddenly, not to say anything.

'Seeing the villa,' she replied, 'and the remains of the temple. It's been overwhelming. And I found a little house I'm thinking of buying, right next to it.'

'Really?'

'Really. Though it needs a lot of work.'

'Really,' he said again. 'How often would you use it?'

'Who knows? But if I accept the invitation from the American Academy in Rome this spring, I can start to fix it up.'

'Sounds promising. And you'd be closer by.'

'I thought of that too.'

'How's the hotel?'

'Very comfortable. Fancy. Expensive. But I figured, just one night. Also, what with its name, I couldn't resist.'

'Athena – after Athens? Was the goddess named for the city or the city after the goddess?'

'The goddess was named for the city. As the patron of wisdom and warfare she was worshipped in many Greek cities, but particularly Athens and her name came from there. But the Etruscans absorbed her, transformed her to their liking, and called her Minerva.'

'Ah-ha. Now I get it.'

'So, I had to stay here, right?'

'Absolutely.'

'Do you know the story of Minerva?'

'No idea.'

'Would you like to?'

'Nothing would please me more. I find these lessons of yours very sexy.'

'She was the daughter of Jupiter, the Roman equivalent of Zeus, the greatest of all the gods. He had lusted after a goddess called Metis, had raped her and got her pregnant. But then he worried she might give him a son who'd become more powerful than him. So he tried to capture Metis and get rid of the fetus. She did all she could to escape until Jupiter tricked her into turning herself into a fly that he promptly swallowed.'

'A fly.'

'That's how the story goes. Anyway, she survived and lived inside his head. Some believe, and I like this interpretation, that Jupiter's wisdom came from Metis buzzing about his brain. As her pregnancy progressed, he got tremendous headaches and to relieve the pain he ordered Vulcan, the blacksmith god, to take a hammer and open a hole in his head. As soon as that happened Minerva was born, emerging as a fully formed adult wearing armour.'

'Where did they come up with this stuff?'

'Hey, they were good storytellers, like the evangelists.'

'What are you wearing?'

'Now what's interesting is that when the Romans inherited Minerva, they didn't make her a patron of war like the Greeks, but of wisdom, science, and the arts.'

'What are you wearing?'

She was clad in flannel pyjamas and socks, because the room was freezing.

'Who says I'm wearing anything?'

Chapter 45

James rarely mentioned Carmensina to Laura anymore. She noticed that he was avoiding further conversation about when or whether he would seek a divorce. And to his relief, Laura had given up asking. She saw no point in nagging him when the opportunities they had to spend time together were so rare. In theory at least, putting two days at risk, or, in this case four days and nights of good restaurants and sensual pleasure, wasn't worth it to her. More telling perhaps, as her plane approached Venice's Marco Polo Airport, she realized that his marriage was bothering her less and less.

As she stepped off a vaporetto into his arms on the Hotel Excelsior's pier, she put the whole issue out of her mind. Here they were, together again and in Venice, fulfilling a dream that had surfaced in New York on the night they first slept together. The opportunity had come about thanks to a small conference he was attending, a gathering of publishing firms that had chosen the luxurious venue as an ideal place at which to grumble about their scant profits and declining influence in the world. His only obligations to the event were that day's inaugural lunch, a few hours of morning meetings on the following day, and the final evening's farewell dinner. She knew all of this before she arrived and was fine with it. Having time to wander about and grab a meal on her own was as appealing to her as the time she could spend with him.

The hotel, a classic five-star behemoth, evinced a Moorish theme, six floors of elaborate, Alhambra-esque window frames and arches overlooking a heated swimming pool and the Lido beach. Their room, predominately beige and brown, was a Junior Suite on the third floor. The bed was enormous and overflowing with shams and pillows. She was disappointed not to see a bathtub, but the walk-in shower was cavernous and fitted with a marble bench to sit on.

James wanted to have sex right away, before his lunch with the publishers. She was not especially turned on by the idea but gave in anyway because it conformed to the fantasy both of them had entertained about how this rendezvous would begin. It was fine, rushed and perfunctory, but it left her troubled. She was actually glad when he hurried out of the room. She tried to minimize its importance, but the taste of it stayed with her. During his all male lunch where he drank too much, she bundled up and took a walk down the deserted beach and ate sparingly at a pizzeria. Exhausted from her travels she was asleep when he got back to the room. They made love again and though it

342

went better this time, for the first time with James, she felt during some of it that she was outside of herself, like she was with a stranger. They showered together and caught up with each other's lives over dinner, again without getting into any details about the state of his marriage. Finally, she felt better being with him until, back in the room and with his phone turned off, just as they had got into bed, a call from Carmensina to the hotel was put through.

She was obviously checking up on him, listening for the slightest sound that might confirm her worries. Laura rolled over and covered her head with a pillow. Then she silently slipped away into the sitting room. She could tell he was doing his best to sound cheerful to Carmensina but, for Laura's benefit, not too cheerful. She stepped out onto the room's slender balcony. Down below the pool was lit up. The beach was dark. Music drifted up from a restaurant somewhere. It was cold and smelled of a winter sea that was calm and black with little lights here and there coming from boats. She went back inside and sat in an armchair trying to resist admitting to the absurdity of the arrangement. She tried to resist getting angry, tried not to listen to him. She didn't want to hear him saying anything affectionate, even if it was just to put the woman at ease.

When the conversation ended Laura stayed where she was. He went into the bathroom for a robe and then came out and found her sitting in the dark.

'I'm so sorry,' he said.

She didn't reply at first. She looked at him standing there in front of her.

'I suppose it's to be expected,' she said.

'She's suspicious of course.'

'And with reason. I wouldn't like to be in her shoes. Then again, maybe she just misses you and wanted to hear your voice.'

'Maybe. But I don't think so.'

She looked down at the floor.

'I don't think I can do this,' she said. It just came out of her.

'I said I was sorry.'

'It's just too vulgar. I shouldn't have come.'

'Laura.'

'I don't think you're going to leave her.'

'You don't know that.'

'I don't think you will, and do you know what's worse?'

'What?'

'I don't think I care anymore.'

'What do you mean?'

'I don't know if it would be worth it at this point. It doesn't feel right. I've been so excited about this trip, about seeing you again, Venice, the whole thing. But the reality of it feels very different.'

The chair she sat in had an ottoman. He leaned over, pulled it to him and sat down facing her.

'Maybe we just need to get some sleep,' he said. 'I'll skip tomorrow's meetings and we can spend the day together.'

He reached for her hand and she gave it to him. She thought back to the first time she'd seen him in Camilla's living room, back to their drink at The Wounded Hart, their meeting at the bar at the Bowery Hotel, their love-making at the cottage in Cornwall. She looked at their hands together in the darkness.

'Come to bed,' he said.

The following morning, she wasn't there. Seeing the note on his bedside table produced a jolt of adrenalin and a 'Fuck.' But the note's contents could have been worse.

James, I've decided to get my own room at another hotel. As soon as I know which one, I'll let you know. You can stay as many of these remaining three nights with me there as you wish, but with your phone turned off. If you choose to go back to the Excelsior to sleep, I'll understand that too. But I need some autonomy. I'm discovering that a little bit of this mistress role goes a long way. In addition, your hotel is too grand and fancy for my taste. I imagined us being somewhere simpler, smaller, and frankly, more elegant. Go to your meetings and we'll catch up later in the day. Love, Laura

In the shower, minutes later, he sat on the marble bench and forced himself to think about divorce again. It felt harsh. Everything felt harsh. Laura should have been there with him at that moment in his fancy hotel, the two of them embracing under the stream of hot water. Carmensina was basically fine. Since she lost the baby things had improved between them. What was wrong with seeing Laura now and then when the opportunity presented itself? No one had to get hurt. They were grown-ups. These things happened and had been happening since the dawn of time. Surely a lie here and there was better than some bourgeois insistence on the kind of honesty that stuck knives into people's hearts. Laura was under no obligation to be with him. She was as free as a bird and could walk away whenever she wished, but why now, after waiting all this time for this holiday, why now just because of an ill-timed phone call?

To make things easier for him she looked at places on the Lido first, but none were to her liking. By mid-morning she found a five-room boutique hotel she loved the look of, near the Grand Canal in the Santa Croce neighbourhood. She checked in and got the only room ready for occupancy at that hour. Though not especially big it had high ceilings, two balconies overlooking the water, and a king-sized bed. Then she headed back to the Excelsior to retrieve the suitcase she had left with the front desk. It was close to lunchtime when she arrived. She preferred not to contact James again until she was fully installed in her own place and she was nervous about running into him. But once she had her suitcase, she found the meeting room where the publishers were gathered and stole a glance through a porthole shaped window in the door.

She saw a lot of men. Men of many ages, shapes and sizes.

Men with long hair, short hair, and men without any hair at all. There were men who were somewhat stylish, somewhat handsome, and many more who, had they passed her on the street, she would not have noticed. To her surprise it took a few seconds to find James among them. At first, she thought that maybe he had skipped the event, or had gone to the restroom and might return and would tap her on the shoulder at any moment. But then she saw him, seated in the middle of it all, listening to the speaker. The speaker was a drab older man and projected on a large screen behind him was a slide of a pie chart depicted in basic colours. The room was drab as well, similar to hundreds like it in large hotels around the world, with floor-to-ceiling divider panels, red carpeting, and folding chairs. She looked hard at James and saw a contemporary professional from Barcelona, a husband, a father of two young girls. It was hard for her to discern the boy who had gone swimming with Camilla in Mallorca, the attractive half-British, half-Catalan man who drank her brandy in the Cornish pub, or the fellow who had lugged a toolbox into the priest hole.

On the vaporetto heading back to the San Stae stop, her arms draped over the retractable handle of her suitcase, and surrounded by selfie-obsessed tourists, she knew that neither she nor James had changed in any significant way. They were still the same people they had been over that first drink at the Bowery Hotel. So why did everything feel so different? Was it a question of context or an upsetting reminder of how capricious human desire can be? All she knew for certain, then and there gliding upon the water, was that for her the love affair was ending. She no longer desired him. And she had sensed it even yesterday, the minute they were alone in his room, hours before Carmensina's phone call.

Back at her new hotel she sat in a chair and stared at her phone. She was uncertain about whether she should follow through on her promise to tell him where she was, or to call and say instead what she was feeling and arrange to meet with him to speak about it the way adults are supposed to. Unable to decide she went out.

When he called her, she was in the Scuola Grande di San Rocco, in the Sala dell'Albergo staring up at the ceiling painting done by Tintoretto, his *St Roch in Glory*. She had forgotten to silence the ringer and the noise it made embarrassed her and annoyed those standing close to her. Answering it was the fastest way she knew to silence it, and as she did, she began to make her way down to the hall on the ground floor.

'Hey,' she said.

'Laura.'

'Hello James.'

'It's good to hear your voice.'

It was good for her to hear his as well, but she didn't say anything.

'Have you found a hotel you like better?' he asked.

'Yes.'

'Good. I'm sorry about how things went last night.'

'Me too.'

A brief silence ensued.

'We're back to saying sorry again to each other.'

He meant it in a nice way, as a way of reminding her of the short but intense history they shared.

'How did your meeting go?' she asked, stalling.

'It was fine. Boring. And now I'm all done.'

'I'm being a tourist. I like it.'

'Good. I'm glad. But when can we meet?'

She hesitated.

'I'm not sure,' she said.

'How do you mean?'

She was standing before Tintoretto's *Assumption of the Virgin*. In the painting, lifted by a gust of wind, Mary begins to leave her son's apostles behind and ascend into heaven. The sensation of weightlessness in play was something Laura could identify with.

'I don't know,' she said. 'I don't know what I mean.'

'You're still upset.'

Again, she hesitated.

'It's worse than that,' she said.

He was back in the junior suite out on the balcony she had escaped to the night before. The day was clear and mild with a grey Adriatic spreading south below him.

'You've met someone,' he said, 'and you're finding it hard to tell me.'

She smiled, but nervously. She thought about Nicola

Carati the archaeologist in Palermo, who was handsome and who she had not been attracted to, but who, in that moment, all of a sudden, represented other possibilities.

'No,' she said. 'I haven't met anyone.'

'You mean you've tired of me all by yourself then. The thrill is gone.'

'I didn't mean for it to happen,' she said.

'But it has.'

'I'm not sure.'

'My my,' he said, 'and we haven't even made it to Harry's Bar.'

'I'm sorry.'

'So, you don't want to see me? You don't think we can put Humpty Dumpty back together again?'

'I don't know.'

He was trying to stay calm, trying not to get or sound too exasperated.

'Well, I'm here,' he said. 'You know how to reach me. I'm here for you. Call me, please, when you feel a bit clearer about things, all right?'

'OK.'

'I do love you,' he said.

'OK,' she said.

He went back inside and sat in the chair she had sat in. He recalled the calculations that had gone through his head on the flight back to Barcelona from Mallorca with Carmensina and the children after they had buried Camilla. He remembered the concerns he had then, that once Laura had finished the translations, she might very well reassess her feelings for him and the situation he was putting her in. He sat there and tried not to face the realization that his marriage only worked because he had Laura. He did not wish to contemplate what would become of him and his little family without her.

Laura had considered this as well and thought she knew what would happen, that he would find someone else, someone more pliable and more conveniently located. Rather than cry she wandered the hall and stopped in front of another painting, *The Adoration of the Magi*. She didn't like it very much and wondered why Tintoretto, apart from being a Venetian native, was so highly valued. The scene was dark and confusing. With the exception of the man on the far left, the one draped in a red cloak that she assumed to be Joseph, Yeshua's father, no one else was actually looking at the infant. And then in the background through a gap in the stable walls there was a group of people on horseback who looked to be contemporaries of the painter. The only thing she liked was the surreal presence of the young, pudgy angels hovering above the manger. She went back out onto the street. The building, Venice, all of Italy and the western world, were filled with churches and images of Christ. Her Joseph of Arimathea would have been chagrined and amazed.

She had a late lunch and went back to her room. She didn't know what to do. Though lonely, she was wary of wimping out and asking James to join her. Either they would end up fighting or make each other feel even sadder than they were already. She forced herself not to call him and while she had dinner near the hotel, drinking a whole bottle of white wine, he called her twice, but she didn't answer or listen to his messages. Then he texted her, saying he understood, and that made her angry.

In bed she got an email from Pierre, her colleague in Paris, with a link to a TED talk he had been captivated by and wanted to share with her. It was an astrophysicist who worked for NASA, a woman who explained how all of the atoms in our bodies had come from stars, some of them located on the far side of the galaxy. She was riveted by it and watched it twice. She thought about Lucretius who had predicted the existence of atoms and who had warned about the dangers of religious thinking. She thought about the miniscule size of the Earth compared with the vastness of the known universe, how relative everything was, how brief human life was. The astrophysicist mentioned how the Earth spun around its axis at a thousand miles an hour, while orbiting the sun at sixty-seven thousand miles an hour, and how the entire solar system was moving about the centre of the galaxy at half a million miles an hour. All of that speed and motion was actually happening as she lay there in her hotel bed off the Grand Canal. It scared her and cheered her at the same time. It scared her because it implied that life was random and meaningless. It cheered her because it was true and wondrous and a clarion call to get the most out of life.

Once again, she regretted having gone back to New

York on that trip when she found Nathan's mistress and James on his own. If she had stayed in Cornwall, Camilla would have too. Camilla would still be alive. She might never have slept with James to begin with. Finn and Bidelia might never have done what they did. The scrolls and the codices and her translations would have been safe.

But what, she thought, was the point of such regret? What had happened had happened. The displeasure and betrayal she felt because of Nathan was just as real as the attraction she'd been possessed by for James. It is, she thought, what life is like. 'First we feel, then we fall.' It might even happen again. And she knew she was fortunate to live in a time when both of these stories with both of these men could be lived through as real and also be experienced as rites of passage. She had not been condemned to chain herself to either one. A more fulfilling love with someone was still possible. Camilla had told her so at their very first dinner together, Jean-Paul Bonnerive had said it too when she came to his apartment.

It rained that night and all through the morning. She changed her ticket, checked out of the hotel, and stepped aboard a vaporetto that went to the mainland. Once there she would take a taxi to the airport and catch her flight back to Palermo where the sun was shining. She would buy the abandoned shepherd's cottage and renovate it into a little house from where she could contemplate the villa and the remains of Daphne's temple. She would think further about writing a biography of Eleanor of Castile.

She would go on and try to forget about James. She would try and forget the remains of Christ buried on Camilla's Provence House estate in Cornwall. She would ally herself instead with Joseph of Arimathea, savouring the seasons, savouring her senses, savouring life.

THE END

Acknowledgements

I need to thank poet and New Testament scholar Willis Barnstone for his guidance and advice concerning the 'missing years' of Christ, and Professor Benjamin Rubin for his notes concerning Greek and Roman archaeology. I am also very grateful to Madeleine Feeny for her comments and careful reading of numerous drafts, to my agent Maria Cardona for her unflagging encouragement, and to Charlotte Ledger at HarperCollins for taking this novel under her wing.